Pocket Notebook

MIKE THOMAS

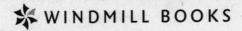

WINDMILL BOOKS

Published by Windmill Books 2011

2 4 6 8 10 9 7 5 3 1

Copyright © Mike Thomas 2010

First published in Great Britain in 2010 by William Heinemann

Windmill Books
The Random House Group Limited
20 Vauxhall Bridge Road, London SW1V 2SA

Addresses for companies within The Random House Group Limited can be found at:
www.randomhouse.co.uk/offices.htm

The Random House Group Limited Reg. No. 954009

www.rbooks.co.uk

A CIP catalogue record for this book
is available from the British Library

ISBN 9780099537489

The Random House Group Limited supports The Forest Stewardship
Council (FSC), the leading international forest certification organisation. All our titles
that are printed on Greenpeace approved FSC certified paper carry the FSC logo.
Our paper procurement policy can be found at:
www.rbooks.co.uk/environment

Mixed Sources
Product group from well-managed
forests and other controlled sources
www.fsc.org Cert no. TT-COC-2139
© 1996 Forest Stewardship Council

Typeset by SX Composing DTP, Rayleigh, Essex

Printed and bound in Great Britain by
CPI Cox & Wyman, Reading, RG1 8EX

For my wife:
'without you I am nothing'

'I, Police Constable 754 Jacob Smith, do solemnly and sincerely declare and affirm that I will well and truly serve the Queen in the office of constable, with fairness, integrity, diligence and impartiality, upholding fundamental human rights and according equal respect to all people; and that I will, to the best of my power, cause the peace to be kept and preserved and prevent all offences against people and property; and that while I continue to hold the said office I will to the best of my skill and knowledge discharge all the duties thereof faithfully according to law.'

The Constable's Oath

ONE

and I yank open the buckled driver's door, look down. Just below her hotpants there's the waxy nub of her splintered femur sticking through the flesh of her right thigh. She's screaming, screaming and looking at me, pointlessly pushing at the engine block that's come through the dashboard after she decided to smash her Clio into a wall on her way home from whatever pub or after-work office party she's been to. Yet another one thinking she was clever enough to drive regardless of however many vodka and Red Bulls she's had. I know she's pissed because I can smell it on her breath, her skin, her sweat as she shudders. People are stupid and they never learn, but I say nothing. Now isn't the time.

I kneel on the wet tarmac, take her hands in mine, smile and calmly tell her everything's going to be okay. *Shhh, everything's going to be okay, it's all right, more help is on its way.*

But it isn't going to be okay because I've seen this so many times before and I know this woman, *girl* really, about the same age as Frank's daughter, just a few years older than my Naomi, she could slip away from me any moment now. Here in the dark, in the rain on this shitty side street while her family carry on their New Year preparations, oblivious that it'll be the last they ever plan because this is the evening their nineteen-year-old never comes home from work. And nothing will ever be the same again.

The girl's shivering, moaning, and I can't make out what she's saying, but I know she's gone into shock. The splintered end of her thigh bone is grinding against the metal jammed up to her midriff and I'm getting her blood on my hands trying to shove the damn thing a centimetre away from the wound. Got to maintain the facade though. Her head has lolled backwards and to one side, her terrified eyes on mine, and I nod to reassure her regardless of what I'm thinking. I turn to Frankie, see the blue strobes of our firearms truck reflected in his glasses, mouth to him, *Paramedics?*

And he shrugs, shakes his head. This is ridiculous, so Frank gets back on the radio, tells ops room to ring the bloody ambulance control again, get an ETA. They tell us it's two minutes away, which isn't good enough. Not nearly.

I kneel again, holding the cold and trembling hands of this young lady, this girl I've never seen before who's becoming quieter by the second, who knows nothing about me. I wonder if I'll be the last person she ever sees. And I wonder if she'll be disappointed.

I keep talking, squeeze her hands, heft my shoulder against the dirty metal of the engine to release some of the pressure on her thighs and pelvis. I hear the sector pandas screech to a stop somewhere in the background, see the Trumptons' wagon reflected in a charity-shop window as it pulls alongside the Clio. The hose monkeys scurry out and start lugging power tools towards us.

When the ambulance arrives I have to prise her fingers from my hands. She sobs, breathes crimson froth, and I know this means her guts are mangled, but still I tell her *it's going to be okay, everything's going to be fine, these people are here to help you now.* I'm lying. I see the faces of the paramedics as I stand to let them at the girl, and know they're treating her just for the sake of treating her. Delaying the inevitable. Going through the motions. Showing willing, like we always do. I walk over to Frank who's stopping traffic in the murk, surrounded by pulsating blue lights. I look at him but don't have to say anything. He swallows and closes his eyes for a second.

'You tried, Jake,' he says.

'Yeah,' I say, and wish we hadn't been just around the corner when the call came out. Wish we weren't the first at scene. I wish we'd never been here at all.

I'm waiting and watching while the water fairies cut the roof from the car and lift the engine block with their pneumatic toys. The medics hunch over the girl while she's freed from the ruined shell, then they draw her out onto a gurney. Still I see the thigh bone poking upwards like a jagged candle. There's something wrong with her left leg, something I couldn't see from the driver's side door earlier. It takes me a moment to realise the foot is missing, probably still wedged underneath the clutch. I think of it lying there. I hold my hands up, my fingers dark and sticky with her blood.

And I hear a drunken voice call from the pavement, some guy shouting that all coppers are bastards and we never do anything right and if we'd got here quicker we could've saved her. I turn and see him looking right at me. This hundred-yard hero, this skinny little fuckstick in his tracky bots and hoodie, a pondlife brawler from some sink estate with his forearms inked full of prison tats, his fingers loaded with Elizabeth Duke sovereign rings straight from the Argos catalogue. He's leering at me, wobbling his shaved head, so I walk towards him and he flaps his fingers and says *come on, come on then*.

And tonight I've had enough of drunks and I'm completely out of compassion or understanding, so I go right up to him, warn him I'll arrest him for public order. He doesn't give a toss, this Stella monster, he couldn't care less and still the lairiness. Now all the other onlookers are starting to gather round to listen. These onlookers, on their way home from work or last-minute stocking-up on beers for tonight, they're crowding me. These ordinarily passive members of the public, these respectable businessmen and shop workers and students, they've got that bloodlust now, their own adrenalin dump at this toe-to-toe developing in front of them and, what a surprise, they're turning on me, on this figure of authority, jostling me, curling their lips and asking where I was when their car was robbed, telling me they pay my wages, that I couldn't catch a fuckin' cold.

And I can't have this, can't lose face, so I take the drunk's arm, tell him he's nicked even though he probably doesn't care or understand. He starts fighting it like they all do, flailing his arms and growling that I ain't locking him up for New Year's fuckin' Eve, bra. He's gone as rigid as a toddler mid-tantrum and the performance carries on. We have to use some of the sector boys to restrain him in front of the crowd. So we cuff and stuff him, escort him to the back of the nearest divisional van where the cage door is open and ready, but his feet are on the footplate, pushing backwards to stop us getting him in there. Then his elbow smashes into my eyebrow and it's all I can do not to kill him.

I don't know how long I've been here or how I even got inside, but I'm in the back of the van with him, in the cage, pummelling the fucker, watching in a detached kind of way as my fists then the heels of my tactical boots land on his scalp and neck and torso. He's cowering under the metal bench and Frankie's dragging me out while someone else slams the cage door shut.

I walk away, feel Frank's eyes on me, feel others watching me silently.

I'm bent over, breathing hard, when one of the paramedics jumps from the back of the ambulance. I'm nodding already as he tells me the girl has gone into cardiac arrest, that his colleague is working on her and they've got to go, though she'll be a Code Blue by the time she gets to Casualty and signed off as DOA by the worn-out junior doctor. Can the police tell the parents, please?

The paramedic walks back to his wagon. They weave through the emergency vehicles and the build-up of civvy traffic and the rubberneckers, then on come the blues and twos and they're gone. The girl's gone.

And it's another one I couldn't save.

placed him in the rear of the van. As I did so, COOPER lashed out with
his right arm, his elbow connecting with my left eyebrow. I
immediately felt a sharp pain in my eye, and COOPER then began
flailing his arms around and resisting my attempts to restrain him.
With the assistance of other officers present, he was placed in a Home
Office-approved hold and handcuffed to the rear in the stacking
method. The Kwik-Cuffs were locked to prevent him causing self-
harm, or harm to any officers at scene. The van doors were closed
but COOPER continued his violent behaviour. I could hear loud
banging noises coming from the rear of the vehicle, and when I
checked through the window could see him repeatedly hitting
his head on the cage door and the side panels of the van itself.
He was then conveyed to Trinity Street Custody Suite. ————
As a result of the DP's behaviour, I sustained a small cut to my left
eyebrow and blurred vision for ten minutes after the incident.
✦ As if anyone will ever read this. Why do I fucking bother. Really?? ✦

1745 Code 30 Trinity Street (admin duties re. arrest of COOPER) ————
Handover package prepared for the Detained Person. ————
Full details of the DP. Dwayne Robert COOPER, 15111986, home address
224 The Waterfront, Bayside BA2 8QE. CRO 133A561014K. ————
PNCId 223/133A561. Matter recorded with Crime Stats Bureau
ref. no. 3300102480Z. COOPER too intoxicated for charge.
Night shift to deal ref. S.5 public order and assault police. ————
1910 Off duty. ————

TWO

Twelve hundred hours.

I'm in trouble. I sense it immediately. Karen's stomping around the bedroom in her slippers, refolding already neat clothes. Picking up the jeans I wore last night. Kicking my shoes under the bed. Cleaning. Arranging. She does this when she's angry. After an argument she can sterilise the entire kitchen in an hour.

I don't really have to speak to her to gauge her mood nowadays: the I-can't-even-bring-myself-to-look-at-you face she pulls ever more frequently is present and correct, so I say nothing and close my eyes again, drifting. My right hand cups my sweaty, shrunken balls and I contemplate stroking myself under the duvet while she clomps about; the sheer cheek of it would be delicious. But no. Instead I think of the old days, when I'd wake and find her lying alongside me. Those times when we'd hangover-fuck, when we'd sweat out the alcohol. Afternoons spent beneath the quilt. Lazy, easy times.

I will her to slip into bed with me now. To stop what she's doing, undress, take the slippers off, ease in alongside me. Painted toenails brushing against my calves. Come on, Karen. Come in.

She knows I'm awake and watching her but says nothing. I wonder what heinous crime I've committed. Last night. Frank's house. I vaguely recall his *faux* grandmother clock chiming from the hallway at midnight, group hugs all round, hollow promises of fresh starts and better times, tumblers of Jack clacking together. The Frankster crashing and burning like he always does, grabbing an emergency kip while the party went on around him. The fifteenth miniature cigar in my mouth, all thoughts of tomorrow batted away because in the moment nothing else matters.

Then Karen's face looking up at mine as we stood in Frank's kitchen, eyes sad yet not a little angry, her mouth moving, talking at me, and I can't remember what she said but after that . . . everything was vague, to say the least.

The party was a stormer, though. Frankie's can be a little hit and miss because of his wife, but even Mel's glacial presence didn't spoil the event this time. I tuned her out anyway, despite the aggravation it's likely to cause me at work tonight.

Karen gives me a strange look, like she's confused or expecting me to say something, but I don't so she huffs, slams the bedroom door on her way out.

'Happy New Year,' I croak after her. 'I love you.'

I listen for any reply, for *Ah loov ya too* in that groovy Manc accent of hers that made me fall for her in the first place. But there's nothing, just footsteps on stairs. I roll over, the left side of my head pressing into the pillow. Feel pain above my eye, curse the countless JD and Cokes I went through at Frank's, because this is getting harder every time. I'm not nineteen any more. Christ, very soon I'll be twice that.

Then I remember yesterday afternoon. That muppet shouting from the sidelines . . . The cut just above my eyebrow. I finger the wound. See nicks and grazes on my knuckles. Dwayne Cooper. Already on the fast track to Magistrates' Court. See you in a few days, Dwayne.

New Year's Day grinds on: repeats of repeats of sickeningly cheerful family films, crass reality shows, That-Was-The-Year-That-Was programmes. I glaze over, think about the money I'm wasting on my Sky subscription, lose an hour staring at the pretty lights on the Christmas tree while Naomi argues with her kid brother over the remote control. Karen and I take turns avoiding each other, use the children to pass messages, ask questions, give replies. Neither of them notices their parents aren't talking and, even if they did, I doubt they'd care.

I'm swallowing bile all afternoon. Spend a little time getting my gear ready, then waste an hour on *Vietnam Encounter* on the PlayStation, finally managing to clear the bunker of Vietcong. It's cathartic. Really it's just me stabbing buttons so my on-screen M16 blazes, but seeing those digital gooks go down after the day I've had makes me feel lighter, somehow.

At eighteen hundred hours I prepare a shake: one pint of skimmed, three scoops of whey protein. Neck it. Eat a large apple. Wait. Give it fifteen for the pre-workout snack to settle. Shut myself in the spare bedroom. It's day two of a high-frequency, low-intensity week. Mass building. Chest, arms, calves and abs. I rack a couple of twenty-kilo plates onto the EZ Bar, start some standing curls. Work those biceps, twelve reps per arm. Veins bulging. Forearms on fire. More plates, another set of reps. Get that light-headed feeling. Switch to the dumb-bells, blast out three sets of lateral raises. Must remember to get a mirror fixed in here so I can watch myself.

My mobile rings. I drop the dumbers, scoop it off the windowsill. It's Sinclair.

'Sorted?' I ask, mindful that anyone could be listening in nowadays. I nod as he craps on in my ear. 'Okay, I'll collect them in work tonight. Later, bra.'

I end the call before he starts nagging me about money. Drop the phone back on the sill. Pick up my leather case, unzip it. Might as well fill up the tank now supplies are on the way. I lock the bedroom door, drop my joggers, sit on the edge of the single bed. Take a clean needle, screw it onto the hypo. Jam the pin into the rubber seal of my last vial of

Testosterone Enanthate, suck out five hundred mils. Pinch the skin above my left hip. Inject.

When I've finished my workout I clean up, rub my left arse cheek where it's gone numb from the gear. I unlock the door, step out onto the landing. Listen to Karen wittering away to Naomi and Ben but can't hear what they're saying because MTV is polluting the lounge. Happy New Year, eh? Happy families. Which reminds me . . .

I'm hungover and shagged from the weights but just thinking about ringing my mother is enough to tip me over the edge. Got to do it, though. Deep breaths. I step into my bedroom, close the door. Bring up the number on my moby. Dial.

'Room eleven east, if you could,' I say when a woman answers.

'Hold please,' she says, her voice flat, uninterested. 'I think it's feed time.'

Feed time. Like my mother's an animal. There's a click and the line rings again.

'Eleven E,' says some guy. Another staff member I've never met. I can hear raised voices in the background.

'It's Jacob Smith,' I tell him. 'I'd like to speak to my mother.'

'She's feeding.'

I squeeze the mobile, press it hard against my ear. 'I *know*.'

There's a pause. Then: 'Fine,' he mutters, and I assume he's handed her the phone because all I can hear now is breathing down the line and still the angry voices from somewhere and the guy's telling my mother, 'It's Jacob, Bernadette. Your son. Remember?'

Fucker. And I recognise the noise now. The shouting. They've got her television switched to Jeremy Bastard Kyle. I picture my mother sitting next to the window with drool on her chin, medicated and rambling to herself after a day spent catching and eating flies.

'Mum?' I say.

She says nothing. Just the TV down the phone line, the rattle of her chest faintly audible when the background screeching stops.

'Mum, I just wanted to . . . wanted to wish you a Happy New Year.'

Still Jeremy. Still the breathing.

'Mum?' I ask. 'Are you okay?'

Then: 'Keith?'

Who? 'No, Mum. It's me. *Jake.*'

'Oh, Keith,' she sighs, and I have no idea who the fruitbat is on about, probably the staff guy who's waiting to finish spoonfeeding her whatever glop they've prepared.

This is going nowhere fast. I kill the call. Lower my head into my hands.

I shower before work, spend half an hour washing away the fug. I think of Jessica as water pulses against my shaved head. She was there last night. Young and unsullied. Clueless about the effect she has on me. It was an effort not to stare. Every time I see her I'm gripped with the urge to tell Karen I'm leaving her and the kids.

I prepare my work bag, start to wonder. Perhaps I was that transparent. Karen must've sensed something. Seen something. Jesus, I was so pissed I could've told her I was in love with the girl.

Point is, I really can't remember anything after Karen speaking to me in the kitchen.

I just hope I didn't tell Frankie I desperately want to fuck his nineteen-year-old daughter.

Tuesday 1st January

2100	On duty. Eastern ARV Office. Tour of duty 2100–0700hrs.
	Callsign FV31. Team Of Two with PC 977 Frank MacReady.
2110	Briefing @ office with PS Hall. Trap-points and sector targets discussed.
	(briefing: 5 mins/tedious discussion of fatboy's latest bloody
	'winter sun' holiday arrangements for Tenerife: 40 minutes)
	Directed patrol – city centre/assist divisional officers.
2135	Mobile patrol. ARV vehicle two. Load: 2 x Heckler & Koch MP5 A3,
	2 x Glock 9mm pistols, L104 A1 Baton Gun, X26 Taser. All weaponry
	securely stored in rear-mounted firearms cabinet as per ACPO
	guidelines. Non-lethal options (CS Incapacitant Spray, F-lock Baton)
	with officers. Firearm cabinet key with PC MacReady.
2155	McDonald's, King Street re. assist divisional officers. All in order
	at premises. Minor dispute between customers.
2220	Fort Square re. disturbance. Matter dealt with by division. Rowdy
	elderly male moved on from front of licensed premises.
2345	Stop-check vehicle on foreign plates, Lloyds Ave. Nissan Micra index
	1884 K326. Driver Khaled AL-BOURASSI, 2705/1979, home address
	86 Hodge Crescent, Mayhill. All in order re. tax. HORT/1 issued
	for production of documents.
0050	St Paul Street – suitable advice given to group of males kicking
	bin bags into carriageway. No offences disclosed.
0135	Parker Place – male advised re urinating in lane. Warned re. future
	conduct. Suitable advice adequate. No further action required.
0245	Operation Guard (intruder alarm) at Dorothy Perkins, Duke
	Road – all in order. Night security on premises had set off alarm.
0310	Mobile patrol.
0600	Eastern ARV office. Code 30 re. paperwork/check-in of weaponry.
0655	Code 100 – off duty.

THREE

I step into the locker room, let the door click shut behind me.

There's no one getting changed to go home, no bleary-eyed afternooners swapping utility harnesses for FCUK belts, or black fatigues for comfortable jeans and a sweatshirt – the off-duty-copper casual look any villain can spot a mile away. No banter, no talk of that imminent first cold pint.

There's nobody else in here because, as usual nowadays, we are it. The 'shift'. Me. Frank. Our old stripy, Tommy Hall, waiting for us in the parade room upstairs. Two hungover plods facing a ten-hour stretch, and probably in no fit state to handle any part of the small arsenal we'll be carrying in the rear of the wagon. It'll be replicated right across the force area. Main stations with four tired young cops to cover a city. Shitty outstations with a lone probationer who hasn't done the driving course yet, so can't go anywhere in a patrol vehicle. None of them with enough service to warrant being left to look after themselves, never mind over a million members of the public. It ain't *The Bill*, that's for sure.

Frank hasn't looked up since I entered. I'm starting to fear the worst.

'Oi, oi, Frankster,' I smile. I can't stop picking at the scabs on my knuckles.

He's bent forward, clipping his thigh holster in place. His wiry arms work at the clasps, fingers pulling hard on the Velcro strapping; he's taking his time, avoiding eye contact. It reminds me of Karen with her angry cleaning. I feel myself start to bristle, so stare at the top of his head and count the pale pink bald patches he's tried to disguise by spiking his hair up with gel.

He straightens, eyes blinking behind those awful square glasses he wears, but doesn't look at me. 'All right, Jake?'

I wait a beat.

'Yeah, mate,' I say. We are Lemmon and Matthau. *The Odd Couple*.

He closes his locker. 'I'll make a brew,' he says, leaving the room. I can't remember him ever being like this. The only thing that takes the edge off it is that he's making the tea. Surely if I'd really pissed him off, he wouldn't have offered?

In the parade room we sit in silence across the table from each other, intelligence reports from the afternoon team spread before us. There's that awkwardness. That looking occupied when in reality all we're doing is pretending to be engrossed in some boring briefing sheet. Swap the paperwork for the Sunday red-tops and you'd have a picture of domestic bliss. The stripy sensed the mood and left, probably to resume surfing for holidays on the office computer.

Frank continues to ignore me. I know I've done something very wrong but the not-knowing what is killing me. I try to distract myself and pull out my mobile, check the pics I downloaded last week. Flip through shot after shot of painted toenails, ankle tattoos, toe rings. It doesn't work. Doesn't calm me down.

'Look,' I say, and having to break the ice first hurts even more. 'About the party . . . about what I said . . .'

Just what did I say? *'C'mon Frankie . . . juzzt half an hour with yer daughter . . . pleeeazze, mate?'* Surely not. He'd have ripped my spine out by now.

I stop talking when Frank looks at me for the first time tonight. He's angry. Barely containing it. I've seen it when he's about to put the arm on a performing prisoner. Frank's about average height – probably five ten to my six five – but a real hardbody. Can bench over a hundred kilos without breaking a sweat. I lean back in my chair. I know how fast he is across short distances.

'I'm sorry,' I say, then like the best public order prisoner whingeing to the bench in court, 'but I was really fucking drunk.'

Frank eyes me for a second. He knows the drink is no excuse. Knows I'm being a hypocrite. We've talked so many times about how we hate those tossers in the dock who point accusatory fingers at the twelve cans of Spar Super-strength Wifebeater lager they'd necked before shattering their girlfriend's jawbone in six places. And yet, it's true. I *was* really drunk. I can't remember what I did.

'You bloody demolished my kitchen door, you donut,' he says. 'Mel's not speaking to me.'

I blink several times, quickly. Glance down at my knackered hands. 'I . . . what?'

Frank shakes his head. 'You can't wind your neck in for a minute, can you? I don't know what went on between you and Karen, but you just went off on one. Punching holes in the bloody door? What were you thinking?'

I have no idea what he's talking about, but at least it explains the scabs. And it's hard not to break into a fit of giggles. Suddenly, now I know I'm in the clear, all I can think about is Jessica. 'Look,' I say, swallowing a snigger. 'I'll pay for any dam—'

'It's not fucking funny, Jake,' he says to me. 'You know I don't like any aggro . . .'

And then I do laugh. 'You? No aggro?'

'At least not at home, no. And you calling Mel Frosty Bollock all night didn't help.'

Fantastic. I can't remember calling her that but file it away for future use. 'Okay,' I say. 'Sorry, droog. I really am.'

'You're getting out of hand,' he says. Then I see his face relax, his shoulders loosen.

I ignore the comment. 'If it's any consolation, Karen's been blanking me all day.'

Frank sighs. 'I wonder why,' he mutters.

I'm wondering why too, but before I can gather my thoughts or reply to Frankie's little remark, the stripy appears in the doorway, gut straining at the buttons of his uniform shirt, his white hair coiffed into a candyfloss frizz. 'You girls kissed an' made up now?'

'Yeah, Tom,' I say, looking him up and down. 'Whatever.'

'There's a reason I've got these stripes on my shoulders, boy,' he says for maybe the twelve-thousandth time, watching as I neck the cold dregs of my tea.

I hoist my rig from the floor and gesture to Frank. We make our way to the doorway where Tommy stands, not moving. 'Saucer of milk, Tom?' I ask, looking down at the old guy. His piggy little eyes are sunk into the slick dough of his cheeks; I can see blackhead scars and thread veins across the bulb of his nose, smell stale coffee on his breath.

He steps aside. 'What you mean?'

I say nothing. The keys to the wagon tinkle in my hand as I head for the stairs. Tommy's calling behind me: 'What you mean, Smithy? Saucer of milk?'

I hear Frank following. I grin as he speaks to the old fellow. 'He means for you, *Sarge*. The station cat, you know?'

It's a boring shift.

We drive from call to call, backing up the sector lads, and every one turns out to be dross. It's the stuff of heart attacks. I'm adrenalised then flatlining, over and over. That thrill of anticipation. The bitter disappointment that follows. Nothing of any substance, nobody wanting to play.

Street brawls, office dos, family rucks, useless gifts and turkey. It drains people. To fight thy neighbour, to bitch-slap one's wife of a Boxing Day eve – it takes energy to start performing. By New Year's Day, everyone's worn out. I thank Christ for the double-bubble pay cheque I'll be pocketing at the end of the month. Makes the night seem a little more worthwhile. Means I can clear some of my tab, too.

The city centre is like a scene from a Romero zombie film. I keep thinking someone's vacuumed up all the people. There's the odd cluster of hardy lager-merchants staggering along the high street like the undead, but you can only derive so much pleasure from watching lonely crab-walking pissheads as they attempt to traverse that tricky four-inch drop from kerb to roadside.

We stop-check anyone who's about, make sure their mobile phones aren't recording then try to wind them up. None of them bites and by midnight I'm clenching my tattered fists with frustration. There's no firearm calls anywhere across the force. Frank decides on a game of snooker so we waste an hour pulling cars: red first, then any colour from yellow to black, then a red, then a colour . . . We give up when neither of us can find a passing motor in any shade of pink.

At oh-three hundred hours I drift across to JoBlo's as arranged. Sinclair is the lone doorman. He shuffles across, hands thrust into the pockets of his black overcoat, ribbons of breath drifting up in front of his face. Frank turns away as Sinclair leans down and slips his gloved hand into mine through the window I've lowered.

I am the friendly copper doing the rounds, pressing the flesh of the other night-workers. I feel cylinders of cold glass against my palm.

'Jake,' Sinclair says, giving the slightest hint of a nod.

'Happy New Year.'

'I'm awake at stupid o'clock in the morning,' I say. 'There's nothing happy about it. Busy?'

Sinclair laughs, withdraws his hand and waves it at the empty street: 'Dead, bra.'

I see the old ragged scar, his war wound, running from his left ear to the side of his nose, a mottled pink fissure on the black of his skin. It puckers and wrinkles as he smiles, like a second mouth. I think of the gypo teenager who gave it to him all those years ago, drawing a smashed beer bottle across his face when he refused the boy entry on his birthday. I remember dealing with them both, putting the kid over the wall for three years – he was released on tag for good behaviour after six months, of course – and how my acquaintance with Sinclair developed. How it became what it is now.

'That should see you right,' Sinclair says, straightening up. 'And about the money—'

'I'll sort it,' I tell him, and pocket the vials. Four Deca-Durabolin, four Testosterone Cypionate. Ten days' worth if I use them sparingly.

Sinclair hovers at the window, mouth slightly open, eyes on me. He sighs.

'You need to sort it, Jake,' he says. 'Truly.'

He walks back to the club door, yawns, and resumes waiting for nobody in the cold.

Frank is looking at me.

'What?' I ask.

'I don't know why you keep using that crap,' he says.

'Because it make me strong like bull!'

Frank shakes his head.

I light a miniature cigar. 'Let's go see the girls.'

He checks the clock on the dash. 'It's ten past three in the morning and colder than a witch's tit. There won't be any.'

I blow smoke out the window, throw the wagon into gear and drive in the direction of the docks.

Frank slumps in his seat, tired. I hear him mumble into his collar: 'Clearly you think differently.'

None of the usual faces on the main drag.

No faces at all, bar a solitary figure meandering along the pavement outside one of the industrial units on Radcliffe Street.

'Told you we were too late,' says Frank.

'What about her?' I ask, and point across to the streetlight the girl has wandered under. She's wearing the classic prozzie ensemble: fur-lined hooded red jacket, short black skirt, tights and Fuck-Me Boots. Her tiny frame is swathed in a cone of amber. The sound of our petrol engine has thrown her, made her think we're punters on the fish. Sector bobbies drive clapped-out diesel panda cars that the old pros can hear from the next county. They're normally melting into the shadows while plod is still ten minutes away.

'Must be new,' Frank says.

'Or desperate,' I say. 'Out on her own, in this weather.'

I pull closer. The girl realises who we are, begins to walk quickly away, her FMBs scuffing the pavement. I smirk, gun the engine. When she realises it's pointless, she stops and faces the passenger window with her hands on her hips. I can't see her face, her upper body, but can hazard a reasonably accurate guess at her expression and what's coming next.

'What you lot fuckin' want?' I hear her say when Frank lowers the window. That accent. She's from up in the sticks somewhere. I can see a patch of red jacket at her midriff, her trembling fingers where they hold a cigarette. She must be freezing. Or petrified.

I lean forward to get a better look at her while she talks to Frank, momentarily tune out their conversation. Because I'm thrown. I sit back, shake my head. This can't be right. I lean over again, look up at her.

'What?' she says, screwing up her face. 'This a staring competition or somethin'?'

I'm thinking of the RTC. The car into that wall in the pissing-down rain. Did you make it after all, girl? But it can't be you. It *can't* be.

I bat the thoughts away because Frank's looking at me oddly. The girl's lost interest, is picking at her bottom lip with chipped red fingernails. Black hair is piled on top of her head, a single curl hanging down like a dark hook across the left side of her face. I guess she must be eighteen, nineteen at most. Jessica's age.

'Are we done here,' the girl's saying, 'or what, piggies?'

It's freaky though. Uncanny. She's the spitting image of the one from the Clio. And like Jessica, she's a very pretty thing. Delicate. Fragile, almost. Beneath the makeup, applied to make her look older, I can see her features are still soft. It'll take a few years walking these pavements before she hardens, before the inevitable smack habit browns her teeth and sucks at the flesh of her face. But for now, she's Little Red Riding Hood.

I wonder what her feet look like. And I wonder who's pimping her out.

'What's your name, sweetheart?' I say. There must be a better life for her than this. She doesn't seem capable of looking after herself.

She glances around, then squats down at the open window, as if she wants to confide in me. Her forearms rest on the doorframe. She has beautiful eyes, like dark marbles. I can see she needs help. I *want* to help.

She smiles, says: 'You pay me enough, you can call me whatever you want when you're fucking me. *Sweetheart*.'

I open my mouth. For some reason nothing comes out.

Frank has turned to me, eyes wide. I swear he's about to laugh.

'That's . . .' I say, still a little stunned. 'That's not really what I was expecting to hear. You're a dirty little cow, aren't you?'

Red Riding Hood pushes herself up from the car. She draws on her cigarette, pitches it onto the bonnet, watches the sparks fly up over the windscreen in the breeze. Exhaling blue smoke she says: 'And you, honey, are a cunt.'

She walks away. I watch her strut around the front of the wagon, sashay across the road, then disappear behind the hedges of an MOT centre.

'She obviously knows you well,' says Frank, tucking his face into his jacket collar.

I can see by his eyes that he's smiling.

It's oh-six fifty-five hours, and in the locker room I slap Frank on the shoulder. 'C'mon. The Elite should be open. You can spot me for an hour on the bench before the stuffed shirts arrive for their pre-office aerobics.'

At the gym I blast my pecs and delts, watching the grey men of nine-to-five land traipse in. The cubicle gimps, they pump meagre amounts of iron before disappearing to their first pointless meeting of the day where they'll talk for hours yet say nothing.

I'm well and truly chinstrapped by oh-eight hundred and sneak back into the house to find Karen and the kids still asleep. I slip into my side of the bed, onto the cold mattress. I'm gone in seconds.

Karen has left for the day when I wake. No note. No food. She's on afternoons at A and E tonight and I'll be on my way to work before she arrives home. I try to engage the kids for a while but fail to divert their attention from the crotch-grabbing rappers blaring on the widescreen in the corner. Naomi occupies one settee, thumb blurring over the keypad of her mobile as she texts whichever new boy's sniffing around her. Ben lies on the other, staring catatonically at the forty-inch screen with his right hand jammed down the front of his baggy black jeans, fumbling with the contents. My film collection – four hundred DVDs, everything from Kurosawa to the Coen Brothers, a cineaste's dream – sits ignored and untouched in the cupboard behind the television.

Children. That gulf. That chasm between you and them.

I think of my own father. Then I try not to.

'You want to watch a movie?' I ask Ben. 'Something decent instead of this rubbish?'

Ben moves his head a little, just enough so he can look me in the eye and make sure I catch the curl of his top lip. I see myself in him, albeit twenty-five years ago and minus the floppy, dyed, jet-black emo haircut. 'Nnnaaah,' he drawls after a few seconds, like a stoner. Then he shifts his head three inches, back to the position it was moments before. Oh, the effort. I'm so thankful.

Naomi gives me one of her I-may-only-be-fifteen-but-I'm-way-cooler-than-you looks, mentally reeling off a list of horrid teenage Americanisms as she rolls her eyes at me. *Yeah, Dad. You loser. Whatever.* She resumes texting, one eye on the whiteboy hip-hop star squeaking out his latest track on the Sony Bravia I'm still paying for but never get to watch.

I can't remember the last time I held a decent, prolonged conversation with my kids. My lack of enthusiasm soon matches their own so I abandon them to their mindless music video channel.

When I ring Rachael her mobile goes to voicemail. I leave

another short message, tell her what a fantastic time we had, ask if she wants to try again because, you know, that night at her flat was just a blip. I try her landline, get the same, do the same. And she leaves for her ski trip tomorrow. Gone for two weeks . . .

I slip up to the master bedroom with a good handful of toilet tissue, lock the door, switch the television on. The DVD tray closes and I silently offer thanks to the CID lad who gave me one of the discs he recovered on a warrant. I lose time watching top-quality Italian foot porn, skipping from one money-shot to the next, hand working my cock, alternating between thoughts of Rachael on her back with her deliciously long toes in the air, and fucking Jessica in a Little Red Riding Hood costume.

Annoyingly, unusually, my mind wanders. I keep seeing the severed foot on the floor of the Clio. Think of the young pro walking the street alone. Then Karen enters my head and ruins everything. We're in Frank's kitchen again, she's talking at me and her face is twisted, is distraught but vicious and I still can't recall what she said to me but whatever it was, now I've got to pay for bloody repairs to Frankie's kitchen door.

It's my birthday soon. I wonder if she'll start speaking to me before then?

	63
1745	Code 30 – paperwork @ Eastern ARV office.
1900	Off duty
	Monday 7th January
0900	On duty. Code 40 (Magistrates Court duties). Tour 0900–1700 hrs.
	Regina v Dwayne COOPER (S.5 Public Order / Assault Police)
0925	Consult with CPS ref. possible plea bargain. COOPER declines offer.
1015	Court No. 3 – contested trial ref. COOPER for above matters.

FOUR

I run the gauntlet of the Magistrates' Court corridors.

It's an animal pen. They wait for you, clumped in groups on stairwells, near the toilets, outside the very court they're about to appear in. They bring their friends, their families. Despite the draconian ban, the air is thick with smoke. Soggy roll-ups, or if they're flush it's Lambert and Butler, the underclass's pre-rolled cigarette of choice. It's a blur of hoodies and cheap Asda trainers on cream tiles. These Burberry fools. These walking abortions. The aroma is fags, sweat and stale lager-breath from their pre-court piss-up. You walk past, uniform pressed, eyes fixed on somewhere ahead but not really looking, pretending to ignore them when they tell you what they plan to do to your wife and children. How they hope your father dies of cancer, you fuckin' truffle-snuffler. That they're going to rape your mother as soon as they're finished in this joke shop of a building.

This zoo. This kennel stuffed with stinking, yapping dogs.

They don't care. They have no fear. It's a social event for them.

I hate coming here. Wish my Glock was strapped to my thigh. How many of them would goad me to fight with the threat of a nine-millimetre hollow-point drilling through their sternum? No wonder ordinary, decent folk don't want to appear in court to give evidence.

In the police room I nod at Frankie, at the two plods I don't recognise but who were apparently there the night I took an elbow off Dwayne Cooper. One sits reading a three-day-old copy of the *Sun*, light from the overhead fluorescent gleaming off his bald scalp. The second gazes out through the window, playing with the wiry ends of his moustache like a hamster with mange.

The Crown Prosecution Service solicitor is a short and nervy fifty-something, his lank blond hair swept awkwardly across his forehead like a Hitler Youth swish. The suit he wears is three sizes too big and hangs from his skinny frame like a shire horse's empty feedbag. The sight of him hardly fills me with confidence.

He thrusts out a hand. 'Greg Cadwallader,' he says.

I'm worried Greg's arm may snap as I shake it. His palm is soft against the calloused skin of my own, as if he moisturises regularly. I look at Frank, see his eyes flick between me and this weedy runt of a solicitor. He knows what I'm thinking – is thinking exactly the same.

Crown Prosecution Service. The CPS. *Crap Police Solicitors. Can't Prosecute, Sorry. Criminal Protection Service.* My stomach knots as I listen to this CPS drone give his opinion of our case and in doing so demonstrate how little he knows of it, how he's probably just picked up the file this morning and given it a perfunctory going-over.

'So,' I say. 'What about job and finish?'

Greg looks at me. He doesn't understand.

Frank steps forward. 'Y'know, get Cooper to duck his nut? If he pleads guilty we can all go home. Two hours in work, rest of the day on the Queen.'

I'm nodding away, thinking if this is put to bed sharpish I can scoot across to Rachael's, spend the afternoon while Karen thinks I'm still in work. But Greg, he pulls a face, like someone's offered him a turd 'n' onion baguette for lunch.

'There are complications with this case,' he says, fingertips flicking at that fringe.

The case is airtight. I can't believe I have to be in court for it. 'Such as?'

'There's been a complaint of assault,' Greg says.

I laugh. 'That all?' I remember what my old tutor constable told me all those years ago: *if the public don't complain about you, you're not doing the job right* . . . 'Goes with the territory, mate.'

He looks up at me. There's something in his eyes, like they're shining as he stares. It's bizarre but I think he might be attracted to me. I check his left hand, wrapped around the case file: no wedding ring. Hmm. Do you sit at home endlessly watching the DVD of *West Side Story*, Greg? Wrestling over whether those Jets do it for you, or those Latino Sharks? Or is it *Philadelphia* on loop? Weeping while counting the lesions on Tom Hanks's chest, then cooing over Antonio Banderas as you imagine comforting him in his time of loss? Do you?

'There's an allegation of . . .' he says, neatly polished fingernails picking through the case file. He looks up quizzically. 'Ah . . . There's an allegation of . . . *black-dogging*?'

Black-dogging. Damn right.

I think of the red mist that descended after Cooper smacked me with his elbow. Close my eyes, try once again to fit the pieces together, to fill in the gaps from the point where I was clouted to finding myself standing over a squealing Cooper, chest heaving, Frank hauling me out of the van by my body armour. There's nothing. A void. A blue cinema screen with a title card: *we apologise for the temporary interruption to the main feature*.

And then the paramedic telling me the girl was going to snuff it, Frank groaning, me snatching the van keys from an anonymous open-mouthed sector bobby and climbing into the driver's seat. After that . . . after that it was foot on the accelerator as I drove towards the custody suite, listening to Cooper call me from my hole to my pole through the segregation wire, Frank following in the firearms wagon while Cooper screamed and I screamed back, my throat burning, spittle on my chin, blaming him for the accident, for the girl dying, for making me have to arrest him and fill in seventy stupid fucking forms when I should be getting ready for Frankie's party, blaming him for what happened with my parents and what this shitty job's made me become, for 9/11, 7/7, SARS, Aids, Bird Flu, Swine Flu, blaming him for not finding any damn WMDs in Iraq, for all those grunts who lost their lives in 'Nam, blaming him for pretty much everything ever . . .

And then there it was, that old black dog, that mythical beast, running right across the road in front of the police van. I remember checking the speedometer: nudging sixty, rev counter redlining, diesel engine straining.

Perfect.

I slammed on the brakes, like I always do when I see that old dog. Like every copper out there has done at one time or another, prick of a prisoner in the cage, no witnesses about, usually under cover of darkness.

Cooper carried on moving at sixty. Right into the segregation wire.

He didn't make a sound for the rest of the journey.

And that old black dog was gone once again.

All that was left to do was get our heads together back at the nick and make sure everyone's pocket notebook entries tallied. Credit to Cooper, he can't have been completely out of it while Frank prisoner-surfed him on the floor of the custody suite. He must've heard us laughing about doing it as he was booked in. About black-dogging him. How else would he complain about it, or even know the police-only phrase?

'Not guilty, m'lud,' I say, and grin. Frank raises a hand to his mouth.

Greg sighs. Clearly we are not on the same page, humour-wise. 'So would you care to explain what the term means?' he asks.

'I have no clue,' I say.

'Well, the defendant would have his solicitor believe otherwise.'

I place a hand on Greg's upper arm. It's like a bamboo pole wrapped in chicken fillets. Sinewy, knotted. Weak. 'I know nothing about it, simple as.'

Greg narrows his eyes at me. 'So you weren't involved in this "black-dogging"?'

'No.'

'Sounds like something sexual to me.'

I bet it does, sweetie. 'Sorry to disappoint you.'

Greg flushes. He riffles through the file again, embarrassed. 'And you know nothing about any assault?'

My face is expressionless. 'He can complain as much as he likes, but we all know how much he was thrashing about in that van. It's bollocks. Any injuries were self-inflicted and the four of us here will testify to it.'

Greg waits a moment, studies me. He turns to Frank, to the bald cop, to the bobby with the moustache who's still lean-ing against the windowsill. 'Okay,' he says, finally convinced. 'So be it.'

Another fine performance. Ladies and gentlemen of the Academy . . .

'So anyway,' I say. 'The guilty plea?'

Greg chews his bottom lip. 'I can speak to his solicitor, if it makes *you* happy,' he says, obviously not happy about it at all.

'Do it then,' I say. Test his mettle, right?

Greg's upset at being spoken to in this way, and for a second

I think he might have a hissy fit. Then he gives a little shoulder-shimmy and slides out of the room.

'How to lose friends and irritate people,' Frank says.

'Ah, he'll get over it,' I shrug, and drop into one of the orange plastic chairs lining the walls of the police room. I reach into the chest pocket of my shirt. Pull out my notebook, flick through it, an idea forming. I'm chuckling to myself as Greg stomps back in.

'So?' I say, standing up to look down at him.

'No,' he says, and offers an I-told-you-so smirk. 'He wants a trial.'

I look at Frank. 'Game on,' I say with a smile.

I'm last on.

Officer in the case. The OIC. Everyone else has given their evidence, been cross-examined. They're sitting at the back of court number three when I enter. Frankie throws me a look, rolls his eyes in an amused, you're-not-gonna-believe-what-just-happened kind of way, and I've worked with him long enough to get it: Cooper's already fucked. Convicted. Tucked up before I even walked into the room.

Might as well enjoy myself, then.

There's nobody else at the back of the court other than a guy in his mid-twenties. His bespectacled eyes watch me over silver frames, the tips of his bleached blond hair artfully teased skywards. He holds a spiral-bound pad in his hands, pen jammed into the rings. I peg him straight away: journalist. Or at the very least a trainee solicitor, as if the world needs any more of those. But it doesn't matter if this non-event case makes the papers. Clearly all that remains is for me to add the icing and the Cooper-cake is well and truly done.

'Your worships,' I say, bowing in the doorway as I'm supposed to.

The court is pathetic. Striplights clipped to polystyrene ceiling tiles. Bland cream carpet. Bench and witness box constructed of MDF and screened with fake beech like a B&Q kitchen. All that's missing is a range cooker. The black-caped clerk hunches over the statute books on his desk, pulling at the skin on his neck and mumbling to himself. Above him there's the magistrates lined on the bench: two tubby guys in cheap polyester suits, a frumpy female in her early sixties. Three wise monkeys. Laypersons with no knowledge of law and relying on the Alzheimer's-addled clerk to steer them to a verdict. I would have preferred a stipe, a legally trained stipendiary who knows what they're talking about, but you can't have everything. Anyways, thank fuck it's Magistrates'. Imagine Crown. Putting myself in the hands of twelve people too stupid to get out of jury duty.

Dwayne Cooper sits behind the defendant's desk. I don't remember him but he clearly remembers me. I feel his eyes on me as I walk to the witness box and catch him fidgeting in his chair, fingers scrunching up pieces of paper. I know it's barely contained fury: not *Twelve Angry Men*, just one agitated tracksuit.

Cooper's defence brief sits in the adjacent chair. Another sick-souled money-grabber in a slick suit. How he can sleep at night, looking after these turds, is beyond me. And there's no way Cooper could afford him in a million years, but that doesn't matter when people pay taxes that go into the Legal Aid kitty. Cooper got his services for free, via me.

I get the impression Mister Super-slick is far from happy. He's slumped over the desk, looking like he wished he was anywhere but here. Looking thoroughly pissed off. Strange.

I take the stand, lift the Bible, hold it in my right hand. The clerk snaps out of his stupor, asks me to introduce myself to the court, so I go through the usual spiel. My face is blank, professional. My voice clear and emotionless: 'I swear by almighty God to tell the truth, the whole truth and nothing but the truth . . .' I say, and glance at Greg. My left hand hangs down against my trouser leg, fingers crossed.

It's good to know you've got some leeway in these situations.

Greg does his bit for the cause then sits down. We're finished in three minutes: straightforward, boring. Nothing the fatbodies on the bench haven't heard a thousand times before. I wait for Mister Super-slick to slither from his chair to cross-examine but he doesn't move.

Instead, Cooper bumps his own chair backwards and gets to his feet.

I look at Frank. He shrugs. There's a cheeky glint in his eyes.

Greg half rises. 'I'm sorry, PC Smith, I forgot to mention. The defendant has discharged his solicitor of his duties. He's now representing himself.'

Cooper's brief wilts further.

I start to wish I hadn't crossed my fingers. If you exist Lord, thank you.

'Whorrit is, righ' . . .' Cooper begins. He rolls up the sleeves of his tracky top. Damn, doesn't he mean business! 'You, bra, are the guy wot smashed me up in that van, ain't you?'

And he's off on one. There's no logic or train of thought to his line of questioning. He has no clue of the finer points of law, seeming to base his legal arguments on snippets he's picked up watching *Judge Judy* reruns on some ropey satellite channel. He struts back and forth like Kevin Costner in *JFK*, gesticulating and grandstanding. But this ain't no Oliver Stone movie, *bra*. Black-dogging rears its head but I am poker-faced. The clerk repeatedly orders him to return to his seat and calm down but Cooper, in his own tiny little mind, is on fire.

I stand quietly, knowing I've won, and remember the idea I had in the police room.

'Your worships,' I say, my hand on the chest pocket of my uniform shirt. 'Would it be in order for me to refer to my pocket notebook for this matter? The defendant's cross-examination is confusing me a little.'

The clerk nods immediately. 'Indeed, officer,' he says with a withering look at Cooper. 'I understand entirely.'

Cooper watches sullenly as I take out my notebook, flip through the pages. I choose one at random, some nonsense diversity training I endured months ago where the notes I made consisted of names I already knew I wasn't allowed to call black people or the handicapped but the holier-than-thou condescending civvy prick tutors forced us to write them down anyway. I clear my throat. The magistrates lean forward in unison. Cooper's jaw clenches.

'Go ahead, officer,' says the clerk.

My eyes flick over my handwriting.

> No-no — coloured, half-caste, darkie, jigaboo, mechanical digger —
> — Spastic, spaz, scopey, window-licker, shoulder-muncher, Joey Deacon
> 1235 | Code 50 — Ref's (Curry — thank fuck!) —

What a waste of time that day was. Cracking tikka masala we had free for refreshments, though. Then I give the bench my version of events as I recall them, not from the notebook at all. I make it up as I go along, embellish it just to tighten the screws on a now purple-faced Cooper. I see Greg quickly flipping through his file, confused. Nobody even bothers to stop me and check the page I'm reading from.

Inside I'm laughing so hard I could soil myself.

Cooper is apoplectic. I think he's about to have an aneurysm.

I turn to Frank, check the young journo sitting a few seats away. My hand taps my notebook back into my shirt pocket. Job done.

Then: 'Officer!' the clerk squeals.

I swing my head around. Cooper is running towards me. It's full-pelt stuff, fists pumping air, his hundred-quid-an-hour ex-brief wide eyed and mouth agape behind him.

'I'mgonnafuckindoyoubra!' Cooper squeaks.

The clerk is freaking out, paging security. Out the corner of my eye I see Frank bolt from his seat. I boot open the door to the box; it flies backwards and there's the short sharp *squee* of screws nearly pulled from woodwork.

Cooper's almost upon me as I step down from the dais. Everything slows. Slows down enough for me to check him out properly: he's probably five seven, twelve stone in his keks. A shaven-haired lager-merchant with man-boobs wrapped in a shocking-white McKenzie tracksuit. I'm almost a foot taller, six stone heavier. I could bench-press him if he stopped moving long enough. Must've been something wrong with me the night we met; how this wimp ever stuck one on me I'll never know. But why, oh why does it always have to be this way? What's the matter with these people? I'm so tired of all this.

Then everything speeds up again and it doesn't matter if I'm tired because it's always been like this and always *will* be like this, so I smash a forearm into Cooper's windpipe, watch him drop to the floor. He writhes with his hands clutching at his throat.

'Aaag,' he says. His chest hitches, bloodshot eyes fixed on me.

Frank is beside me. I hear his faint snort of laughter.

Time to end it. I flip Cooper over, know by now that all eyes are on me. Baldy and moustache-man are standing at the back of the court, shaking their heads. At Cooper or Frank or me, I can't be sure. Frank does the necessary, places himself between me and the clerk, the bench, shielding me from view. I go through the motions, pull out Kwik-Cuffs and Velcro restraints, truss Cooper using Home Office-approved techniques. Within a minute he's on his front in a figure-of-four, legs strapped and hands cuffed at the base of his spine. A good old post-Christmas turkey, ready for stuffing. He's still fighting it though, craning his head around, gobbing thick lung butter in my direction, and it's disgusting so I kneel on his neck, grind his face into cream fibres. I think of New Year's and Karen as I carpet-burn his cheek.

Security arrives, carts him away. After that it's formality time. The bench find him guilty. A fine, probation. Hundred quid compensation to me for the eye injury. I'll never see it but couldn't care less – I'm not even listening any more. Not listening as the bald cop grumbles that I went overboard with Cooper. As Greg berates me for flowering up the evidence. My hands, for the first time ever after a ruck, they're trembling. I stare at them. I'm squeezing them into fists as Frank pats me on the shoulder, asks me if I'm okay, guides me out of the court. I pass the young blond guy at the door, see him scribbling notes into his pad. He looks up at me, squints behind his glasses as if examining some lab specimen.

'Seen enough, fucko?' I say, and the kid's right eye twitches.

Twitches just like my hands.

My hands. I can't make them stop.

	Property booked into store at Eastern ARV office. Ref **ZZ/20/778**.
0700	Off duty.
	Saturday 19th January
	Rest Day – Birthday!
1225	Code 35 (training @ The Elite). RV with The Frankster for a sesh. My arms, man!
1350	Home address. Discuss action plan for the day.
1440	Foot patrol city centre. Acquire halter top for wife.
1915	Code 50 – refs @ The Tidal restaurant. Didn't really go to plan, did it Jake? If you'd just listened to her on New Year's Eve you wouldn't be in this situat

FIVE

Thirty-eight today.

I'm starting to feel it. Thirty-eight: my father's age when it all happened. On this date, exactly twenty years ago. Some birthday this is likely to be. Some anniversary. Only five hours' sleep after a night turn, just so I can squeeze in some training, blow off some steam, before the endurance test that is Karen continuing to ignore me and the kids whining – I guarantee it – about what they'd rather do on *my* birthday.

To top it all, Rachael still hasn't replied to my texts or calls. I've had no messages and I need her. Where is she? Her shift ski trip ended three days ago and they're back in work tonight. I know this, I've checked.

I'm simmering already.

Finished, I unscrew the twenty-kilo plates, rack them. Four, six, eight of the things. The bar weighs fifteen at least and clangs as I drop it to the gymnasium floor. High-tensile steel, crosshatched for a better grip, thicker than my wrist to support whatever ridiculous amount I've been lifting. I bend over at the waist, nauseous. Ten sets of six reps. Increasing the load as I went, curling the bar to failure, curling it until my delts, my burning biceps, they just gave out.

Frank laughs as he watches my bent-over frame in the wall-length mirrors. The Elite is quiet, just a handful of regulars – monsters, pin-freaks, and I'm glad Sinclair isn't one of them because I don't have his money – lifting massive amounts behind me. Frank looks tiny in comparison. Jesus, *I* look tiny compared to some of the Human Growth Hormone giants in here.

'What's funny?' I ask him, looking upwards. Sweat hangs from the end of my nose.

'You. *"Eeeyaargh!"*' he says. 'What was all that about?'

I straighten, strip off my gloves. 'Effort.'

'It looked like an effort,' he says, slapping me on the shoulder. 'You is getting old, bra.'

Old? Don't be a cheeky bastard. Not today . . .

'Got to get the work in,' I say. 'Make the most of the gear. I'm on a bulking cycle.'

Today's stack: fifty milligrams of Dianabol. Half a mil of Arimidex to combat water retention and tender nipples. I've already got five hundred mils of Testosterone Enanthate and four hundred of Deca-Durabolin floating around in me.

Frank rolls his eyes. 'False economy, mate. Soon as you stop sticking needles in your arse you'll deflate and be like the rest of us. 'Cept you'll be covered in acne scars and your balls'll be half the size of mine.' He walks over to the bench press, slips medium plates onto each end of the bar.

I inspect myself in the mirrors. A couple of other lifters check me out, eyes on my torso. I move and twist at the waist, flex my forearms and see the welts across my deltoids and triceps under the torn fabric of my tatty vest top. Purple boils at my neckline, down my latissimus dorsi: they give a glimpse of themselves before darting back under cover. I didn't realise they were so prominent, so angry-looking. Must've been mixing up the dosage. It's embarrassing and, thanks to Frank, everyone in here knows about them now. But how does *he* know about my bollocks?

I'm vaguely aware of my nails digging into the flesh of my palm, but I don't feel pain, just dull and distant pressure as they pierce the skin. Frank lies back, begins quickly pumping about fifty-odd kilos over and over. Quick and clean jerks. Toning himself. Pussy style.

I whip off my weight belt, eyes on Frank as he stares at the ceiling. He puffs out air, puffs, puffs, puffs. I wrap the belt around my right hand, timing the loops to Frank's breathing. The thick leather covers my knuckles as I curl my hand into a fist.

Acne scars. Small bollocks. Getting old.

Where's Rachael? What's wrong with Karen? And why won't my bloody kids just *communicate* for once? It's my birthday after all. My fucking *birthday*.

I have static in my ears. All I see are Frankie's lips moving as he exhales.

His lips moving . . .

You cheeky fucker, Frank.

You cheeky, dirty . . .

'You going to spot me while you stand there, or what?' he asks suddenly.

I blink. The belt feels tight around my knuckles, buckle facing outwards, the chipped metal ready as the first point of impact.

'Jake?'

I'm right next to him – almost standing over him at his feet – but can't remember getting here. I find my arm drawn back, fist aimed squarely at Frank's throat. I look at the belt, at my knuckles, as if they belong to somebody else.

'Come *on*,' he says, eyes still on the ceiling. The tendons on his ripped forearms are wire cables beneath skin. 'Let's get this out of the way. I've got your birthday presents in the car. You're going to love them, mate.'

I drop my arm before Frank notices. Raise my belt-covered fist to my mouth. Bite down so hard my teeth cut through half a centimetre of leather.

Frank doesn't look at me as I move behind his head, lift the barbell from his hands. That trust. He gives himself to me. If

I wanted I could drop it, all seventy-odd kilos onto his windpipe. Crushing it.

It clangs as I drop it onto the rests.

'Thanks,' he says, sitting upright. He frowns at me. 'You okay?'

I swallow. 'Yeah,' I say, not really sure if I am at all. 'Like you said: getting old.'

Vietnam Encounter II: Charlie Don't Surf, two hundred Café Crèmes and the brand-new issue of *Foot Worship Monthly.*

A PlayStation game, duty-free box of miniature cigars and a fetish mag for my birthday. I *like*. Frank certainly knows what floats my boat. I felt a small pang of guilt as he handed them to me in The Elite car park then hugged me in a *Brokeback Mountain* style.

I wish my family were as enterprising. As thoughtful. I'm standing in the kitchen near the central island, waiting as Ben argues with his big sis over what they'd rather do for my birthday. I knew it: what *they* would rather do. Neither has asked me what I want. Karen's sitting on a stool at the breakfast bar, idly flicking through a newspaper, chocolate hair hiding her face. In eighteen days she's spoken precisely twelve words. Or rather, she's said *no* twelve times to questions I've asked: variations on: *are you speaking to me yet?, will you tell me what's wrong?* and *are you going to tell me what I've done?*

'But I want to go shoppiiiing,' whines Naomi.

Ben shakes his head. 'Nuh,' he says. 'You just wanna meet up with your mates or your boyfriend . . .'

'No I don't.'

'Er, *yeah.*'

I glance at the clock on the cooker: thirteen fifty hours.

This is going to be a very long day.

Karen drops off the stool, folds the newspaper and throws it between them. I can barely believe it when she speaks. 'It's y'dad's birthday,' she says. I note she doesn't look anywhere near me. 'Let him decide.'

Naomi and Ben look at me expectantly but I'm caught off guard. Karen walks back to her stool, slides a magazine from the rack near the bread-bin, resumes reading.

Is she starting to relent just because it's my supposed special day? Whatever the reason, I lose control of my faculties for a moment. Five minutes before she spoke my brain was thinking of a few hours in the pub watching Sky Sports with Frank, then out for a pizza with the *fambly* before back to the house, Karen to bed and me on the PlayStation while chain-smoking cigars. Simple, cheap, unfussy. Put Karen ignoring me to one side and just get on with it.

Now I'm thrown. Now I'm thinking: shopping, new clobber for Karen, pizza and film for the kids, swanky restaurant tonight – *sans* teenagers – where we'll bury the hatchet over several bottles of *vino* and she'll forgive whatever it is I've done. We'll laugh together for the first time in as long as I can remember. We'll come home, Naomi and Ben asleep, and fumble around on our bed like the good old days when we were just-married twenty-one-year-olds. It'll be top-up sex of course. That marriage-saver. Fucking to maintain equilibrium. To sate each other's appetite so neither goes a-wanderin'. At least, that's what it's meant to do.

'Yeah, let's go shopping,' I say, and pull out my mobile. Oddly, I'm quite excited.

Naomi shrieks with pleasure.

'Don't worry, mate,' I say to Ben. 'Domino's for you tonight.'

He brightens. 'Really?'

I nod, look towards Karen, her face still hovering over the

magazine. 'Your mother and I are going out for the night,' I say, and start searching dialled numbers on the mobile. At this she does look up. I can't tell if her open-mouthed expression is one of pleasant shock or mild horror. I decide on the former, but that could be misguided optimism.

The voice in my ear is East European. I bark the booking into my mobile, carefully enunciating each syllable so the clown'll understand: *eight pee em, tay-bull for two, Smith*. It's The Tidal. Seafood, wood floors, stark furnishings, low lights. Expensive. Karen's kind of place. I took Rachael there the week before she disappeared on her Christmas ski trip and the number's still in my phone. How convenient.

As I end the call I feel a flicker of anxiety: what if they recognise me? And now I'm with a different woman, ring on my wedding finger rather than looped on the dog tags around my neck for the night? I weigh up the odds. The Polish workers in there can barely string a sentence together in English anyway; Karen'll hardly be able to understand them, even before her regulation three drinks begin to take effect.

'Shopping at . . .' I say, and check the cooker clock again. 'Fourteen ten hours. That gives you twenty minutes.'

'That means ten past two to you, loser,' Naomi says to Ben.

He ignores her. There's a lot of that about in this house.

Karen sighs. She's off the stool, pulling her hair into a ponytail; a black hair-bobble is gripped between her teeth. She says nothing, follows the kids out of the room.

Think I'll get her something new to wear tonight.

Something red.

SIX

We are that couple you see in restaurants.

That couple tucked in one corner: her studying the menu for the thirteenth time; him sitting rigid and miserable with his hand cupping a warm tumbler of JD and Coke, its ice long melted, a glazed look in his eyes. Neither will speak, other than to thank the waitress as she offers them another chunk of granary bread from her wicker basket or pours more Sancerre.

You pray it never happens to you. You hope your relationship never reaches that depth, the one marked rock bottom. It's purgatory. A waste of time. The fun is . . . well, the fun is beginningless.

I never thought we'd end up this way. We never used to be like this and I don't know when life became a marriage-go-round of fractious mundanity. This is pointless. Karen and I could be at home ignoring each other. It'd be a damn sight cheaper and a lot less public.

The Tidal is full. I feel eyes on me. On us. Karen's not spoken a word since we waved goodbye to the kids an hour and a half ago, and she doesn't seem bothered in the slightest. Our empty dessert dishes are swept away. I can't bear this any longer.

'So?' I say and down my drink. The Coke is flat, like syrup. I signal for the Polack waitress to get me a refill.

Karen exhales. Checks her watch, says nothing. She's wearing the red halter top I bought this afternoon but has covered it with her favourite black cardigan, buttoned up to just below her neckline. Beneath our table, her feet are encased in dull leather boots.

'This is ridiculous,' I say. 'What was the point of coming here?'

She stares at me. 'I thought there was a very good point.'

Jesus. A sentence.

'Yes,' I say. 'It's my birthday. We're supposed to be—'

'No,' she interrupts, and I notice her teeth are grinding together. Her Northern accent is more pronounced, always a sure sign she's pretty miffed. 'Not *we*. It's nothing to do with *we*. It's supposed to be *you*. I need to know you finally *understand*.'

'I do understand. It's because you haven't spoken to me for three weeks.'

She sits back, eyes wide. 'So it's my fault?'

Yes. 'No.'

'You think it is, don't you? You think this . . . this miserable effort of a marriage is all down to me. Right?'

'I didn't say that. To be honest I have no idea what the prob—'

Karen jerks forward, jaw jutting out. There are scarlet blotches in the centre of her cheeks. Her neck is flushed. 'That's right, Jake. You have no idea. No bloody idea whatsoever.'

I find my fingernails scraping at the underside of the table. Scratch, scratch, scratch. I'm sure the hubbub of conversation from the other diners has lowered in volume. I don't want to turn around. One pair of eyes. If I see one pair of eyes looking at us . . .

'If this is about what you said at New Year's . . .' I say. 'I really can't remember. I'm sorry.'

She looks at me sadly. I detect a hint of disappointment, of incredulity there too. And her bottom lip is trembling now. She hesitates. I'm not sure if she's about to cry right here in the restaurant or if she's so angry she's choosing her words carefully.

'I can't do this,' she says then, and looks upwards, almost as if she's talking to somebody else. 'I'm not going over it again. I won't.'

Scratch, scratch. My fingernails scrape at the wooden table. It's starting to hurt but the pain seems a million miles away. 'What the fuck is it, Karen?'

She blinks, her head recoiling a little. 'It's just *you*, Jake,' she says finally. 'You've changed. You're not right lately. I really think you need help.'

It's as if she's suddenly deflated; the stiffness goes out of her. I feel blood trickling down my fingers and gathering in my upturned palm. I wipe it on the fringe of the tablecloth. Let the Polacks deal with it.

'Well that's really helpful, sweetheart,' I say. 'The usual one hundred per cent sound advice. Ninety-nine per cent sound, one per cent advice.'

The waitress, a reed-thin mousy blonde with a drawn and hollow-cheeked face, she's at my shoulder and coughing in that oh-so-polite way. I don't answer her when she asks me in her broken English if everything is all right.

'Oh, bravo,' says Karen. 'Know what? I bet you're just like your father.'

There's that white noise in my ears again. I swear I feel a nail tear loose. My hand comes up to my mouth and I bite down on the ragged skin at the tip of my middle finger. My blood in my mouth. Salt and iron and lukewarm heat.

The skeletal waitress is gone from my side. The restaurant is silent.

Karen is sitting opposite me with her jaw slack and mouth a perfect O.

I didn't even realise I'd screamed.

I don't know how I got here.

Twenty-one twenty hours, I'm at Rachael's nick with a bloodied white cloth wrapped around the tip of one finger. I tap in the entrance code, step through the rear door. Breathe in that old police station smell. Damp. Grime. A healthy dose of apathy, of weariness. With each step I'm more lucid. Calmer. These places are my sanctuary. My real home.

It's a hive of inactivity. Probably five plods on night duty if they're lucky. Jesus, when I used to work here on sector, we'd turn out fifteen bodies and go kick some arse. I honestly don't know where we've all gone. All the clueless bosses – those self-congratulatory politicos masquerading as police officers, those minority group schmoozers and politically correct hand-wringing pseudo-liberals who've ruined the job – they're tucked up in bed, preparing themselves to bollock someone – anyone – when they come into work after an untroubled night's sleep to find the wheel's come off.

I trawl the corridors and offices on the ground floor and there's nobody, just dust motes, forgotten files, radios gurgling to themselves like R2-D2, pieces of kit lying around that I think about stealing. Rachael's nowhere to be found, so I head upstairs, along the corridor to the parade room.

I stop in the doorway. Swallow. Watch.

Rachael's filling in some endless Home Office pro forma, probably because she had the temerity to stop-check an ethnic and now has to cover her back. The place is a dump. Tired, dirty, disorganised. The Police Farce in microcosm. Third-hand desks and antiquated computer equipment. Faded A4 information posters, most of which had already been hanging ignored for months when I last worked here years ago. *Stress management. Voting for your Union rep: twenty facts to get it right. Correct Posture: avoid back pain!* Home Office crime-recording procedure which changed before the flyer went up. *Neighbourhood Watch* crap. Information for the strawberry mivvies, the civvies who think they run this job, about ways to increase their earning potential. None of it relevant to front-line workers. Not one poster dedicated to the grunts.

There's mugshots of local sector targets pinned to a corkboard: so-and-so the prolific autocrime merchant, whats-is-name the dwelling burglar, Kyle-who-cares the street robber of students' mobile phones. All fresh turds from the factory. Scowls and cheap haircuts, fucked-up teeth and sunken eyes. Juvie scrotes, sons of men I was locking up on this patch a decade ago. Offspring of their useless villain fathers, taught nothing other than to suck at society's teat while wailing *they* are the victims.

Behind Rachael, typing away on a computer keyboard, is the FNG on her shift.

The Fucking New Guy. The sprog, proby, YTS cop. I've had the misfortune to suffer his small-talk when he's been on cordon at firearms jobs. He's cocky. Smart-mouthed. A three-month-in cherry who talks like a seasoned veteran, typical of the new breed of arrogant plods. I've got bloody biros with more service. And I never could remember his name at first, just referred to him as Seal Pup because all I wanted to do was club him to death.

Clive Someone-or-other. Your straight-off-the-production-line clone we get nowadays. Standard height, weight, temperament. A pretty-boy, all hair gel and soft good looks, can reel off word-perfect policy and procedure, law and statutes learned by rote, but no *feel* for the job. Nothing warm about him at all. Fifteen years younger than me – nearer Rachael's age – but give it time and I'll probably be calling him 'sir'.

I stand in the doorway for a minute. My breath stinks of bourbon.

Rachael's blonde hair is pulled back into the regulation bun, pen tucked behind her ear. She's tanned, has caught the sun on the slopes. Looks healthy, relaxed. But now it's time to get back on track.

I think of the run-up to Christmas. The screaming matches with Karen. The finger-pointing; telling me this obsession with my parents was dragging the family down. How she didn't want to hear it any more. That I should get over it or leave her alone until I did. Then the night out with the Tac Team. The beer. So much beer. Bumping into a drunken Rachael at her shift do. Flirting with the newbie policewoman, dazzling her with tales of specialist ops, knowing she'd made the classic mistake of becoming bewitched by an older, glamorous officer. I was flattered, got carried away, knew it was wrong but couldn't stop myself as we staggered here after I told her it'd be easier to book a taxi from the nick. I needed the company. I needed *someone*.

I glance across to the radio room. Picture Rachael bent over so I couldn't see her face, so she could be anyone, my hands pulling her backwards and onto me by the hem of her party dress, by her skinny hips, her black high heels clacking on the floor, fingers clawing at the chipped desktop, at radio cables, gasping in dust from a pile of unopened boxes stuffed with obsolete force paperwork as I cried quietly behind her.

And the next night, at her flat after The Tidal, more comfortable with the guilt now, pushing the envelope a little, letting her know what turned me on, her face wary as I told her what I wanted to do to her feet, her gamely letting me suck her toes as we fucked, then going the whole hog and asking her if she'd trample my balls while I masturbated – but it was a too-much too-soon, too big a thing for her to handle on a second date, and it didn't end well . . .

Rachael's finished the stop-check chitty, leans backwards in her chair to look over it. Clive stops typing at the same time, arches his back. *Pop-pop-pop* goes his spine as he stretches, yawns. I hold my breath: their shoulders, an epaulette each, are almost touching.

'Is that you?' Rachael asks him, not looking away from the pro forma.

Clive gives a weird sort of half-laugh, half-gasp. *Tcheheh*. 'All that exercise on the slopes, I'm suffering,' he says. 'Maybe I'm getting old.' He's rolling his shoulders and neck as he witters; I note he doesn't have his tie clipped on, the scruffy bastard. If I was his stripy he'd be in the disciplinary book, quick-time.

'Believe me, I *know* old,' Rachael giggles, still not looking at him.

Still not noticing I'm in the doorway.

'This is all very cosy,' I say. It's like I've shot my Glock into the ceiling.

'Jake,' says Rachael, quickly shuffling paperwork.

'Hello, stranger,' I say. 'Nice holiday?'

'Ah . . . hey, Jake,' says Clive. I note with satisfaction his Adam's apple is pistoning.

'Cliff,' I say, without looking at him. I'm staring at Rachael. Her wide blue eyes, darting around to avoid mine.

'It's Clive, actually,' he says, and I know this but don't care.

Cliff. Cheeky Little Insignificant Fucking Faggot. Know your place, boy.

'You got two minutes?' I ask Rachael. 'Got to discuss that . . . case file with you.'

She nods silently, follows me out into the corridor. Clive, Cliff, he watches her go.

I close the door to the writing room. Rachael looks up at me; she's agitated, nervous.

'I'm really busy, Jake,' she says, her voice low and breathy and quite possibly irritated, as if my unannounced visit is rather bothersome.

'Why haven't you answered my calls?'

'Why've you come here?' she says in her fabulous tough-girl voice. 'Did you drive in that state? You could get yourself into trouble. You could get *me* into trouble.'

Bless her for caring. But I shrug anyway. 'Who's going to tug me for a breath test on the way home? You? Every copper in this city knows who I am.'

Rachael shakes her head. 'What's . . . what've you done to your finger?'

My finger? Ah, my finger. I raise my hand, unravel the bloodied cloth, see it's a table napkin with a name printed along one edge in tasteful font: *The Tidal*.

The restaurant. I've abandoned Karen. Shit.

'It's my birthday,' I say, as if this will explain somehow.

'Congratulations,' Rachael says flatly.

I flash the napkin again. 'Remember going there?' I say. 'Good times, right?'

She sighs. 'Yes. Good times.'

Ah, a chink of light. I could salvage the evening here. Got to be worth a go: 'I thought maybe we could disappear to the toilets for five minutes,' I say, smiling. 'Replay that night before Christmas?'

'Jake . . .' she hisses, checking around. There's just the two of us here in the corridor, though I'm pretty sure Cliff has his standard-sized, perfect-hearing ear pressed up against the other side of the writing-room door.

My fingers toy with the zip on my trousers. 'Well, get your boots off then,' I say, and lower the zip, slip my hand inside my boxers. 'I'll give you a quick foot spa.'

'I'm not into that, Jake. I told you. It's . . . you're not what I thought.'

She's lying. 'We're good together. Come *on*, Karen.'

'*Karen*? Who . . .? Is that your wife? And will you please take your hand out of your pants?'

This isn't going well. I've already clearly buggered it with Karen and any designs I had on a bit of nonsense with Rachael are swiftly going south. I recalibrate, think what I could do next if this pans out as I'm expecting. You've always got to have a Plan C.

'I've slipped away to see you,' I say anyway, going for the emotive approach as a last resort. 'To see *you*. Don't you know how hard that is for me? Who d'you think you are, blanking me? Blanking *me*?'

Her face is twisted, as if she's revolted. 'Leave it, will you, Jake? Please? It was a bit of fun. Christmas fun . . .'

Blown off. On my birthday. If it wasn't for Plan C I'd be getting a little more agitated than I already am. 'I'll call around the flat tomorrow then,' I say, zipping myself up.

'Don't,' she says. She's shaking her head, shaking it over and over with her eyes closed. 'It was just a bit of fun . . .'

'Tomorrow,' I say. 'For my birthday.'

Eqa Enquiries at Clinton Street station.

Attempt to speak with Rachael but obstructive/uncooperative. Just what is going on with her now? Four weeks. Over four weeks since we spent time together. ~~And that fucking weasel off~~ = I could beat that tosser to a pulp, I really ~~could~~ Appointment made to RV at her home address tomorrow to discuss matters and clarify state of our relationship/reason for complete lack of respect/understanding.

SEVEN

'What's up, bra?' I say.

It's twenty-two fifteen. Plan C is in effect. Frank swings his front door back with a groan. He's wearing some strange baby blue towelling T-shirt-and-pants combo with leather moccasin slippers. It's very fetching.

'You're drunk, Jake,' he says, eyeing my wagon and then the items I'm carrying. His eyes taper behind his specs.

I glance down. Tesco carrier bags in both hands, bloodied napkin hanging from my left index finger. Empty Stella bottles chime against the I-can't-remember-how-many unopened ones inside the bags. I'm not sure why I brought the dead ones with me.

'I always said you should be a detective,' I say.

'Mel's going to go nuts.'

'Ah, Frosty Bollock,' I say, raising the carriers. 'Fancy a beer?'

'For fuck's sake,' he says, closing the door behind me.

His wife is sitting on a sofa in the lounge, wrapped in a matching female version of Frank's ensemble, but in light pink. A DVD is paused, Hugh Grant's cretinous floppy-haired face frozen on Frankie's widescreen.

I recognise the film straight away and despair. '*Notting Hill*,' I say. 'Mmm, nice one, Frankster.'

'Well I like it,' says Mel. 'And we *were* enjoying it.'

Mel's feet are bare but she's got bunions and freakishly long little toes; I have to clamp my teeth together and swallow as my mouth floods with saliva. How Frank can even be with this woman is beyond me. It's all I can do not to retch.

'Frank,' she says, waving a hand at the television.

'Oh,' I say, clinking my lagers. 'Am I interrupting?'

Frankie looks at his wife, pulls a *what-can-you-do?* face. 'It is his birthday, hon.'

'So why isn't he celebrating it with Karen?' she asks.

'Good point, Frosty,' I say.

Frank rocks his head back, rolls his eyes. It's a tumbleweed moment.

Mel's not a happy bunny. 'Here to smash up some more of my house, are you?' she says, and stands. 'I think I'll call it a night.'

'No,' I say. 'Please stay.'

Please go. Your feet are making me ill.

Mel tugs at the neck of her flannel T-shirt. She looks at Frank and I see his eyes doing the same as Rachael's in the writing room. Evasion. He's in trouble just for letting me in here so might as well go the whole hog. Might as well get rid of Mel and deal with the consequences in the morning.

She waits a few seconds. I say nothing, let this mini-drama play out. Frank is looking at the carpet, the television – anywhere but Mel. I know he wants one of the bottles I'm carrying. I know him better than his own wife does.

'I'll go to bed then,' Mel says.

'Cool beans,' I say.

She bristles but I ignore it. She knows I'm ignoring it.

'Just make sure Jess is home at the time we agreed, Frank,' she says, and glares at me. 'And make sure *he* doesn't smoke those stinking cigars in here.'

Frank nods. I can tell he's holding his breath.

Jess. Jessica. 'She not home, then?' I ask.

Frank shakes his head. 'No.'

'Oh,' I say, and try not to look as gutted as I feel.

'She's out with friends,' says Mel, yanking open the

lounge door. 'Which gives you pair of idiots plenty of time to get drunk and swap war stories before she comes home, doesn't it?'

She slams the door. I'd mentally dismissed her some time before.

'Oh,' I say to Frank. 'This going to cause you problems?'

He sits. Stares at the floor for a few seconds. Then: 'Just give me a bottle.'

Twenty-three twenty-five hours.

We're slugging Stella and watching *Platoon*. Watching those sweaty GIs yomp through the jungle and we're whooping and yelling, deep in the boondocks alongside them, just as hot and sticky as they are but thank God we've got the booze to cool us down.

Me and Frankie, we're tunnel rats. Specialist grunts, just waiting for Charlie to show his little face, for the call-up from the top, from the LT – the lieutenant – to send us in and sort out their unholy mess, to save everybody else. I wish I'd brought my PlayStation. We could've doubled-up on *Vietnam Encounter II* after the film.

'Let's clear this LZ motherfucker,' I say to nobody in particular, hoping it's loud enough for Mel to huff and puff upstairs. 'Get our skinny GI asses into those ratholes and flush 'em out. Into the open so we can bust some caps, man! Clear the *ville* of the goddam Vietcong!'

I turn to Frankie but he's flagging on the opposite sofa. He's drunk one lager to every two of my own, is on the verge of dozing off in his baby-gro. Lightweight.

I'm about to go shake him when I hear keys in the front door.

I chug the last of my bottle, shove it onto the glass-topped coffee table, nudge it across to Frank's side where the rest of his empties stand. You awful drunken father, you. I tense my pecs. They bulge against the tight fabric of my shirt. Pumped. Swollen. Ready. Hold the pose.

'Hey, Jake,' she says. 'How's it going?'

Sweeeet Jeeesus.

I hear the swell of choral music. Something like Bach's *Saint Matthew Passion* at the climax of Scorsese's *Casino*. She's at the lounge door and everything drags. A movie cliché. Slow-motion time. I smell alcohol and citrus perfume. She's drunk; not stupid binge-drinking drunk but enough to qualify as pleasantly mullered. Eyes slightly bloodshot. She's had strange red-purple streaks layered into the dirty blonde hair that falls around her shoulders.

'Hey, Jess,' I say, trying hard to sound nonchalant. She looks at her slumped father as I drink her in.

Jessica's wearing a glittery silver vest, the minuscule straps looped over her tanned and bony shoulders. No bra, small breasts moving freely beneath the cloth, a glorious nipple-on from the cold. Belly-button piercing, some dull metal bar with balled ends. Black shorts that would be hard-pushed to qualify as anything other than underwear given the amount of skin covered, they cling to her rock-hard thighs like they're sprayed onto her flesh. Despite the sub-zero temperature she hasn't bothered with tights. While she studies Frankie – who's now snoring quietly on the sofa – I sneak a look downstairs to see she's wearing a fabulously funky pair of black diamanté high-heeled mule sandals.

I've never seen her feet before. I thank the Toe Lords she hasn't inherited her mother's gnarly monstrosities and fall in love with her all over again. They're tiny, slender – about a size five by my eye – and I imagine how soft they would be to rub my hands against, how enjoyable it would be to lick and kiss her teenage heels. Her big toes coil upwards, the nails painted a deep black. I could suck those things right now. Give them a good old shrimping.

'Why don't you let me help you with that?' I hear her say, and follow her gaze down to my lap.

It's so sudden.

My trousers are undone, my hand on my erection. This is better than the script of the worst porn film. Minimal exposition. Straight action. All it needs is a Barry White song to cap it off.

'Yeah,' I say, *Platoon* running in the background. I can barely breathe. 'Finish me off, baby. Put your feet on it.'

Jessica moves towards me, kicks off her sandals. They fall against the legs of the coffee table with a quiet thunk. She's at the edge of the sofa, calf brushing mine, lifting one foot into the air. It drops gently and she places the heel at the top of my thigh, works her toes into my pubic hair.

'Why've you got a hankie on your finger?' she asks.

I shake my head. No, no, no. This isn't in the script. I hear Frankie snoring somewhere nearby. 'That's right, Jess,' I urge her. 'Good girl.'

'What?' Jessica asks. I can tell without opening my eyes she's amused. 'Are you drunk, Jake?'

I heave my eyelids upwards, glance around. Frank's copping zeds on the opposite sofa. *Platoon* is still playing. I look up, to my right. Jessica hasn't moved from the doorway, is standing there studying me, her eyes cat-like, the long lashes thickened with black liner *à la* Raquel Welch in *One Million Years B.C.*

'I said, are you drunk?'

My napkin-covered finger is on my crotch, the buttons still done up. Where was I?

'It's not a hankie,' I say, and lift my left hand to show her. 'It's a napkin from a posh restaurant. *Actually*.'

'Jess?'

There's phlegm and a cough. Frank's awake. He shoots to his feet and I lift my right hand from my groin just in case. Jessica's still watching me, eyes narrowed.

'You,' Frank says to me, finger waggling in accusatory circles as he blinks behind his glasses. 'Sleep on the sofa again. No driving tonight.'

I lob him the keys to my truck, look at Jess. 'I'm not going anywhere.'

Frankie. My good friend Frankie. Leave me here for a while. Get thyself to bed so I can root your daughter.

He gives a bizarre salute and walks towards the lounge door. I watch as he kisses Jessica on the cheek in that way fathers do; she proffers her face to him and half grimaces like any good teenage daughter would. I can't remember the last time Naomi let me do such a thing.

'So,' I say as the lounge door closes.

'So,' says Jessica, standing over me.

The film's still running in the background. In work, at home, with Frank, I always know just what to say. Now, I have no clue.

'D'you want to . . . y'know, watch this for a bit?' I ask, pointing at the widescreen. I am a teenager trying to unclasp his first bra. 'It'd be nice if you stayed for a while.'

And then I watch those cat-eyes move slowly down to my crotch, where my hand was when she walked in. 'Yeah,' she says, and there's no hint of embarrassment; more coquettish confidence. 'I bet you think it would.'

I don't know what to say. I've had this scenario in my head for so long and now . . .

I slump deeper into the sofa as she paces around me, kicks off her sandals for real and walks barefoot across the lounge. It's torture. She goes into the kitchen, gets a glass of water, crosses back in front of me.

'Stay, Jess,' I say, trying for casual but probably well wide of the mark. 'You could catch the end of the film . . .'

She's at the lounge door, half in the hallway, ready to go upstairs. Hand on the door handle. 'No,' she says, and tips the brim of her glass towards me with a wink. 'Because if I did . . .'

And I want her to finish the sentence. I want her to move this scenario along because I don't have the balls to. I wish I could say something so she'd stay just a little longer and I could take something from this miserable day.

Instead I watch her go, the door closing, machine guns and explosions sounding quietly behind me on the television. I hear her soft footsteps up the stairs and then I'm alone again.

So I wait for ten minutes, make sure the house is asleep. Get up from the sofa, check the shelf beneath the coffee table, remove the item I've seen so many times before. The fail-safe.

Because the pluses to having a foot fetish are legion. It can be a flesh fair, especially in summer. A myriad paint jobs on toenails. Ankle bracelets, toe rings. You walk around looking and none of them knows. In work, off duty, whenever. They just don't think you'd be checking them out in that way. That you're feeling the first stirrings of an erection while waiting in the queue at the cigarette counter, staring down at the twenty-something's feet in front of you. That you're at a call, some crock-of-shit drugs warrant where you're the firearms entry team, where the young girl in the flat is cuffed, sitting barefoot and cross-legged on the sofa while her place is searched and all you can look at is the curl of her big toe.

Then there're the visual aids. The shoe section in a Marks & Spencer catalogue is pure porn, negating the need to embarrass yourself buying top-shelf smut in the local newsagent's. Go home, flip it open in the comfort of your bedroom, choose a selection of slingbacks picturing smooth fleshy heels, a range of open-toed sandals that show bright red nail varnish, a choice of ink-black stilettos to provide a hint of bony skin at the top of the foot.

Slip some real porn into the DVD player if you wish. For ambience.

I get myself comfortable on the sofa, flip through Mel's Next Directory. Find the women's shoe section. Thank Christ it's the spring/summer edition. Bare feet aplenty.

I think of Karen. Of Rachael, Jessica. Of a girl in red on a frozen street at New Year.

	Sunday 20th January
	Karen incommunicado — 19 days?
1100	Recall to duty (less than three days notice so look out guys, here comes another failed fucking overtime claim) re. Operation Attleboro
	Controlled drugs warrant/arrest of murder suspect Tang YEH on behalf of Metropolitan police w. firearms team.
1120	Briefing @ Headquarters. OIC DCI Harrison, Drug Squad North.
	Callsign FX11 — team of two with PC 977 Frank MacReady.
	ARV vehicle one. Load: 2 X Heckler & Koch MP5 A3, 2 X Glock 9mm, L104A1 Baton Gun, X26 Taser. Method of entry/distraction inc.
	percussion grenades (4) and Remington 12-gauge shotgun w. breaching rounds. Less lethal options (CS Incapacitant Spray, Friction-lock baton)
1210	RV point, outer cordon. Tactical team briefing.
1515	* Retrospective notes completed after entry/search of premises * At 1225hrs Sunday 20th January, in co. with PC 977 MacReady, I forced entry to premises at 94 Chapel Row, Canningtown using dynamic entry technique (two rounds of shotgun ammunition to breach locks). Necessary/appropriate to maintain element of surprise/ensure security of evidence. Upon entering I noticed multiple rows of what appeared to be cannabis plants, along with full hydroponic equipment. All rooms on the ground & first floors were in a similar state re. plants and lighting. I then entered the rear second floor bedroom to find

EIGHT

Today's outfit:

ATLAS Assault coveralls with Namex III flash-resistant fabric and Kevlar reinforcement patches on the knees, elbow and groin; Damascus Imperial neoprene knee pads; Damascus Imperial 'Hardshell' elbow pads; 5.11 Tac-Ak Tactical Application gloves with Kevlar; spare Blackhawk HellStorm Light Operations gloves; Lava Combat GTX boots; Web-Tex Cross-Draw Vest for cartridges and percussion grenades, along with Maglite LED 4D cell torch, plasticuffs, Velcro leg restraints, Gerber multi-tool and normal Kwik-Cuffs in a Fobus cuff-case; 5.11 'Field Ops' Sniper Watch; Viper 3-point rifle sling, modified to hold my pump-action; Bianchi UM92 Military Holster for the Glock; Blackhawk HellStorm Poly-Pro Tactical Balaclava; Bulldog customised ballistic body armour; Avon FM12 Respirator coupled with an Anson ATLAS flame-retardant Avon Respirator cover; ATLAS Ballistic Helmet which offers ballistic *and* blunt trauma protection; Gorilla Bar for method of entry and a collapsible 'Quickstep' ladder, both strapped to my back.

All in black. I look cool as fuck. Imposing. Intimidating. A futuristic street-warrior. RoboJake, and you've got twenty seconds to comply. Only problem is I can barely move.

I glance around the industrial estate car park. The gang's all here. Full Tac Team for dynamic entry. Dog handlers. Beat bobbies to clear up the mess after we're done. Drug squad and CID, half of them suited in their Primark polyester best with so-called bulletproof ties flapping in the wind, rest of them scruffed up and smoking hand-rolled cigarettes to, y'know, be down with the junkies.

Paramedic wagon, a guy 'n' girl team of two sipping tea from a flask, chatting away with a Pointlessness of Police Community Support Officers.

Fire crew, the Trumptons, the little water fairies in their shiny red truck looking pissed off about being called out in the middle of their Sunday roast.

And there's some bewildered electrician with his plans and schematics, his meter readings for the target house where the power consumption is higher than the rest of the street combined. Bet he never expected this when he tipped us off about a spike in the readings. Let's hope the sparky's not Brazilian, or a de Menezes sympathiser. Just make sure you cut the power, matey. Don't want to be fried by a booby trap when I blow the front door off its hinges.

All these people. All this fuss. Christ, even Tommy Hall's managed to drag his lardy behind out into the fresh air.

These last-minute jobs. Cobbled together so the self-important detective wallahs can create a bit of excitement when they have to work a rare weekend. For a stupid cannabis factory run by a Triad gangster's lackey. If this goes tits-up with no booty recovered or body in the cells at the end of all the expense, some ESSO, an Every Saturday and Sunday Off desk jockey from the Senior Management Team, will refuse my overtime claim. Just because they can.

When my mobile went off at oh-nine hundred, I thought it might be Karen. Instead I got Dave Collingwood, the Firearms Inspector, calling me into work on a rest day. I don't know what I was more disappointed about: that it wasn't Karen offering her humble apologies for shooting her mouth off about my old man, or the fact I had to get myself into work – still drunk – with Jess catching zeds. Would've been nice to see her before I left.

My lungs feel swamped with oil. Must've smoked about twelve miniatures on Frank's patio last night after Jessica went to bed and I'd finished with Mel's catalogue. A sofa's no substitute for the king-size at home and my back's in no fit state to carry this weight. My stomach's doing flip-flops. I don't feel right. Not sure if it's anticipation, nerves or the protein shakes I necked at the station while I was kitting up. One chocolate. One strawberry. Then a pint of powdered creatine and six tablets of branch-chain amino acids. The cocktail isn't sitting well with last night's Stella, that's for sure.

Collingwood's droning on but I'm barely listening.

Every one of you up to speed on the intelligence, floor plans and entry?

I've got a bad feeling about this.

Have any of you been drinking in the last twenty-four hours?

Shake your head, Jake. Make it match your hands.

Are any of you experiencing problems in your private life that may be stressful?

Life's a ball at the mo, Dave. I wonder if I've got lager cancer?

And then it's through the I.I.M.A.R.C.H. system: information, intention, method, administration, risk-assessment, communications, human bloody rights. Health and safety. Weapon procedure. Which team's on where. What's expected of each duo. Protection of any suspects is paramount. I tune him out, adopt the default position: nod, frown, look like you're sucking it all in. Then just do whatever the fuck you want to do.

'Are you clear, Smithy?'

What? Oh. 'Yessir,' I say, saluting.

The Inspector's looking right at me. Everyone's staring, even Frank.

'You taking the piss?' he asks.

'Erm . . . sorry,' I say, lowering my hand.

He's ex-forces, is Collingwood. Small and hairy but rotund and with an air of menace. The sort that looks like he beats his wife, if he has one. Reminds me of a walking testicle. Heard a whisper long ago he might be ex-Special Air Service, but of course he'd never admit it. All I know is he barks at everyone like he's under heavy fire and needs artillery support ay-sap, even when he's ordering pie 'n' mash at the station canteen. Get over yourself, sonny. This isn't *Bravo Two Zero*. This ain't Khe Sanh or Saigon. Let's just get this freak show on the road so I can go home, pull a quilt over my head and pretend the world doesn't exist.

'You and MacReady,' he says, gesturing at me. 'You're on white. Understand?'

Front of house. Door-knocking duo. I nod again. Frankie's ducking his nut next to me.

'Sir,' Frank says, 'do we even know chummy's in there? I mean, all this performance for one bloke . . .'

Collingwood swaggers over like Frank's his other half and he's about to give him a shoeing for questioning his washing-up prowess. 'Have you been listening at all this morning, you pair of mongoloids?'

Mongoloid? If it wasn't for mortgage payments I'd stick my head on his nose.

'Course we have, boss,' Frank says.

'This guy,' he says, and checks to make sure everyone else is listening. 'This guy Tang Yeh is *serious*. The Met have been looking for him since last October after he shot an ex-business associate through the eyeball. The weapon he used hasn't been recovered. That's why there's . . .' and I wince as he gives us air-quotes with two fingers of each hand. ' . . . "*this performance*". All right, Smithy?'

No. No I'm not. If I'm honest with myself I feel a little . . . off-kilter.

Collingwood's in the groove, really selling it, polishing the turd to buggery. 'Plain clothes have done drive-bys so there's no need for an investigative assessment by us,' he says, stepping from me to Frank to the other members of the contact team, jabbing a fat and hairy little thumb at each of us as he goes. He begins counting off on his stubby fingers: 'A car we know Yeh's rented is parked outside. Our informant has given us the nod and puts him at the premises alone as of now. Chopper's done a flyover, plenty of heat from the house. And intelligence says this fella has been parachuted into town to look after the family cannabis business until the London fuss dies down.'

I say nothing. Think of the oxymoron that is police intelligence. Raise my gloved hands a-ways. Just a little, so nobody else notices.

Even though they're enclosed in Kevlar, I can see they're trembling.

NINE

I speed through Canningtown towards the target house in an unmarked car with Frankie.

This hillside village was built around a coal mine that died thirty years ago and nobody seems to have noticed. Street after tired terraced street, houses blackened with rainwater mould, refuse sacks stockpiled against front doors like sandbag defences. The satnav girl robot-talks her directions and I follow, but I could be anywhere. Everything's the same. I wonder what people do to pass the time: no shops, no pubs, no cinema. There's nothing, just an eerie sense of abandonment, of an extended death rattle where no one's bothered to tell the fools living here that the gig is up.

Frankie checks the satnav display. 'Nearly there,' he says, taking off his glasses and rolling down his balaclava. He winks at me through an eyehole. 'Nearly *Big Fun Time.*'

I'm so damn hot in all this kit despite the January weather. Just wrenching the steering wheel about makes sweat bead on my temples. The tip of my still-bloody finger chafes against the inside of my glove. Both hands are at it again. Trembling. It won't go away. It's pissing me off. Unnerving me. I whack up the air-con, swerve towards a couple of mongrel dogs fighting over a shit-stained nappy lying in the gutter.

'What a rush,' Frank's saying. 'What a *buzz.*'

'Yeah,' I say, swallowing.

At least he's getting a kick out of it. Of being tooled up and screaming about like *The Sweeney*. We're lead vehicle. In the rear-view I see the support cars, three of them, following in convoy. I'm starting to wish I was back there. Even back behind the cordon.

'Da-dum-de-dum-daaa-daah, dum-de-dum-DAAAAAA-DAAAAH!' hollers Frank, and I jump as he punches the roof of the car and hoots with laughter. He eyes me through the lenses of his respirator. 'It's *Apocalypse Now* time, buddy!' he shrieks, voice high and muffled by rubber. 'We're Lieutenant Colonel Kilgore's Air Cav choppering out of the sun! Get me to that Vietcong village, Jakey-boy!'

He's loving it. And so he should be, right? This is how it normally goes. What we usually do. These places are our jungle. Our rice paddy. Our bunker complex. We're jolly green giants walking tall through the boonies and nobody can ever stop us. Except something's not right. I don't feel like walking tall anywhere. The shake in my hands has spread to my thighs.

Frank's checking comms in his headset as I yank the gear-stick down into second, drop the clutch, spin into Chapel Row.

'Keep going, keep going,' says Frankie, urging me on with a gloved hand. 'The house is at the block end.'

I double-park. Yeh's hooch sits near the edge of this miserable old identikit row of terraces. I adjust my radio earpiece, unclip the Remington 870 from the door panel, pull down my balaclava. Jam the respirator over my head, listen to the sound of my breathing.

I'm a bad-ass asthmatic Darth Vader. A black-clad angel of death with a touch of emphysema.

There's a burst of static, then Frankie's tinny voice is inside my left ear.

'*Foxtrot X-Ray One-One to Gold Command,*' he says. His MP5 sub is butt-down in the footwell between his knees. '*We are closed at scene, over.*'

'Roger One-One. Target has been placed in upper floor of premises. Policy is still Priority One. All teams in position. Proceed to contact.'

Frank screams: 'Yippee-ki-ay motherfucker!'

Engine off. Door open. Ballistic helmet on. Shotgun cradled and safety off.

Breathe. *Breathe.*

Frankie looks at me, transmits: 'Confirm this is a go, Gold?'

Come on, Collingwood, you dick.

In my ear: 'Confirm, Foxtrot X-Ray One-One. This is a go. Proceed to white.'

Cher-chuk. I pump the bottom-loader on the 870: one breaching round feeds into the pipe from the tubular magazine. Lock 'n' load, right?

It's slo-mo time again. A movie scene, something from John Woo or Michael Bay or that reliable ol' fruitcake Olly Stone. A sideways tracking shot perhaps, following Frank and me as we round the unmarked car, all sweat and low sun and cooler-than-cool outfits, surrounded by fluttering skybound white doves, and then we swing our weapons towards Yeh's hidey-hole, mount the pavement.

Quick cut to handheld camerawork at normal speed, chasing behind as we sprint to the front door, kinetic wobbles for that visceral feel so the audience think they're in the thick of the action.

It'd be pretty awesome but for the tightness in my chest.

I throw my body against the front wall of the target house; Frankie flits across the doorstep to the opposite side, presses himself against the mottled brickwork. We look up. Second nature. Training. Autopilot. The blacked-out window directly above the front door. Always watch for that friendly neighbourhood fridge being dropped on your noggin.

And so this is it. I blink behind the eyepieces of my

respirator, feel sweat on my chest. My roiling, choppy stomach is full of sweet milkshake and old lager, of sickening adrenalin. Scorched lungs. Crusted fingertip. A domestic outcast.

It hits me.

I'm in no fit state to be here. But it's too late. I've let myself get swept along with it again. Just got to keep up the facade, Jake. Got to keep plugging away. Got to keep—

'Let's go!'

Frank's voice over my ragged, metallic breath. My gloved fingers tighten around the synthetic stock of the shotgun. I'm flat against the wall, Gorilla Bar digging into my shoulder blades, the pump-action across my sternum.

'Jake?'

Faces in the house windows opposite. I'm taking too long. The natives are curtain-twitching. Soon they'll be out on their doorsteps and Gold'll pull the plug. And it'll be my fault.

Collingwood, in my ear: '*Foxtrot X-Ray One-One, power to the premises has been cut. Foxtrot X-Ray One-Five is on plot at the rear and covering black. Can you confirm breach?*'

I'm not breathing. Houston, we have a problem.

The support cars block the road behind us, set up as the perimeter group. I look towards Frankie, his Heckler & Koch submachine gun raised, safety off, black leather finger looped through the trigger-guard and pressing on the trigger itself. His eyes are wide and on me.

'*Hoo-aaaah!*' he shouts, thumping a fist against his chest. '*Go, go, go!*'

The house is covered front and rear. Everybody's ready . . . except me. I can't get my lungs to work. My quads, my thighs, they're spazzing out uncontrollably, shivering like I'm squatting two-hundred k to failure at The Elite.

This is new. Something for the mobile-phone cameras

behind the net curtains: a shotgun-wielding six-foot-five stormtrooper falling to his knees and blubbing like an anklebiter that doesn't want to play any more. Just imagine that posted on the web. My career flushed down the YouTube.

'Jake,' Frank hisses, and he lunges for me, grabs the edge of my body armour. 'Get a grip, bra. We gotta get in there . . .'

Collingwood's caught the transmission. Along with everyone on the open channel. 'What the hell's going on down there, Smithy?' he shouts, his voice stabbing at my eardrum.

'Frankie,' I say. 'What . . . what am I doing?'

Frank's looking up at me. His hands are curled around and behind my ballistic vest, pulling me down to him so I can see his bugged-out eyes through the fogged glass of his breather.

'C'mon, Jake . . . not now,' he says. 'Not in front of the whole world, mate.'

Breathe, lungs. Please breathe.

'Foxtrot X-Ray One-One, I repeat, I want an urgent update. Immediately.'

Update: I'd like to shoot you, Collingwood.

'Jake, let's do this,' says Frank, pulling me closer. We are mask-to-mask, eyepiece-to-misty-eyepiece, nuclear-fallout lovers. 'Think of the 'Nam. A real man's war, right? Isn't that what you always tell me? What would those grunts do, eh? Wouldn't they just walk on into the ville?'

He releases me. Please don't let go, Frank. Never let go.

''Nam . . .' I say, and force a breath. 'Hoo-aah . . .'

I swing the Remington around to Yeh's door.

Frankie watches me for a second. 'Atta boy,' he says.

'Rock 'n' fuckin' roll . . .' I say, and try to make my eyes look like I'm smiling.

The recoil. It slams the butt of the pump-action into my right pec, throws my shoulder backwards, makes me stagger. I steady myself. Stare at the first ruined door hinge. My ears ring as if with tinnitus. I shuck the bottom-loader, feed in another breacher. Aim. Fire. The second round takes out most of the top of the door; shrapnel splinters ping off my helmet.

Frankie transmits, his screeched words bleeding into one another as he shoes the wrecked door, makes entry at a crouch with his MP5 shoulder-ready: '*Foxtrotxrayone-oneconfirmbreach!*'

I hear notes from a bass guitar, a hypnotic rhythmic finger-plucking.

The opening bars of Jefferson Airplane's 'White Rabbit'. Psychedelic, man. *Platoon* time.

I am calm.

I follow Frank into the house.

Oh yeah.

This must be what it was like for them.

Gloom. Greenery. The smell of exotic alien foliage, your heart pumping like a cokehead who's just done five lines and needs peeling off the ceiling.

Those GI boys in the 'Nam. Terrified but getting on with it. That's where I'm at. That's where I am right now. All I have is the light from the broken front door, Frank squatting and sweeping in front of me, my own breathing in my ears.

The stench of the plants feeds through my breather.

And the music in my head.

The guitar's been overlaid with a rolling military drumbeat. I pan the Remington back and forth, looking for the suspect. The intelligence was bang on for once: there must be at least two hundred cannabis bushes on the ground floor alone.

Ganja. Weed. Blow. Puff. If it was Stanozolol or Trenbolone Acetate or Equipoise, some synthetic I could inject into my quivering thigh, I'd start filling my pockets; instead it's just hippy happy shit I couldn't give a toss about.

I'm surrounded, engulfed by the admittedly pretty jagged leaves. Unlit hydroponic arc lights hang overhead, dead due to the cut in power. I duck into the foliage, let them brush against my breather, caress my body armour. Pretend I'm in the forested wetlands north of the Perfume River waiting for the 'Cong offensive.

The windowsills are prickled with mantraps beneath the blacked-out glass, ten-inch metal skewers set in cement and covered with cardboard waiting for any plod stupid enough to clamber through an opening. Booby-trap wires snake from a cupboard to the window frames, front door and door handles; I know from previous jobs they're plugged directly into the mains and would've given Frank and me enough voltage to fry us on the spot. Bless the sparky who killed the juice.

I immerse myself in the jungle of this lounge, knees bent, pump-action arcing in front of me. Nobody here. Might as well enjoy the game. Have some fun.

'*Room's clear,*' says Frank in my ear.

My head-music plays on. The song's mesmerising, undulating. Creeping onwards, rising in volume. A noodling guitar intro peeks its nose in. Frankie signals for me to take the stairs to the first floor with a sharp flick of his right hand.

I hear Grace Slick over the music, singing about a pill making you larger.

Doesn't it just, sweetheart.

'*Gold to Foxtrot X-Ray One-One, any update, over?*'

Collingwood. That bollock on legs.

'*One-one to Gold,*' I hear Frankie in my ear. '*Commencing slow search to contact.*'

Good on you, Frank. Stall him. Keep the other teams out so we can play soldiers.

We climb the stairs. The first floor mirrors the ground.

Neat rows of cannabis plants everywhere. Lighting equipment jerry-rigged from the ceiling.

Grace is singing about chasing rabbits, but I ain't after any rabbit, lady. I'm flushing out the Vietcong.

'Think there's any dinks hiding in here, Frankie?' I transmit.

He jerks his helmeted head towards me, eyes goggling behind his mask.

Jefferson Airplane lay it on, the vocals louder now. I suck air through my breather, follow Frank up the last flight of stairs. The top floor, where our supposedly reliable informant saw somebody moving not fifteen minutes ago.

The uppermost landing has two doors: one ajar, the other closed. Frank takes the last step up, swings the MP5 around, heads to the front of the house where the door is open. I shuffle into place behind him to provide cover with the 870, can see the tiny bedroom is jammed with samey-same.

'There's nothing in here,' I say. 'Just more plants.'

Frank doesn't turn around. He's squatting at the doorway, weapon raised, shoulders hunched. 'Gotta make sure . . .'

I check behind me, to the closed door. 'It's just plants, brother. What about back there? It's the only sealed room in the entire building.'

The only closed door.

Frank doesn't reply, edges forward.

'White Rabbit' is building to a crescendo. There's an urgency to the surging drums, the rhythm guitar, the looping bass notes and the otherworldly echo of the vocals. It's spellbinding, galvanising. I watch Frank work his way into the room. Nothing happens. Nobody else there. He lowers his weapon, looks at me. Shrugs.

I turn to the closed door.

Look at Frank.

Back to the closed door.

Later, Frankie. It's glory-boy time.

'*Jake . . .*'

I sprint across the landing towards the back room, the pine door closed.

Load up the Remington with a few pulls on the slider.

Come on, you NVA mothers.

Grace is yelling over the music now, screaming at me to feed my head, feed my head, feed my head, and then the song crashes to an end. What timing. What synchronicity.

My boot connects just beneath the door handle and I lurch into the room. No time to lob a flash-bang. Seconds to take everything in. Quick tactical visual sweep. Shotgun barrel tied to my line of sight. It's small. Dingy. Stained mattress on the floor. Solitary unlit bulb hanging from discoloured ceiling plaster. Bin bag taped awkwardly across the sealed window, letting in a thin shaft of daylight.

It's taken just over two minutes from breach to get here.

I've stopped breathing again.

And I recognise him from the mugshots.

Tang Yeh stands in front of me, eyes wide, unsteady hands held up in front of his sunken chest. He ain't all that. Small, sinewy, buzz-cut black hair. But then who needs muscles when you've got a handgun to shoot someone in the face?

Yeh's weapon. The Met never recovered it.

'Hey, hey, got me,' smiles Yeh, raising his hands as if in surrender, and I'm pretty sure a pistol isn't in either of them but I bring the butt of the shotgun down on his nose anyway.

He drops to the floor. The hiss of interference fills my skull.

'*Are you Vietcong?*' I scream and hit him again.

I raise the shotgun. Hit him.

Raise. Drop. Raise. Drop.

My voice across the airwaves: '*Are you VC? Are you? Are you*

VC? There's enough fuckin' rice here to feed a whole goddamn gook regiment!'

I'm vaguely aware of others in my head. I hear Frank, that irritant Collingwood, other jumbled words hissing in my left ear. My chest heaves, breathing heavily now, the eyepieces of my mask fogged to obscurity, I can feel my arms lifting and dropping whatever I'm holding but can't remember why I'm doing it.

I can't even remember where I am.

'Jesus Christ!'

That voice. So familiar.

I feel a pair of hands pull on the back of my body armour. Then I'm on the floor, the Remington skittering away from me. I snap to my feet in a crouch, draw my Glock. Wish my respirator would clear so I could assess the threat. I get rid of my ballistic helmet. Yank off the breather, the balaclava, then I'm sucking cold air and pungent cannabis fumes.

Frank's standing over me, his MP5 levelled at the centre of my face.

I can see a crumpled shape on the floorboards behind him; a pair of disgusting bare feet stick out of tracksuit bottoms. Crenellated blood-spatters cover the wall and floor. Next to the feet I see something metallic sticking out from under the mattress.

What have I done?

I look up at the business end of Frankie's submachine gun, see his finger against the trigger. Behind the weapon his large eyes glare at me through the clear plastic of his mask. His head moves, the rubber around his respirator disc shifts. He's talking but I can't hear. My earpiece was attached to my breather.

I drop the Glock back into the Bianchi holster and point to my ear, slowly. No sudden movement. 'No comms,' I say.

I look down again as Frank pulls off his headgear. I know where I am now. That's Yeh lying motionless behind Frankie's tactical boots. And I know I need an 'out' here. Something. Anything. Quickly. Or I'm going to end up as somebody's prison bitch.

The metal object is still there, jutting out from the mattress at Yeh's feet.

'You're fucking crazy,' I hear Frank say, but ignore him and squint. I can see rivets and crosshatched etching on the object. I tilt my head. The object catches the tiniest chink of daylight from the bagged window.

And I've found my out.

I sit back on my haunches. Look up at Frankie. 'He pulled a shooter on me, mate,' I say, and puff out my cheeks with a shake of my head. 'That was a close one, I tell you.'

Frank's eyes are narrowed. His MP5 is still pointed down at me. 'What?'

'Check by his feet,' I say. 'There's a bloody gun there. Aimed it right at my eyepiece when I came in. Shit meself, I did.'

I hold my breath as Frank kicks Yeh's legs away, toe-pokes the side of the mattress.

Hallelujah. It's a revolver. Nickel-plated. A .38 to my eye.

I know my guns when I see them and I'm gladder than hell I saw this one.

'You were supposed to be covering me,' he says, lifting the piece from under the mattress. He slips an evidence bag from the thigh pocket of his coveralls, drops the revolver inside.

I sit on my backside, lean against the wall. 'And you're the second person in the last five minutes to point a loaded weapon at my eyes.'

I pull my best hurt face.

Frank presses his lips together and looks at me for a long time.

Then he unhooks his spare Tetra set from his body armour: 'Foxtrot X-Ray One-One to Gold. Premises secure. Suspect in custody and weapon recovered.'

He looks back to me. 'If we'd stayed together I could've tasered him, Jake. Now we've got to deal with *this*.' He gestures at the groaning Yeh, transmits again: 'Can we have the standby paramedics at scene, please? The suspect has injuries after drawing his weapon on Smithy.'

Good on you, Frankie.

'I'll cuff him for you, shall I?' I offer with a smile. 'No hard feelings about threatening to shoot me, eh?'

I am unavailable for calls. Unavailable for calls. Code 45. Code 45 for a while. Unavailable.
Can't think. Can't think. Got to think. Got. To. Think. Got to ~~mae~~ make this right.
Make the bosses think it's okay. Make my hands stop shaking. Can't let the troops
down. Let Frank down. I'm Code 45 and unavailable while I think about this, about

---

TEN

I sit alone on the rear footplate of a prisoner wagon, drawing on a miniature cigar.

Too many people here. All eyes on me. I hang my head, hope they think it's down to my hastily contrived brush with death-by-revolver and leave me alone. That I'm in shock. That I need a little space. No questions or congratulations for bagging the bad guy at the moment. Because I need time to think. I need to get things right.

This one'll go straight to the IPCC for investigation. I've got to fill in the blanks. So many blanks. Got to explain every-thing I said – can remember saying – over the air.

I look up. Frank's standing on his own, fifty feet away and outside the cordon, blue and white police tape fluttering against his midriff. He's just watching me, eyes slitted behind his spectacles. He hasn't said a word to me since I cuffed Yeh.

'Smithy?'

I turn, see Dave Collingwood at the side of the van. His face is stony and pale, a telltale sign of barely controlled fury.

Beside him is a big-boned woman in her early thirties; she has thick ginger hair which she's unsuccessfully tried to disguise with blonde streaks. Her face is peculiarly flat, like a dog that's spent too much time chasing parked cars. She says nothing, just stares at me with her puffa-jacketed shoulders hunched up against the wind.

I dump the cigar. 'Sir?' I say, and look down again.

Collingwood's perfectly bulled boot kicks the cheroot away from him. He speaks slowly. 'Take your firearms car. Follow the prisoner van to the cells now,' he says. 'Book Yeh in and get yourself looked at by the med examiner. Leave MacReady here so I can speak to him. Clear?'

I nod silently, glance over at Frank again.

'What about the debrief?' I ask, looking up at the Inspector and Ginge.

'Fuck the debrief,' he growls. '*I'll* debrief you at HQ first thing tomorrow. Alone.'

I lower my head. Don't scream, Jake. Don't say anything.

I walk to the firearms truck, look to Frankie who doesn't move, just stares at me in a way I've never seen before and which makes me feel strangely sad. I climb into the driver's seat, close the door. As I start the engine, one of the Tac Teams from down west walk past the front of the wagon. They haven't seen me. They're laughing uncontrollably.

'"*Are you VC?!*"' one of them shrieks.

'Yeah, what's this thing about the rice? What is he, the Chinese takeaway police or something?'

'I thought he was going to bottle it at the start. *Tosser.*'

My fingers squeeze the steering wheel; I contemplate flooring it. Instead I pull forward slowly until I'm square with the prisoner van containing Yeh. Let's go, I gesture to the driver. She hesitates, looking at me with an expression of mild distaste. Then she nods, moves off towards the perimeter tape and I follow.

I've nothing left except my coveralls, boots and the notebook hidden in my back pocket.

Collingwood must've been on the blower before I arrived. CID and some of the Drug Squad were already milling around the cell block, muttering and eyeing me while I booked Yeh into custody. Once I'd given the spiel and the stripy granted detention, the Detective Sergeant and one of his token pretty-girl plonk DCs collared me, shoving a dozen clear plastic evidence bags into my hands as Yeh was dragged away by the civvy jailer, shouting something unintelligible at me as he went.

'We need all your kit bagged up, city boy,' the DS said, his ruddy face expressionless. 'Y'know, chain of evidence an' all that.'

'You can strip in the rape suite out back,' the plonk offered.

I would've argued the toss considering most of the stuff wasn't personal issue but gear I'd bought over the 'net. But I sensed the atmosphere was less than jovial and the DS looked in no mood for me to kick up a fuss. I knew what it was all about, just as much as they did. Chain of evidence, my rock-hard arse. They wanted my stuff to hand over to Professional Standards for the investigation when Yeh makes his obligatory complaint.

Fuckers'd better be careful with my kit. I want it all back, soon as this nonsense is cleared up and I'm on the road with Frankie again.

'And the knuckles, please?' the Force Medical Examiner says coolly. I'm squatting on a wobbly plastic chair in the med room at the front of the custody suite. My coveralls stink, a vile mixture of cannabis and stale sweat. The FME is attractive yet tiny; her face is barely level with my chest.

I turn over my outstretched hands. You won't find anything there, doc. Maybe some old nicks from New Year when I fell out with Frank's kitchen door, but I usually try to keep my hands clean on the job.

'What happened to your fingernail?' she asks.

'That's not from today,' I say.

'I'm aware of that,' she says. 'This wound is a day or two old.'

'Freak nose-picking accident,' I say.

'Indeed,' she says, and pulls off her latex gloves. 'We're done, thank you.'

'No, thank *you*,' I say with a smile, but she ignores me.

In the custody suite the bulletproof ties have left and there's nobody about but the bored sergeant behind the booking-in desk. The noise is deafening and the place smells worse than I do: cells full of Sunday afternoon White Lightning drunk and incapables; crackhead hookers with their crotch-rot and equally foul mouths; unwashed scrotes brought in on warrant the previous morning and waiting for Monday's court where they'll be set free on bail again by the magistrates. And always the 'banger'. Some muppet who knows his rights, wants a fag, wants his *farkin' slisittor*, and'll hammer that cell door for nine hours straight until he gets them.

I'm looking around and feeling sorry for myself, wondering what's going on at the debrief, hoping Frank doesn't sell me out to Collingwood, when I catch sight of a prisoner's property bag hanging from a hook on the wall behind the sergeant.

There's a bright red hooded coat sealed inside the clear plastic. Fur-lined. Fuck-Me Boots squashed in behind them.

I stare at them for what seems like five minutes.

'Mind if I just take a last look at my boy, Sarge?' I ask the stripy, but he's engrossed in his newspaper and waves me away.

The bagged coat has a yellow label fixed to the white plastic seal.

Cell 5 (F), it reads.

'I'll just log the visit on the computer, okay?'

The sergeant doesn't even respond, eyes never leaving the sports pages.

I round the counter, take a seat on the spare terminal behind him. Log into the custody board for this station. Cell five. Cell five. Come on. Where is she . . . ?

And there you are. In for shoplifting. How mundane. How beneath you.

I bring up her details, slip out my pocket notebook, snatch a pen from the desktop.

I thank the sergeant, don't listen if he acknowledges, make my way down to the female block. At pokey number five I lower the suicide hatch, peek inside.

She's sitting on the bench, knees tucked up under her chin, socked feet pressed against the wall. That hook of dark hair is still there, hanging across one eye as she turns and looks at me through the hatch.

'Yeah?' she says, curling her lip. 'Where's my fucking tea, piggy?'

Ah, yes. Red Riding Hood.

I smile. Feel warm inside.

'Hello Lowri,' I say. 'Remember me?'

73

'Red Riding Hood'—Full details: Lowri Clare Horton, 12 Valley View, Gravesdale, DOB 18/05/1990. PnCId 989/744C681. CRO 744C681/04 2M. Pre-cons: theft (12), criminal damage (2), soliciting (1). Resides with parents(?). — mobile tel number:

There's no reply from the intercom but I know she's home.

I move out from under the entrance, carefully take a couple of steps down to look up, check I wasn't seeing things when I arrived. Rain makes my eyelids flutter. The arc light above the apartment-block doors leaves retinal imprints when I blink.

The second-floor window is lit. Her lounge window. The blind's down. Rachael's all for the environment, Little Miss *An Inconvenient Truth*. Never leaves appliances on if she's out for the evening.

I pull out my mobile, hold it a few inches from my face. Shake my head. Shake away the whisky fug. I'm wobbling on the step as I search for her number, decide I'm going to end up on my arse in the gutter so climb back up to the entrance porch. Concentrate, Jakey boy. One thing at a time. One thing. The floor's level here so I scroll through my contacts, miss Rachael's house number three times, keep trying. Have to keep blinking then widening my eyes to focus.

Got it. I press dial, exhilarated that I even completed the task, hold the phone to my ear. It rings and rings and I clear my throat of cigar-induced grot, will her to answer. My guts clench when I hear her say hello so I say hello back then she's still talking and I realise this isn't a conversation, only her answerphone message.

I kill the call. Kick the wall beneath the entry intercom. Wish I hadn't because even though I'm wearing my tactical boots it's agonising; I'm going to wake tomorrow to find I've probably fractured something and won't even remember how I did it. Another UDI. Unexplained drunken injury.

Squinting and swaying, I try to find Rachael's mobile number. Focus, Jacob. I fight with the buttons on my phone keypad, find the number, speed-dial it. Hear the automated voicemail message.

'Hey,' I say, and it's an effort to stay pleasant, to make my lips work. 'Know you're in there. Why you no' answer the door, eh? Or your house phone? Lemme in, yeah? F'me birthday?'

I say nothing else, just hold the phone to my ear and breathe. Maybe she'll hear this message right now, not tomorrow. Maybe if I wait on the line she'll sense something, pick up her mobile, turn it on and – like magic – I'll be there so we'll talk then she'll let me in and everything will be all right again.

I wait. And wait. And it's just dead air in my ear.

I end the call, drop my mobile into my pocket, wish I'd made some effort to go home and change because I reek of weed, body odour and cheap spirits, but then what's there to go home for?

My finger dances around the intercom, the lines of raised buttons and square panel reminding me of some gigantic metallic Lego block sticking out from the brickwork and I don't know why but this makes me laugh, throw my head back and giggle until I overbalance and have to flap my arms to right myself.

I can't get my eyes to settle on the right buzzer. 'Just do it', like the Nike man says.

I jab a finger at Rachael's intercom and hear a faint monotone hum. I hum along with it for a few seconds until there's a crackle and then:

'*Hello? Rachael?*' I say. 'Lemme in.'

Silence.

'Karen . . . I mean Rachael, s'me,' I say, and I'm so relieved she's answered that it just gushes out of me. 'I miss you.' I nod, agreeing with myself even though it may be a lie but I really can't remember. 'No, honestly, I do so can you please let me in? Just t'see you for me birthday? Promise I won't ask for anything more than a foot job, I swear.'

I sign a cross over my heart and I know she can't see me but don't care.

'*Mmm, tempting,*' says the voice. '*But you've got the wrong flat.*'

'Rachael?'

'*No, mate,*' says the voice, and I note the sarcasm. '*It's not Rachael or Karen or even your wife. But they sound like lucky ladies with the foot thing.*'

'Hardy-har. Just lemme in,' I say. 'I can find my own way to her apartm—'

The voice cuts me off. '*I don't know who you are and I'm not letting you in anywhere, you bloody pervert. Go away before I call the law.*'

Crackle, hum. She's gone.

'I *am* the law!' I bite down, grind my teeth and begin stabbing fingers at buttons, feel unpleasant numb pressure on the circle of skin where my nail used to be, keep going until I'm leaning into the intercom and hitting those small raised discs with the knuckles of both hands.

I'm spent. Gulping in air. I hobble towards the steps, fish out my keys and return to the truck. As I start the engine I glance up at the front of the building.

The lit blind, the lounge window of the flat. Silhouettes there. *Plural.* Two figures, one curling their fingertips around the side of the material to peek into the street.

How fucking dare she? This needs to be addressed. Right now!

I open the car door, place one foot down onto the wet tarmac, start to climb back out.

I am rage personified. I picture pummelled heads, splintered bones, deep red blood sloshing across the laminated floor of Rachael's lounge, a torrent of crimson, a viscous wave driving and rolling through each room before exploding in red spray like the elevator scene from *The Shining*.

I hear the faint wail of sirens. See distant blue strobes in the rear-view mirror.

Weigh up the odds. Quickly. Self-gratification or self-preservation.

The door slams shut by itself as I shove my ruined foot down on the accelerator.

I'm gone.

~~—————————————~~

~~—————————~~ ~~————~~

~~————~~ ~~————~~

~~——————————~~

~~————————~~

~~——————————~~

Wednesday 6th February

Karen incommunicado — 36 days? 34 days? ~~————~~

2100 On duty again. Same old office. Tour of duty 2100–0700hrs. ~~——~~

Callsign FV31. Team Of Two with a fuckin' FnG. Where's the Frankmonster??

2110 Briefing @ office with PS Hall (if I have to listen to this cuntypollocks

describe Tenerife's varied & volcanic landscape one more time I'm going

to grab my H&K and pop some caps into his doughboy arse, I swear)

2215 Mobile patrol. ARV vehicle two. Load: 2 x Heckler & Koch MP5 A3,

2 x Glock 9mm pistols, L104A1 Baton Gun, X700 Taser. All weaponry

securely stored in rear-mounted firearms cabinet as per ~~ACPS~~ ACPO

guidelines. Non-lethal options (CS Incapacitant Spray, F-lock Baton)

with officers. Firearm cabinet key with the FnG. ~~————~~

2235 Assist sector officers re. disturbance @ Athena Kebab, Caldy Street.

Cancelled en route. Shall I get some food while I'm here??? ~~————~~

2250 Alpha 4 call to Victoria Street Petrol Station re. male threatening

staff with knife. Cancelled en route (again!). Sector officers dealing.

0005 Robbery, Parker Place. Culprit already in custody upon arrival.

0035 Violent domestic, Christine Street, Mayhill. Back up sector ~~————~~

officers due to intel on male occupant (warnings for firearms, violent).

Cancelled en route as male already in custody. For fuck's sake!!! ~~————~~

0155 Concern for occupant, 4 Princefield Place, Fairborough. 999 call

received from premises and screaming/gunshots heard by emergency

operator. Deployed for investigative assessment. Upon entry discovered

ELEVEN

I'm losing the will to live.

Seventy-seven years old, living alone and watching *Bad Boys II* at maximum volume at nearly two in the morning. I pity her neighbours. The woman's almost completely deaf: all *ay?* and *you what, dear?* from the settee when I explain she's been trying to change channels on her television using the house phone. And this is the high point of my night.

I'm standing over her, rigged up and cradling my H&K. 'You've been pressing the nine button on your telephone, sweetheart,' I say, pointing to the cordless in her waxy right hand. 'We thought there was something wrong.'

She looks at me blankly, then back at the screen. It's bigger than the one I've got at home, probably fifty inches and dumped there by her relatives to keep her occupied so they don't have to.

'He's lovely, innee?' she says, and I turn to the FNG who shrugs.

'Who?' I shout at her.

'That Will Smith,' she says, and sucks at her chops.

There's nothing for me here. There's been nothing all night, just a stream of human garbage calls which we've blue-lighted towards only to be called off as we turn into the street. And to top it off, Collingwood's doubled me up with someone from the northern sector, some skinny FNG who's fidgeting with his MP5, a jittery cherry whose name I don't even want to know and who's only been on the Tac Team for weeks. Frankie's crewed with someone else for the shift and I have no clue why.

I have to leave. Immediately. I'm so glad I'm not a tit-head. Those lowly sector plods can make the tea and fill in the forms for the useless Social Services while this old crone gurns at Big Willie.

I crawl around side streets in second gear for ten minutes, then slip the wagon into a lane. Turn off the engine, lower the window, feel chilly air rush into the cab.

'What a night,' the cherry says, staring ahead.

I nod, spark up a cigar. 'Yep.'

I don't say anything else. Why encourage small talk? I don't even know you. I take a puff on the Café Crème, exhale, settle back in the seat and let him suffer the awkward silence.

We're surrounded by terraced houses, the lives of others. I listen, feel the mild thrill of a peeping tom. From somewhere behind the firearms truck I hear raised voices, muted by thick walls but undoubtedly a couple in the throes of a drunken quarrel, and I wonder how long it'll be before we get a call. A few houses further along I hear a woman panting and *yeah*ing, zone in on the noise and see a rear first-floor sash window propped open. I smile yet feel oddly sad. Then a male groaning, muttering a name I can't quite make out but it could be Bev or Beth but it doesn't really matter because he gives one last guttural grunt then he's spent and there's nothing more to listen to.

Neither home resembles my own at the moment. We're a DVD on pause. It's been so long since Karen and I spoke, the silence seems normal. Own cars, spare bedrooms, own toilets: all the trappings of comfortable suburban life which allow you to stay apart. We're two single parents living under one roof.

I glance at the cherry. See the wedding ring.

Do you wake in the middle of the night and fuck your wife, newbie? Does Mrs FNG sense you're awake and aroused and know what you want in that way a good woman always does?

Allow you to paw her hips and thighs, grab roughly at her breasts from behind her without so much as a by-your-leave? Do you lift her leg with your knee then shift closer, enter her; she accepts you and you fuck then finish, roll away, back to sleep and it's okay because you love her, she loves you and that's all that matters?

Do you, cherry?

'Do I what?' he asks. He's looking at me, confused.

'Do you . . .?' I say. 'D'you reckon Frank'll be back after tonight?'

The cherry shrugs. 'Dunno. The boss rang me out of the blue this afternoon, says I'm crewed with you until further notice.'

Then he's bumping his gums about what a pisser it is with all the extra travelling he'll have to do now but I've stopped listening. Because nobody rang to tell me about the change. I think of the debrief I had with Collingwood, when he bawled at me for an hour in his cramped little office and I just drifted in and out of the moment, glazed over, dismissed him out of hand and sat there while he huffed and puffed and got it out of his system.

Did I miss something?

I slide by JoBlo's to RV with Sinclair. Leave the cherry in the wagon; tell him it's a witness I need to speak to about an extremely important case I'm dealing with.

'Wh'appenin, blood?' Sinclair says, looking uncomfortable as he palms me this week's vials. I check they're right. Testosterone Propionate. Trenbolone Acetate. Anavar and Arimidex. Good for the cutting cycle. Get rid of some of the Christmas flab. Get ripped. Get better.

'Something wrong?' I ask, looking past him. The club is kicking out.

He forces a smile of brilliant white teeth; the scar on his face is hideous. 'Look, been checking the ticklist,' he says. 'You owes for the last nine months, bra. And most of that juice you been buying ain't cheap.'

I'm scanning the crowd when I see a flash of red coat. 'Yeah,' I say, not really listening. 'Just add it to the tab, amigo.'

'No, Jake,' he says, and I'm wishing he'd move out of the way. 'You gotta pay now. I owe my supplier much dollar for the gear and you holding up the line. He leaning on me and don't care who I am or what you do for a living. Five-oh, MI5 or even Batman, he want his money. One way or another.'

'I'm good for it. I'll square with you at The Elite.' My eyes on the bodies spilling out onto the pavement. Was that Lowri? I blink a few times, search the teenagers milling around the pavement. I can't see her anywhere. I will her to appear at the club doors.

'Jake, you don't get it,' says Sinclair, and his voice is a whine in my ear so I dump the vials into my cargo pocket, grab his forearm.

'*You* don't fuckin' get it, *brother*,' I say, looking into his eyes. 'I'm the sheriff and I say what goes here, and what goes is I'll pay you at the fuckin' gym, right?'

Sinclair pulls his arm from my grip, straightens up, the smile gone. His face is expressionless, unreadable. He's bigger than me, a real beast.

'I hope so,' he says.

'Now I've got important policey stuff to do,' I say. 'Stuff you wouldn't understand. I'll settle up later today.'

I walk back towards the firearms wagon.

'Problems?' the cherry asks, looking across at Sinclair. As if the bag of bones would be of any use if that monster decided to kick off.

'None,' I say, getting into the driver's seat. I'm gunning the engine, waiting for the FNG to buckle up and all I can hear is Sinclair's voice from across the street, calling after me as I ease away from the kerb and work the wagon through the pockets of clubbers.

'Six Gs, Jake,' he's shouting. 'Six thou, bra. Serious.'

I wish he'd shut up.

I raise the window, drive towards the docks.

It's oh-three oh-five hours.

Me and the FNG, we're trawling the industrial estate watching the handful of streetwalkers plying for trade, the desperate scags looking to perform that last ten-quid suck job for a post-club punter. I can't find Lowri anywhere. This pleases me *and* pisses me off. If she's not here she's safe at home, but then I'm not going to get the chance to see her. Not going to spend time with her, finish off the conversation we had in the cells.

Fuck it. I unclip my mobile from my body armour, dig out my pocket notebook, flip to the entry I made in the custody suite after the raid.

'Who you ringing at this time of the morning?' the FNG asks.

'A friend,' I say, as if it's anything to do with him anyway. And I'm not sure if Lowri is a friend but I know I'd like her to be. I can't stop thinking about her. I picture her, this girl who knows nothing about me, this teenager who reminds me of everything that's missing in my life.

It rings for an age and I think I'm going to be speaking to her answerphone when there's a click then a voice and I can't believe it's her on the other end of the line.

'*Hello?*' she says groggily, and it's clear I've woken her. I smile just hearing her voice; am happy because if she's asleep she's at home, not servicing someone in the back of a car or being defiled in some shithole B&B or swallowing anybloke's DNA underneath the railway arches that border the city centre.

I say nothing. Breathe quietly.

'*Hello? Who is it?*' Lowri asks, and I press the mobile tightly to my ear, gently rub my thumb down its side, stroke the corner of the plastic. We could do so much for each other, Lowri. So much. I see it in you just from the little time we've spent together. You could fill all the voids. I close my eyes, imagine her lying in bed with her mobile up to her ear, that dark hook of hair falling across her face, and I'm there; just like with the girl in the Clio I'm holding one of her hands and telling her everything's going to be okay, shhh, everything's going to be okay, it's all right, I'm going to help you. And I know this time it's the truth.

This time, with her, everything's going to be all right.

'*If you're not going to speak then go fuck yourself,*' she says, then cuts me off, and I sigh, can't help but grin.

'Goodnight, sweetie,' I say into the mobile, close my notebook then turn off the phone. I'm clipping it back to my vest, see the cherry staring at me, shaking his head a little and just staring at me.

'*Girl*friend, you mean,' he smiles, nodding towards my ring finger.

I look at the figures skulking in the doorways of the business units, the walking clichés in their fishnets and itty-bitty skirts calling out to us, laughing and gesturing that we're wankers, knowing we can't be bothered to stop and in reality it's just a game. They're on it, we're part of it.

'Got to have a few aunties on the patch, haven't you?' I say, and think of Rachael. Of the night outside her apartment.

The two silhouettes.

Of unfinished business.

	Tuesday 12th February
	Karen — still incommunicado (Days? Stopped counting)
1000	HQ — training / assessment day @ Firearms Unit. Method of entry / negotiator /
	room clearance (sudden change of training plan?? I bet they all blame me for it.
1315	'meeting' Inspector Collingwood's office. Also present (and I can't believe it was

TWELVE

We're doing room clearance in pairs and I know it's because of me. Because of Yeh and ditching Frankie to check the rear bedroom. Nobody's said as much but today's original training plan has been abandoned and now we're doubled up in full kit with blank 5.56 ammo loaded into the G36 carbines. The warehouse is stifling despite the subzero temperatures outside and no one's happy. The other AFOs are sitting about the training facility with their rigs ready to go through this stupid apartment mock-up and they're looking at me. Not all the time but I see the sideways glances, hear the whispered curses.

I'm with the cherry again and he's so excited to be here – actually *thrilled* to be doing a full training exercise in this heat, the tool – and I can't bear it; wish I was doing this with Frankie, but he's sitting on a bench near the tea makings on the other side of the hall and chatting into his mobile phone.

I haven't had time to speak to him, put the arm on him to find out if he's heard anything, and this FNG is at my ear wittering about how awesome the G36 is but he much prefers the C-Compact model variant because the barrel's shorter, it's got a four-prong open-type flash suppressor, the carry handle's got an integrated Picatinny rail plus of course the hooded front post and flip rear aperture on the rail-mounted iron sights. I want him to shut up, please shut up, you're making my ears bleed, you weedy little runt . . .

'All right, I was only sayin,'' he says, stepping away from me sulkily, and I've done it again – maybe I should apologise, but before I can decide if I'm bothered, here comes whats-is-name, the firearms medic from down West, Paul or Phil or Pete, I can never remember but we all know him as Thrombo because he's a slow-moving clot.

'Boss wants you in his office,' Thrombo says, and I'm nonplussed but glad for the opportunity to be out of this heat and away from the rambling FNG.

I look at Frank. He's finished talking on his mobile and is watching me. In fact, everyone has turned towards me, even the cherry.

Everything is still.

'What for?' I ask.

Thrombo shrugs. 'Dunno. Collingwood just wants you in there ay-sap.'

Ay-sap. Ay-fuckin-sap. He's even got the grunts saying it. I take a breath, suck on the warm air in this sweltering building and stare at Frankie who's slumped back in his seat, not looking at me, not looking up at all but has his head in his hands and is scanning the concrete floor.

I walk across anyway. Take a seat beside him.

'What've you heard, droog?' I say to him. 'Come on.'

He looks at me. Looks at me for a long time before he says, 'Why don't you go see your father, Jake?'

Just the mention of it makes me want to puke. There are days when I wish I'd never told him. It's involuntary: my hands ball into fists and then I'm rubbing them on my thighs, back and forth from knee to groin and there's the *ssshhh-sshhh* of skin on cotton and my collar is suddenly too tight.

'Don't say that,' I tell him. 'Don't say that, Frankie.'

'It could help, y'know,' he says. 'If you talk to him, do your thing, just get it out of your system. Mel agrees.'

Static. That hiss, building in my ears. 'You fuckin' told her?'

'I tell her everything. Why d'you think she puts up with so much of your crap?'

I shake my head. 'It's pointless.'

Frank shifted his body towards me. 'But it's that time of year, isn't it?'

'Right,' I say. 'The great anniversary. The date of all dates. Except this one's a little more special, isn't it? I mean, how old am I this year?'

I turn to him and see he doesn't understand for a moment. Then it dawns on him and his mouth opens slightly. He grabs my left wrist to stop my knuckles kneading my thigh. His fingers clamp around my skin. 'You ain't your old man, Jake,' he says.

And I think about that. I think of my life and what I've become.

'I'm not sure what I am any more,' I say.

'Collingwood,' Frankie says, squeezing my forearm. 'You'd better go.'

'Okay,' I say, standing, looking at him and feeling a little odd, anxious maybe. I glance around the warehouse, at the target range and staging area, the briefing corner where I've spent so many hours on Gold command procedures and negotiation techniques; the rows of plastic chairs where I've sat with Frankie and Thrombo, even Tommy Hall, and shot the shit for hours about gigs we've done and doors we've jemmied and that one time when I had to rappel down the side of a pie factory after some kid went postal with a meat cleaver and took the whole sausage-roll production line hostage.

'Okay,' I say again, and leave the building.

Collingwood's your typical boss with a my-door's-always-open policy just as long as what you've got for him isn't griefy. I'm sure the piles of boxes are a recent addition to the polished desk and empty in-tray and those sad little foreign-police-force plaques he collects every time he goes on holiday.

He's lumped behind the desk, squat in his leather swivel chair, and eyeballing me as I walk in. I'm surprised to see the ginger woman from Canningtown making tea in one corner. I didn't know he'd been given a secretary. I'm slightly nervous: he obviously thinks he needs one to take the minutes of what I now know is clearly a formal meeting.

'Take a seat, Jacob,' Collingwood says. He never calls me Jacob and his voice is gentle, all touchy-feely, not like him at all. My guts are suddenly loose as he gestures to one of the hateful bucket chairs in front of his desk. They're stunted little fake leather things, low enough for him to look down on whoever's sitting in them.

I sit anyway, look around at the cardboard boxes. 'Deliveries, boss?' I ask, and try to smile, but the muscles around my mouth are quivering annoyingly and it comes out wrong and I think I leer at him.

'No,' he says, and looks quickly at Ginger, who's turned around and is stirring her mug of tea and hasn't offered me so much as a cup of cold piss. He looks back at me and says: 'Packing. I'm moving on to pastures new.'

'Promotion?' I hadn't heard any whispers about him getting his third pip.

'Office job,' he says, and I'm confused because I thought he already did one. 'I'm off to learning and development. Training school.'

'Yeah, *right*,' I say and laugh, then stop because he doesn't.

'We've all got to move on sometime,' he says, and I detect a tone there and he waves a hand at Ginge and then he smiles and says: 'Jacob, while you're here I'd like to introduce you to the new Firearms Inspector.'

Ginge, she places her mug on Collingwood's desk, steps towards me, proffers a hand. For a second I can't move, want to laugh out loud and bat her fingers away, ask Dave if he's joking, but I turn to him and when I see his face I know he's not. He's serious. This doesn't compute. I watch my hand rise as if of its own volition, move towards Ginger's meaty fingers and then I'm shaking hands with her and she's looking down at me with a shit-eating grin, that shovel-face of hers is so close it fills my vision, I can smell her lemon-tea breath, I'm counting the freckles across her pug nose and wondering what the hell is going on here.

Too fast. This is happening too fast. Let me take a breath, here. Let me . . .

'Inspector Howells has excellent credentials, Jacob,' I hear Collingwood say. 'I'm confident I'm leaving the place in very safe hands.'

'Pamela Howells,' she says, pumping away.

And I can't let her hand go. I feel her trying to pull away, I'm looking up at her and she's stopped shaking it but my fingers just won't work, won't open. I've been doing this job for years and never clapped eyes on this woman, which tells me all I need to know. She's an office dweller, some fast-track promotion plonk with a third-rate uni degree. Someone whose shoes have barely touched the street in the few years she's been working. One of the new breed who knows the buzzwords but can't cut it operationally. Probably has friends in high places, too. The good ol' police casting couch.

'Pleased to meet you, ma'am,' I say, but I'm not. Not in the slightest.

'You can stop now,' she says, and narrows her eyes at my hand, so I do as I'm told because it's been bred into me to obey anyone with stripes or pips even if they're a total dick. Respect the rank not the person, right? I release her. She brushes her hand on the front of her suit. 'I've heard a lot about you, Jacob,' she says, slurping at her mug.

I glance at Collingwood then back to her. 'All Marmite.'

'You've lost me,' she says after a moment.

'Well, you'll either love me or hate me, y'know?'

Ginge, Pam, she takes a deep breath, lets it out very slowly. 'Personally I can't bear the stuff,' she says. 'Leaves a horrible taste in my mouth. *Y'know?*'

I'm looking up at her and trying to absorb all of this when Collingwood clears his throat. 'Ah, which kind of brings me on to the reason you've been asked to come in here, Jacob,' he says. 'As I said, we've all got to move on sometime . . .'

And I look at him and see his expression, which is a strange mixture of smug self-satisfaction and malice and not a little fear, and suddenly I know what's coming and I can't believe it. Why Frank's been avoiding me, why they've kept him away from me since the cannabis job. Pam wants to hit the ground running. New broom syndrome. A hatchet woman. Setting her stall out, because when the rest of the guys hear about this they'll cream their coveralls and be nodding dogs for as long as she's in charge. My heart thumps so hard against my shirt, my body armour, I worry it's about to rupture my sternum like the chest-burster in *Alien*, spew onto the floor where Pam can stamp on it and twist her heel before hawking a loogie and gobbing it onto the flattened muscle tissue just for good measure.

From somewhere in the wind tunnel between my ears I hear Collingwood tell me my performance has been less than satisfactory since December and the organisation is worried, that I'm considered a liability at present and as a result they're withdrawing my firearms ticket.

They're kicking me off the team.

'It's just a temporary measure,' says Pammy, but that's what they always say. I can't bring myself to look at her as I'm bent over at the waist, dry heaving at the nice thick carpet – *her* nice thick carpet – and part of me wants to spill my breakfast onto the lovely cream woollen fibres as a joint farewell/welcome present.

And Collingwood's still talking, telling me there's a slot on one of the reliefs in the city centre and he thinks it'd be good for me to go back to basics and do some sector work and get my hands dirty while I work things out with the force therapist and y'know, she's really good at what she does and you never know, Jacob, in six months, once everything's blown over you'll be back here with Frankie and the guys and it'll be like you've never been away . . .

And then the telephone on his – *her* – desk rings.

I'm still swallowing saliva as Collingwood uh-huhs and okays then says, 'No problem, send him in.'

When the door opens I look up and just when I thought things couldn't get any worse I see a twenty-something guy with glasses and carefully spiked bleached blond hair and for a second can't recall where I've seen him before. Then it clicks; it's the fella who was sat at the back of the court the day I potted Cooper and I remember what I said to him as I left.

And I know I'm really in trouble.

'Jacob,' Collingwood says. 'This is Detective Inspector Ewing from Professional Standards. He's here to see you.'

And I don't know where they're getting these bosses from nowadays because this guy is way too young to be a DI, but it doesn't really matter what I think because he walks towards me in his neatly pressed slacks and metallic purple tie and holds out a sheet of paper that I reach up and take without thinking.

It's a Regulation Nine notice.

'PC Smith,' this man-child detective says in a voice that tells me he's done this many times before. 'You're being investigated for allegations of assault on two prisoners and harassment of a female colleague. Do you wish to say anything?'

He cautions me. Cautions *me*.

I look at the sheet of paper in my hand, then up at this DI Ewing. Across to Collingwood. Over to Pammy. All so serious. All so damn holier-than-thou.

What a carve-up.

'I just want to say fuck-you all very much,' I say, and screw up the piece of paper.

all those motherfuckers. You carrot-topped cocksucker. That's what you are lady, a gold-plated hundred per cent knobswallower. Fuck you, and that Judas boy Ewing with his little Reg ~~Nne notei~~ ~~notit~~ ah FUCK IT FUCK YOU ALL YOU HAVE NO IDEA WHO YOU JUST ~~FUK~~ FUCKED WITH TODAY, DO YOU? DO

THIRTEEN

I'm home and don't know what time it is but it's dark so could be anytime after seventeen hundred and everyone's upstairs, I can hear them in their rooms, and it's just noise and bright light down here; even the television's on and playing MTV or TMF or The Hits or whatever it is to nobody and why the fuck can't people turn anything off around here?

They've asked for my pocket notebook. And I can't remember what my reply was exactly because all I could think about was not being there any more and how I was going to dodge this bullet and explain to the investigating officers tomorrow that I haven't exactly been following the evidence recording rules in the strictest sense so I just muttered something about losing it.

Losing it.

I climb the stairs and my legs feel drained, muscles shaky like I've given them a good going-over on the squat machine and I'm coming unglued, yes I am, I'm coming apart at the seams here. I'm back where I was ten years ago as a bloody beat bobby and beneath the dread, flickering but still present and correct, is the faint knowledge that everything I know is slipping away from me. My family, my job. Frank, Rachael, Jessica. My status. My *place*. I close my eyes, urge my leaden legs up each step, try to work out when this all began, when everything started to go wrong, I think about it as I lift my feet and climb towards the landing where every door is ajar, Karen and the kids in their own rooms, cut off in their own little worlds, getting on with their lives; and then I stop thinking because I know when everything started going wrong, it was the night of my eighteenth birthday. And it's been building since then. Growing inside me like a tumour.

And now everything's going too fast.

I need to press rewind. I need to go back. I can't let history repeat itself.

So I tap on the door of our bedroom, step in, and Karen is sitting at the vanity unit brushing her hair, lips rouged, jet-black eyelashes curled and thickened, dark grey satin camisole covering her upper body, lacy hold-ups stretched over her beautiful feet and stopping midway up her thighs. I shuffle forward. She looks so good. A little black dress I've never seen before hangs from a wardrobe door and I wonder for a moment if all this effort is for me so try to smile but she doesn't even look my way, doesn't even stop what she's doing, hand rolling at the wrist, brush bristles working through her ebony hair, and then I see the beige card on the tabletop and it's an invite of some sort, gold leaf around the edges, *Nurse's Valentine Ball* embossed on the front.

She hasn't mentioned it but I'm too tired to be angry. All I feel is a sense of defeat, of humiliation, of emasculation. And even though it may be too late I try to tell her: Karen, I'm sorry, I wish we could talk about this, I'm losing everything here, it's all running away from me and I don't know what to do and I don't want us to end up like my parents, y'know? I'm floating loose, I'm all alone here and I need you.

I really need you.

I see myself in the mirror and my mouth hasn't moved because I don't say any of it. Big macho man Jake with your granite abs, your shrunken testes, you've bottled it again. So I take a breath, say to her: 'They've booted me off the Firearms Unit.'

Karen stops brushing. Doesn't turn around. Just looks at

me in the mirror. Says nothing but pulls a face, an expression that says just how low we've sunk and makes me want to claw at my own eyes. Disgust.

I leave the bedroom.

I stop at Naomi's door because maybe I can find solace here, reconnect with her somehow, and I'm about to knock when I hear her voice; she's talking on her mobile, talking to some guy by the sound of it. *Nah*, she's saying, *I don't know where he is, none of us know where he is most of the time, y'know, it's just so much hassle here at the moment. He's, like, really freaking us all out and keeps going off on one like he's stoned – what? yeah it was great, Finch brought a couple of joints – where was I? Yeah, my old man he's such a dick and to be honest I'm not surprised my mother's had enough he's, like, totally pissed her off, uh-huh, uh-huh yeah cool, well pick me up at eight. Love ya . . .*

I'm breathing at the door. I hear my fifteen-year-old daughter, my baby, this stranger moving around inside, then there's the tap-tap-tap of a keyboard and I wait five whole minutes before pushing open the door to find her sitting in front of her computer.

'Hey,' she says, and smiles.

'Hey,' I say. 'What's up?'

'Nothing much,' she says, nodding at the PC screen. 'Just Facebooking. Catch up with the girls sort of thing.'

'Okay,' I say and can't move.

'All right with you if I go to the cinema tonight?' she asks. 'Lucy wants to see the new Orlando Bloom.'

'Okay,' I say again. My face feels weird and numb. I may be grinning.

'You okay, Dad?' Naomi asks.

'Okay,' is all I can say, and shuffle backwards, her eyes narrowing as I close the door.

I walk into Ben's bedroom without knocking, find him

sitting on his queen-size, eyes closed, knees hugged to his chest, floppy emo hair hanging over his face like a black frill. He's wallowing in misery, isn't he? And it's my fault. I'm ruining my son, just like my father ruined me, and this makes me nauseous so I step to the foot of the bed. I have to speak to someone tonight to tell them why I am like I am. Because Ben and Naomi don't know. And they need to know, I need to tell one of them before it's too late, before I lose them once and for all. So I hold nothing back, gaze at my son as I recount what happened to me – to my parents – when I was just a little older than he is now, when my father was the same age as I am now, and Ben might not be looking at me as I talk, his eyes might be closed as I say don't end up like me kid, but he's nodding so it's obviously sinking in and suddenly this is so *cathartic*, I can't stop myself, I'm disgorging it all, spewing the poison out, my son's nodding like he understands everything and for the first time in as long as I can remember I feel like a human being once more.

Then I've finished, tell him he doesn't have to say anything, not yet, just absorb it, the magnitude of it all, and I thank him for just *being there*. He's still eyes closed and nodding but I feel like I've shed a hundredweight so walk to the door, turn around, see he's shifted on the bed, hair flopped to one side.

And I see the iPod 'phones wedged into his ears.

So I leave and think how I really need to speak to my father.

	Wednesday 13th February **9**
	K — still nothing. Valentine's Day tomorrow. What if? Maybe. You never know... ♥
♣	Got to hide this thing. Going to go with the story that I lost it somewhere.
	Maybe if I tell them it was around the time of ~~Gang~~ Canningtown they'll drop it and
	just issue me with new one. Got to keep own record for the investigation, when it
	all comes out in the open. Just in case I need to prove anything, or put a grievance
	in about how this job's treated me or something. Who the ~~fuck~~ do they think they
♦	are, sending me back to division? ————————
0930	RV with Jermaine Sinclair @ The Elite. ————————
1130	HQ, Professional Standards dept re taped interview with Det. Superintendent Jones and

FOURTEEN

I've got a busy day, things to do, and I don't know what's happened but I woke this morning at oh-five forty-five, still dark outside, two hours' sleep, and I had this terrific rush of energy, of optimism, bordering on euphoria, and I don't know where it came from given yesterday's events but suddenly it was clear to me I obviously *needed* a fresh start and now I'm holding on to this feeling and hoping it lasts.

I really hope it lasts. I need to get on the front foot.

It's time to do some joined-up thinking, Jacob.

So I'm up early, pressing my uniform in the spare bedroom, my bedroom, steaming those creases into my trousers as if it's my first week in the job, starching the sleeves of my white short-sleeved shirt, bulling my boots and burning the gloss with my cigar lighter until the tips are shiny as the nose cone on a cruise missile. I won't let the fact that Karen didn't come home until one in the morning dampen my mood.

Got to sustain this energy, make it a high-protein, low-fat day. After a dose of Trenbolone, breakfast is a pint of skimmed milk with two scoops of whey protein and three whole raw eggs. Then I neck another three egg whites and eat a plain bagel. It's going to be a long day and I don't know if I'll have time to eat at headquarters so wrap six wholewheat crackers spread with peanut butter in tin foil and put them in my rucksack, add a sealed tub of low-fat cottage cheese mixed with pineapple plus half a packet of rice cakes – salt and vinegar flavour of course. Then I grab my utility belt and leave, get into the truck, try Frank's moby but it goes to answerphone. I leave a message asking him to ring me, then try Lowri's number, which I've added to my speed-dial list, but her mobile's turned off.

Not a problem. Everything's good.

I drive towards the gym and on the way realise this will be the first occasion I've gone there with any other intention than to rack plates and pump weights. The first time I've ever been there in uniform. The only time I've ever been there on official business.

It doesn't take long, I just stride in and it's full of the usual midweek morning musclehead shitbags because none of them has got anything better to do except come here or burgle people's houses while they're at work. Or maybe come here *then* do the burgling, I can never remember which way it goes, but the thought is lost and I'm working my way through the obstacle course of fixed-weight machines looking for Sinclair while the crowd stops what they're doing, every last one of them, because they didn't know what I did for a living and they can't believe it, I'm the *fackin' filth* – I've bought juice from some of them, how amusing is that? – and somewhere in my head I know I'll never be able to come back here. I feel a stab of sorrow but will *not* let it ruin this good mood so force myself to think: does that really matter? We've all got to move on sometime.

Sinclair's in the middle of a set of reps, blasting his triceps, kneeling on a bench doing dumb-bell kickbacks. He sees me, stands and drops the weights, and I watch them roll from his feet a-ways on the rubber mat; see he's got Christ-knows-how-many kilos on the bars, Ivanko plates too. He's an animal, this guy, ripped and vascular, but this is police work and I'm in full uniform so size doesn't matter, as they say.

'What the fuck you doin' here in that fancy-dress outfit, you prick?' Sinclair says. 'I got to do business after you gone, Jake. Who's gonna want to deal with me now?'

And I flip out my pocket notebook and say to him *you do not have to say anything but it may harm your defence if you do not mention when questioned something which you later rely on in court, and in fact anything you do say may be used in evidence. Do you understand,* brother?

'What?' he says, and I'm not sure if he's going to laugh at me or knock my front teeth out. He blinks several times like he doesn't quite know what to do, which I consider to be an appropriate reaction given the gravity of the matter. 'You cautioning me?' he asks, the scar twitching. 'For what?'

So I tell him I am good for the money I owe and I will pay it *ay-sap* and if he ever *humiliates* me in such a manner in front of a colleague again he will feel the full force of the law because I am a sector bobby now and I will straighten out my patch and my patch happens to be the city centre where he *does his business*, am I clear?

'You threatening me?' he asks, confused but getting angry.

'No,' I say, 'I'm telling you off this time. Consider it a verbal warning about your behaviour. I've made a record of it in my pocket notebook, see?'

And I hold it out to him to show my handwriting.

'You don't come here and tell me off, Jake,' Sinclair says. '*Ever.*'

I pause. Look at him. So that's how he wants to play it.

'Fine,' I say, and slip a Fixed Penalty ticket from the document pouch on my nice new belt. 'You had your chance. How would you define your ethnicity?'

'Eh?' he says.

I tilt my pen to the Fixed Penalty. 'For the form. What are you, White European, Black, Asian, Mixed Race? There's quite a few to choose from . . .'

'Are you serious?'

'Of course I am,' I say, and wait a few seconds, but he

doesn't say anything else, just sort of goggles at me. 'I'll just tick "refused", shall I?'

I sign, time and date the ticket and hand it to him. He doesn't take it, so I let it drop to the floor and he lowers his head to stare at it for a short while then looks back up at me.

'You're giving *me* a Fixer for disorderly conduct?' he asks.

I nod. 'I tried to warn you but you continued with a course of action that caused me harassment, alarm or distress. You left me with no choice.'

And then Sinclair does laugh, bends over at the waist and slaps his huge hands on his even bigger thighs, calls me a crazy motherfucker and I think I might agree with him but I'm too busy to discuss this today. I make my way back through the various exercise machines, ignore the pig noises, the calls of *babylon* and *filth* and *cuntstable,* walk out of The Elite for the last time, get into my truck in the car park and drive away, quite proud of the fact I've just successfully completed my first Fixed Penalty notice for public order with the minimum of fuss. I should really make an entry in my Personal Development Profile.

I've been waiting here more than an hour and run out of things to occupy myself with.

This is so unprofessional considering they're supposed to be Professional Standards. A real case of bad manners. Don't they realise I've got a job to do? I could be patrolling the city centre instead of sitting here on their plush little royal blue couch waiting for them to finish whatever it is they're doing upstairs.

The brassy receptionist, some old hawk dripping with pearls, a name-tag I can't be bothered to read pinned to the left breast of her royal blue force blazer, she gives me her pinched and knowing smile.

'Won't be long now,' she says again. This is mental abuse, surely. I'm being softened up here. Guantánamoed by a receptionist ready for those vicious little people from the Complaints department. Those fast-track slickies, the rubber-heel squad that you can never hear coming after you, the types who'll fuck you over given half the chance, no matter how many good things you do in your career.

I swivel around, tell hawk woman I'd really rather she didn't speak to me for a while, in fact never again please because I'm not very happy about being treated in such a rude manner by the organisation. She waits a beat then looks down, picks up the phone and pretends to dial somebody. I'm wishing I wasn't sweating so much because my armpits are damp then the doors to the inner sanctum of headquarters hiss open and three men walk out, head for the exit, don't notice me in the corner.

'Hey,' I call after them; I don't know why but it seemed the right thing to do for some reason. I step forward as they turn to look at me and there's something vaguely familiar about all of them, like I've seen them in a film: two plods and some skinny little guy in his fifties, a civilian in a baggy single-breaster with a blond fringe that's pasted sideways across his forehead. The civilian does a comical double-take and one of the cops, a bald fella, he sighs and resumes walking towards the exit ramp.

I take a few steps closer but the civilian steps away and the other plod, some old sweat with a frazzled handlebar moustache who reminds me of a Seventies porn star, he places a hand up to my chest and says: 'We can't talk to you, you know that, Jake.' And I have no idea what he's on about or how he even knows my name and I start to ask him when the civilian reaches out with an arm the thickness of a Twiglet and pulls at porn man.

'Let's go,' he says. 'We've given our statements.' Then he looks at me and says: 'You need help, PC Smith. If I'd known the full facts of the case I never would have prosecuted Cooper for you.'

Cooper. Cooper? Ah, yes! *Cooper.*

It clicks but they're walking away, following baldy down the ramp. A sweat rivulet traces its way down the side of my torso from my left armpit. I reach into my shirt pocket, wish my hands would stop shaking, pull out my pocket notebook, need to check it now I remember what I'm here for. I hoist my rucksack off the floor, don't look at the receptionist but tell her I'll be in the urination station if anyone wants me.

I don't need a piss but lift the toilet seat anyway, drop my trousers because I'm so damn hot then sit on the plastic ring. I flip through the notebook pages and can't recall writing half the stuff in there to be honest. Cooper. I check my prisoner list in the rear, trail my trembling, nail-less finger down the rows of names. *Where are you?* I say. And my voice bounces off the walls of the windowless toilet so I say *Cooper Cooper Cooper*, and suddenly I'm singing it and that's okay because the acoustics in here are pretty damn good.

Page fifty-eight. Dwayne Robert Cooper. I turn to the entry, speed-read my notes. It makes me laugh. I laugh so hard I'm doubled-up, trousers around my ankles, sitting on the loo with my boxer shorts still on and I sing his name again and I love that echo, man, that reverb, it's awesome. I'm sweating worse than ever now. I think I might be in a spot of bother here. Unless there's some minor miracle, I could end up smoking Lamberts and watching Jeremy Kyle all day.

I stand, dress, unlock the door and step out. I'm walking across to the mirrored sinks when I hear a toilet flushing. I didn't think to check the other cubicles when I came in, so turn around, see the door to the far left is closed and there's someone in there; now it's opening and I think about legging it out of here but I won't have time. Then out steps some ranker. It takes me a second to work out where on the ladder he is, but there're crowns on his epaulettes and it's a superintendent, of all people.

He eyes me for a long time, hands hanging at his sides, his left eyebrow arched in a Roger Moore stylee. Then he says: 'What's your name?'

'MacReady, sir,' I say. 'Frank MacReady.'

And he looks me up and down, shakes his head a little, and his beady, slitty eyes are on me for an eternity before he finally decides he's seen enough and without saying anything steps past me, uses the sink to wash his hands, gives them a once-over under the dryer and leaves.

I wait a few minutes then go out into the foyer. 'They're ready for you,' the receptionist says, and her hand hovers over the switch that buzzes open the double doors.

I pull out my notebook and pen. This isn't too clever a move here, but it's necessary to keep an accurate record to prove this conspiracy.

'Your full name, please?' I ask the hawk woman.

'Barbara Williams,' she says without thinking, years of conditioning, of being a prole, causing her to blurt it out when asked by a figure of authority. Then she realises her mistake and cocks her head.

'Why did you want to know that?' she asks, frowning.

I sigh. Try to be patient. I tell her I'm taking her name because her behaviour has been unacceptable and her inability to provide me with sufficient detail about when I would be allowed upstairs is tantamount to obstructing a police officer.

'I am warning you on this occasion,' I say, actually starting to enjoy this sector bobby lark. 'Don't let it happen again.'

This woman, she places a hand on her chest in an *oh-my* gesture, and I hear the rattle of her jewellery beneath her fingers.

'Nice pearl necklace,' I say to her. 'Buzz me in.'

And for the first time since I arrived this morning, she does as she's told.

FIFTEEN

I'm relieved to see Frankie even if the conversation is minimal.

As I reach the top of the stairs he's coming down the corridor looking over his shoulder, all furtive like, as if to check for any rubber-heelers sneaking down the lovely thick HQ carpet. Nobody's following him so he takes me by the arm, pulls me into an empty office. I'm just glad to have some sort of contact with him even if it's being dragged about.

'I've missed you, honey,' I say. 'Give us a kiss.'

He just peers at me over the rims of his glasses, looking tired. 'You've got to take this seriously, Jake,' he says.

I slap him on the arm. 'I'm good,' I say, and even though I've never boxed in my life I find myself bobbing and weaving, throwing air punches. 'I'm ready for 'em.'

Frank swallows. 'You'd better be. They could do your legs good and proper. Is it true about this plonk you've been stalking?'

I stop mid-punch and think about Rachael, about Cooper, about all the other stuff swirling around in my head. I can't latch on to anything tangible, any solid recollection of the last few weeks. I know Karen isn't overly keen on me at the moment, but that's about it.

'I . . .' I say, but nothing more comes out. I open my clenched fists, hold my hands up in front of my face. They're shaking again.

Frank steps closer, takes hold of my upper arms, and then I worry he really *is* about to give me a kiss, but he simply looks up at me and there's something in his eyes, the tight expression on his face, that I've never seen before and can't quite describe.

At a push I suspect it may be pity.

'If they see me talking to you before you go in I'm in more trouble than you,' he says. 'I just want to tell you I've done all I can.'

'Where've you been, Frank?' I ask.

'Where've *you* been, space cadet?' he says, smiling awkwardly. 'Spoken to your father yet?'

I shake my head slowly. 'Later,' I say.

'After this,' he says.

'Yeah,' I say, but this might be a lie. 'After this.'

Then he nods, wishes me luck, and walks out of the office.

The red LED timer on the machine reads 43, as in minutes, and I'm watching the little brown tape coil around the spools as Ewing drones on in the seat opposite and I'm thinking, Christ, how much more of this?, because this is the fourth three-quarter-hour cassette they've slotted in there and they don't appear anywhere near done. I calculate: one hundred and seventy-eight long minutes I've lost for ever.

If this runs over my hours of duty, can I claim overtime? I make a mental note to check the regs.

Today Detective Inspector Ewing is looking pretty slick: metallic black-and-white chequered tie, gunmetal satin shirt that's been starched to buggery, platinum cufflinks which match the expensive-looking diver's watch on his left wrist, though I suspect he's never strapped an oxygen tank on his back at any time in his short little life. No funky glasses or spiked hair; contacts and carefully coiffed locks are the order of the day. He looks the business, means business. And he has not *stopped*.

Next to Ewing is Superintendent Doug Jones, Deputy Head of the Professional Standards Department. I haven't been able to look him in the eye, even when he's asked me questions, and he must think I'm weird *and* a stinking liar now because he's the dude from the toilets. I almost fudged my underwear when I walked in and saw him sitting there and I'm still wishing I'd just given my own name when he appeared from the cubicle and asked me who I was.

This is just endless. They've wittered on about Dwayne Cooper and the Vietnamese or whatever-he-was chap from up the sticks. They've thrown in the usual open questions, closed questions, leading and oppressive questions that even a junior solicitor could argue out of the room. But then I didn't read the Reg Nine notice properly and forgot I could ask someone from the Federation to come here and represent me as a 'friend'. So they've been pretty much going for it hammer and tongs and I'm sick of it now and do they really think I can remember every tiny irrelevant scrap of information, each single moment of every incident I've been involved in since New Year?

Ewing checks his posh watch, announces the time and presses the stop button on the recorder. 'D'you need a comfort break, PC Smith?'

I'm playing with my dog tags through the cotton of my shirt and not really listening because I'm too busy thinking of other things like Karen, Frank, my parents, the fact I haven't had sex since before Christmas, where I'm going to get my juice now I've ditched Sinclair, how I'm going to find six thousand pounds to settle my debts, how on earth I'm going to clear the cave section on *Vietnam Encounter II* because I've saved my position but I'm running out of ammo for the M16 and my energy bar is pretty low. Maybe I should log on to the 'net and find some cheats for the game?

Coolock Branch Tel: 8477781

'PC Smith,' Superintendent Dougie says, and he doesn't sound very happy. I look up but not at him. The clock on the wall shows fifteen fifty hours, I've been up since oh-six hundred or so, only slept for a couple after waiting in my uncomfortable single bed in the spare room for Karen to come home from wherever she'd been and I'm so tired I could weep.

'No energy or ammo,' I blurt, then close my eyes and my hand is against my mouth, I'm gnawing at the skin on the knuckle of my thumb.

'*What?*' asks Dougie, his voice rising an octave.

'Sir?' I say and sit back, my head kind of fuzzy, stuffed with cotton wool, and I still can't bring myself to look at the Superintendent so my head is rolling around on my neck like Stevie Wonder's. I see Ewing has inserted another cassette into the machine. 'Aren't we done yet?' I ask, incredulous. I have a horrid sinking feeling in the pit of my belly.

'I said, do you need a break?' Ewing says. 'Cup of tea, stretch your legs?'

'I want to go home,' I say. I wonder if welling up might do any good then decide against it. Ewing looks the sort who'd capitalise on any display of weakness.

'Well you can't,' he says and presses the record button. 'So let's crack on, shall we?'

'Hoorah for me,' I say.

I can't stop my right knee twitching under the table, the heel of my tactical boot jiggling up and down like it has been since I first sat here. I'm exhausted. The fluorescent clipped to the ceiling tiles is making my eyes sting.

Ewing pulls out a handheld Dictaphone and looks at me, almost disgusted, then he says: 'In relation to the final matter of harassment, this message was recovered from a female officer's phone. We believe it to be you speaking, PC Smith.'

His nicely polished thumbnail clicks 'play' and I hear Rachael's answerphone spiel then it's me talking, or trying to talk. I can barely understand most of what I'm saying but the recording goes on and I hear *I needed you, you slag, 'n' you've stabbed me in the fuckin' heart, right, I saw wha' was goin' on at your place tonight . . . two of you, yeah, I saw shadows in the window, Karen, yeah you, no you I mean, Rach, 'n' lemme tell you, let me tell you, hang on I needs a smoke, hang on . . . right lemme tell you I will fuckin' kill whoever you're with now, I swear on my kids' lives I'll take a fuckin' axe to 'im because* and I can't listen any more so place my hands over my ears, ask Ewing to turn it off.

So he does, but not without an exaggerated push, a dramatic click of the stop button. His dark pupils are fixed on me.

I'm fucked, I say under my breath.

'Is that you talking to PC Rachael Gallagher?' Ewing asks.

'Yes,' I whisper.

'Then we're done here,' says Ewing. He reads the time again and stops recording.

'We've arranged for you to see a therapist,' Dougie says, and then I do look at him.

Ewing's nodding next to him. 'Your record up until recently was more than satisfactory,' he says. 'But these allegations are extremely serious. However, the organisation is . . . concerned about you. Hence the suspension of your firearms ticket. We feel you need a period of less intense work coupled with regular appraisals by an independent therapist.'

'I don't believe in all that touchy-feely shit,' I say. 'None of the grunts in the 'Nam did it. They just got on with it. And I've got people I can speak to.'

Dougie, he waits a beat, clearly weighing up whether he wants to prolong this further. Then he says: 'I have no clue what you're on about with this Vietnam thing, Jacob. But this isn't a debate. You're doing it. Twice a week, starting next week. Maybe somebody better qualified than me can work out what's going on with you.'

Ewing's still nodding away. 'PC MacReady has enlightened us a little about your . . . personal circumstances, which of course we take into account. But this isn't going to go away, PC Smith. I'll make sure of it.'

'I'm sure you will,' I say.

'And Rachael Gallagher,' says the Super. 'You steer clear. That's a direct order.'

He's looking pretty serious now, is Dougie.

'Are we finished?' I ask.

Ewing says nothing, starts boxing up tapes. The Super stands, thanks me for coming in, and I tell him it was my pleasure but really I feel like I've been run over, gone the full twelve with an in-his-prime Mike Tyson. I step towards the door, legs a little unsteady so I have to reach out for the handle before I crumple to the floor.

I'm on my way out of the interview room thinking: thank fuck that's over with, and all I want to do is get in my car and smoke when Ewing is at my shoulder, tapping me on my tricep, so I bunch it just so he can get a feel of something he'll never have.

'Almost forgot,' he says, 'your pocket notebook. We need to sign it for today.'

I look down at him, see the all-consuming hunger for greater things in his eyes, the way he'll sell anyone down the river – sell his own soul, probably – just to reach ACPO rank and beyond, the toadying, backstabbing career boy.

'I told you yesterday, I lost it,' I say and hold my breath.

Ewing starts shaking his head, swivelling it from side to side very slowly in a disapproving parent kind of way and he does this for ten whole seconds – I see them tick by on his never-used-properly diving watch – and then he says: 'We'll just add that to the list of incidents under investigation then, shall we?'

'Whatever,' I say. 'I haven't seen it since the raid, when you got the CID to take all my kit off me – which still hasn't been returned. So maybe you should ask that lot what the fuck they've done with my notebook while I just arrange for a replacement from Div Office?'

And I leave the interview room, really not caring any more what Ewing or Dougie or anyone else in this sterilised ivory tower of a building thinks about me. I take the steps down to the foyer, ignore the receptionist. In the truck I pull out my notebook, jot down a summary of today's events and spark up a cigar, thinking: now I'll have two of them to complete.

> ✝ _Retrospective notes_ ✝ Code 45 @ The Big House re Totalitarian State-style grilling. So good to see The Frankster there, despite what I had to endure in that interview. Chuck some pips or a couple of crowns on a bloke's shoulders and he thinks he's some kind of deity. It's bullying, man. That's what this is. I'm being victimised here. And I can't speak to Rachael about it. About the phone calls and shit. To make amends. Ever. They'll grass me up to Karen, man. Dob me right in they

It's already dark when I drive through the entrance gates.

Nothing's changed in three years, not since the last time I came here. Since she was transferred here on a Section Forty-Seven. Can't believe it's been so long.

The driveway is slick tarmac, concrete edging, lush green lawn mowed to a uniform half-centimetre. They've thrown in half a dozen hateful speed bumps along the quarter-mile route. I'm feeling nauseous enough already without my truck lurching over each raised strip. Have smoked six, maybe seven miniatures on the drive over, and my mouth is dry and woody. The skin on my head feels tight, like I'm wearing a swimming cap. A pain in my chest just won't go away.

Mum. I should visit you more often.

The truck rumbles up the wet drive. The closer I get, the worse the twinges in my chest become. I pull over to one side, let the engine idle. The clock on the dash shows seventeen forty hours.

I'm a teenager again. Growing up in the war zone that was my parents' house. Watching from the sidelines for years as they drank and fought and my mother pushed all his buttons, my father shifting from sullen to rage in a heartbeat, the words becoming slaps then punches then the dam was broken and there's no going back, just getting worse because once you start you can't stop and by the end he was just a drunken brawler and my mother his personal punchbag. Until that one night . . .

That one night. My eighteenth birthday. I close my eyes, see it play out like a movie scene for the ten-thousandth, hundred-thousandth time. There's no slo-mo, no orchestral score, no hammy histrionic movie-of-the-week drama, just blunt, shocking violence, so sudden, so unexpected, and it became the night I realised just what we're capable of if we're pushed hard enough.

My eyes fly open. Is this a panic attack? The palms of my hands are glossy with sweat and for a second I can't breathe. I'm feeling like I did outside Tang Yeh's house. I undo my seatbelt, lower the window, pull at my shirt collar. My pulse is maxing out; I can feel it thrum in my fingertips as I grip the steering wheel.

I reach across to the passenger seat. Let my fingers settle on the cellophane, hear the crackle, feel stems through plastic. Tulips. She always liked tulips. Or was it lilies? They'll have to do because I was double-parked and in a rush, but at least the young woman in the florist's looked relieved when I asked her for something other than Valentine roses.

Fuck it. I stamp on the accelerator before I change my mind, drive up to the car park, find a space at the back of one of the redbrick wings. Grab the flowers. Stand outside the truck for a few minutes, cold drizzly air tickling my face. Zip up my fleece to hide my uniform, watch some guy shuffling along in the rain, a blue puffa jacket over his pyjamas.

I take the steps up between two whitewashed pillars, through wooden double-doors into reception. Breathe in the musty, antiseptic smell that reminds me of an old school. Tiled walls, polished floors. Ornate cherubs, rolled cornices on the ceilings of this Victorian building. I wait for the bald guy behind the desk to stop mumbling into the phone, mumbling something that's obviously not job-related because he's chuckling and cooing to whoever's on the other end, so I drum my fingers on the counter.

'How can I help you?' he asks without looking up, his flirting session over.

'I'm here to see my mother,' I say. 'If you're not too busy, that is.'

Baldy jerks his head up then, eyeing me. 'Name?'

'Mine or hers?'

'Hers,' he says, face all pinched and upset.

'Bernadette Smith,' I tell him. 'Ward East One A.'

He waits a beat, watching me. Judging me. Relishing the fact he knows what she's in here for because now it makes him better than me. That my mother's a killer shipped here for indefinite treatment after a prison sentence. And they've always been like it. That momentary pause before they assume the air of superiority. That sniffy attitude. It's one of the reasons I stopped coming.

'Ah, Bernie,' Baldy says knowingly. Smugly. He looks at the bouquet I'm squashing under my arm. 'She'll love those. Bless her. Hang on a sec.'

So I wait for the staff member he tannoys, another staff member with an affably bored expression, an air of weary amusement wrapped in baggy corduroys and comfy shoes. He leads me through rubber doors and past Blu-tacked flyers offering counselling, therapy, drug rehabilitation. This chump in his jumbo cords is crapping away as we walk and I recognise the voice, it's the guy I spoke to when I rang on New Year's Day and he could be saying anything, maybe that he's in love with the hairless fella on reception or how he gets his kicks dry-humping the mad old birds in here after he's given them their medication each night, but I'm not hearing a word, have got my heart thumping quick-time in my ears.

We round the last corner and I almost bump into some old guy.

'Whoops,' he says, stopping. Actually looking down at me. A tall and tanned silver-haired fucker in a blue windcheater with some sailing-club logo on the arm.

I'm about to reply, tell him to bloody well watch where he's going, the Saga merchant, the Ralph Lauren wannabe. Can't he see I'm a little busy here? A little het up because of my situation? But I don't because the guy looks me in the eyes then snatches his head away, towards the wall, the way some of those mental cases do when you make eye contact. I think I know him. He's oddly familiar, and I'm trying to work out if he's some septuagenarian lag I nicked maybe fifteen years ago for thieving council-house boilers, when suddenly he's giving it toes, walking quickly up the corridor. Then he's gone and it doesn't matter any more.

My mother's gazing up at the television bolted to one wall next to the solitary window. Glazed over. Sitting in a bedside chair with a blanket across her spindly legs. She looks older, thinner. Worse than ever. Not eating again, probably. Hiding the food they bring in here just so she can bawl them out for starving her. I'm annoyed to see Jerry Springer on the box, two dumb shitkicker trailer-park sister-fuckers brawling over who's the father of the pig-ugly baby the gurning fifteen-year-old cradles in her arms. My mother stares at the screen.

Corduroy guy, he leans over to me. 'She's having one of those days I'm afraid.'

Aren't we all, matey? I step over. Drop to my haunches and place the flowers on her lap. 'I've brought you some tulips. Your . . . favourite?'

There's nothing. She's staring catatonically at the TV, at the Yanks fighting over Darlene and her inbred kid. And I've had enough of Jerry and Darlene and Wayne and Troy and the bouncers trying to separate the happy family. I stand, switch the television off. Take a seat on the edge of the bed near her chair.

'Mum,' I say.

And then she turns towards me but her eyes, they're not quite there. Not quite focused on *anything*. 'Keith?' she says. 'Are you back?'

I feel a twinge in my chest. She doesn't recognise me and it's all my fault. I turn to the staff guy. 'Are you Keith?'

'No, Bernie, it's your son,' he says, shaking his head, then looks to me. 'She's been gumming her meds. Spits them out when we leave the room. Take no notice.'

So I lean forward at the waist, reach out a hand, just want to touch her for a moment because, despite the glazed eyes and the fact she has no idea who I am, this is my mother. And I need her. My fingers caress the side of her face.

'Don't!' yells corduroy guy.

But it's too late because she's started screaming, is clawing at me, pushing herself away from me and kicking out, the blanket falling from her legs, taking the tulips with it.

'Don't hit me again, Nathaniel!' she's screeching. 'You stay away from me, you hear? Stay away from me!'

I'm leaning back on the mattress, supporting myself with unsteady arms. I can't move. The staff guy, he's pressed the panic button, is struggling to push her back into the chair. I can hear hurried footsteps approaching in the corridor.

'Mum,' I croak.

'I'll do it to you again, Nathaniel,' she's squawking, and I have no idea why she's yelling at my father. It's not like he's going to pop in here on the off-chance, is it?

More staff arrive. I stand, move over to one corner. Squash myself up against the wall and watch the chaos. Watch as they grapple with my mother. As they jam a big fucking needle into her skinny thigh. As she struggles for a few seconds then just conks out, head flopping down, stringy hair hanging over her face.

'You shouldn't touch her face or hair,' Corduroy is saying to me, his breathing laboured, his nice shirt missing a few buttons. 'We can *never* touch her face or hair . . .'

I did not know this.

I wait a while, pressed into the corner. For the chance to explain. But nobody in the room looks at me again, so I leave.

By the time I get home it's nearly nineteen hundred hours and I'm completely chinstrapped, my ears ringing. I dig a Stella out of the fridge and crash.

I'm sitting on the settee thinking about the shitty day I've just had and how it's only through my own strength of character that I've remained so positive. I can't work out what's different for several minutes so glance around, sniff the air, cock my head.

And then I realise: it's quiet. The house isn't lit up like a Christmas tree. There's no lingering aroma of cooked food. And I don't have a music channel blaring on my Sony Bravia.

I drop the lager bottle on the coffee table, check the downstairs rooms. There's a stillness that I'm not used to. I climb the stairs, check the kids' rooms. No one here. I walk into the master bedroom. Nothing. When I check out the window I see Karen's Mini is missing off the driveway. I didn't even notice when I pulled up.

I go into the spare room, to my uncomfortable single bed, and it's there I see the envelope wedged underneath the spare tin of Café Crèmes on my bedside table. Something in me feels like a plug's been pulled, as if all my innards are rushing south. I desperately need to take a piss and my knees have gone again.

I pick up the envelope, pull out the paper, unfold it. Karen's handwriting. Brief and to the point, just like her.

Jacob,

You and I are not working any more. There's been something wrong with you for a long time. Something very wrong since Christmas. I tried telling you at New Year but you just didn't listen. Please don't contact the kids as they don't want to talk to you at the moment. All you need to know is we are safe, especially now we're not around you.

Karen

I sit on the edge of the bed, stare at the letter for a very long time.

Someone please help me here.

Then I can't help it and begin to cry.

Monday 25th February

K & kids gone – 12 days. Area search still being made – neg thus far. Maintaining observations for K's so-called 'chili' red Mini Cooper with black go-faster bonnet stripes.

Contact Frank – also no sightings. Have been receiving threatening messages from Sinclair re. o/s money. Will deal with him in due course. Jessica?? Need to call round to check. Not sighted for weeks and need to pursue this line of enquiry further.

Must check industrial estate tonight. No reply to messages left on mobile & concerned for Lowri's welfare. ⸺⸺⸺⸺

1900 D Relief, Trinity Street nick. Parade with PS 5442 Baker and I'm sitting here writing this up as he briefs us and I'm surrounded by children. Boys and girls dressed in uniform, people I have nothing in common with. I keep reteap repeating it in my head: it's just for six months. Just six months. Like the doc says, take it one day at a time, Jake. One day... (fucking shrink. What does she know???) ⸺⸺

SIXTEEN

'Jake, you're on the car with Laptop,' says the stripy.

I groan inwardly as everybody around the table laughs at Baker's joke *yet again*. I've only been on this shift a week after the powers that be gave me five days' compassionate leave to get my head together but it clearly hasn't worked. It's lucky I don't have access to guns any more because it's quite possible I'd take them all out before swallowing a bullet myself.

The guy I've been doubled-up with is some midget twenty-year-old probationer and they call him Laptop because he's just a small PC. It's so fucking hilarious.

'Woot!' says Laptop and shakes his tiny fists in the air. Then they all do it. Their little in-joke. Their way of dealing with unpleasant news. They giggle among themselves and I close my eyes, measure my breathing like the doc told me to do, imagine myself in the firearms car with Frank doing real work instead of listening to these muppets.

Inhale. Exhale . . .

My new shift. A sergeant with four years in. Nine other plods, male and female, with a combined service that doesn't even add up to my own. Everything they do is at full pelt, laced with excitement and wide-eyed amazement. Everything's so nauseatingly jolly. They're fresh-faced young puppies and surely I was never this green-looking? And the nicknames – I can't bear it.

There's Laptop, of course. Two Backs, a flat-chested rake of a filly. Some lazy bastard called Gurkha because he doesn't take any prisoners. A gurning idiot who can't drive properly known as Chi-Chi due to all the pandas he's fucked. BMX, a girl who's allegedly done a few of the Senior Command Team so everyone thinks she's the station bike and easy to ride. Some jug-eared halfwit predictably called Plug. Gravity, a miserable bastard who's always bringing everyone down. Three Amp, this wiry fellow with a short fuse. Then there's Roid, an irritating, opinionated chunk of a girl, a sturdy little wench with strawberry-blonde hair she consistently fails to keep in a regulation bun. Her first name is Emma and, of course, you put it with 'roid' and you've got a pain in the arse.

I struggle to remember their real names because I care so little. And what's wrong with plain old Frank or Jake?

Nobody's labelled me with anything yet – at least not to my face – but I suppose it's because I just sit and stare, not talking to anyone unless I have to, while they slurp tea, talk shop and try to work me out. There's stuff I just don't understand. Computer systems I just can't get my head around. Job-speak that rolls from their mouths, like sanctioned detections, street bail, special population groups, corporate approach to hate crime. They may as well be speaking in tongues.

I'm lost. I haven't been on sector for ten years. I don't belong here. I get the feeling they don't want me either – I see it in their eyes. I'm an outsider, a cop on a disciplinary, someone who's been booted off a specialist unit. When it's like that your length of service, whatever you've accomplished, it all counts for nothing. Everything rewinds to the year dot.

Laptop is sitting next to me and I'm trying to write up my pocket notebook when he nudges me with his elbow. 'Ready for some action then, Jake?' he says.

I shift my notebook so he can't see. I don't look at him. 'Does your mother know you're up so late on a school night?'

I ask, and I can sense I've hurt his feelings. Don't care in the slightest.

I listen to the burble of my Airwave handheld, the nonstop chatter of the channel as the dispatchers in control send plods flying about the city. I know what my night has in store. Shitty calls with a proby who wets his drawers over a simple shoplifter.

And the real pisser is they've unintentionally stuck me on the same shift pattern as Rachael. I'm bound to bump into her at some point. And what am I supposed to do if that happens? Hide in the panda with my tit covering my face?

Then I hear my callsign blurt from my radio and Laptop's on the case and answering; it's a domestic in the street next to the athletic stadium, some shaven meathead giving his missus a tuning. I picture my father pummelling my mother and feel numb.

Laptop's shouting *code fifteen* into his handheld to tell them we're en route and I snatch the panda keys from his hand.

'I'll drive,' I say, gathering my kit as slowly as I can, planning on tootling down there at fifteen miles an hour and hoping this battling couple will be gone before we arrive because I can't bear the thought of getting a prisoner out of this one, of spending the next eight hours in a stinking custody suite with this child copper at my heel, listening to his endless questions. And most of all it's because I don't know if I'll be able to contain myself if I get my hands on the bloke who's doing it.

Baker smiles at us. 'And so it begins,' he says sagely. I almost laugh at him.

'Woot!' says Laptop and gives a little shimmy.

'Woot!' says everybody else.

I clench the keys in my hand.

Inhale. Exhale . . .

*

The mundanity of it all makes my head reel.

I'm neither surprised nor exhilarated by anything I've done or any call I've been to in the last week. Just constantly shocked by the pettiness of it all, how the people I'm supposedly serving are so inept as to be virtually incapable of looking after themselves. I'm society's garbage man, just here to take out the trash, to spoonfeed these spastic sink-estate dwellers, the trolls and inbreds in their shellsuits with their state-funded cinema-sized surround-sound tellies, these women – these *girls* – who think spewing out babies by different and now absent fathers qualifies as an occupation.

Already I'm sick of being used by these fakers – these underclass chavs who take and take and never give anything back – to run their lives for them when I should be out there fighting real crime. The poor genuine members of the public moan about never seeing us and now I know why: I'm too busy mediating between Chantelle's new boyfriend's brother's girlfriend Shazza and Letitia across the way because Letitia knows Shazza's been calling her a slag behind her back and that's why she and Shazza have been exchanging abusive text messages for the last three days. I'm their referee, their personal plod now they've latched on to my name.

I spent the whole day in the custody suite with them both yesterday, interviewing and fingerprinting, taking photos and submitting paperwork to the CPS, all the time knowing it'll never go anywhere and both of them will be back at it in a few days. Either at each other or some other plebian resident who's failed to show them *respec'*.

I can't get over how busy it is on sector. And I can't believe how much shit we have to deal with nowadays, like we're doing everybody else's job as well as our own. I'm some strange hybrid of policeman, fireman, paramedic, teacher, social worker, parent. I'm Frankenstein's public service monster.

Laptop loves it and I know Frank's on a night turn as well tonight so I'm driving around the city centre willing him to pull up next to me in the firearms wagon just so I don't have to listen to the overexcitable midget in my passenger seat for twenty minutes. Just to catch up, talk real work, find out if he's heard anything about my disciplinary. But I know as soon as I see him kitted up with someone else riding shotgun I'll want to weep. Or throttle the FNG next to me. I can't even have a Café Crème because Laptop's a nonsmoker and a newbie who'll drop me in it if I spark up.

It's twenty-two fifty hours and my companion's constant wittering is like someone gouging my eardrums with toothpicks.

I'm parked up doing my unofficial notebook so everything's recorded properly when the complaints people finally make their decision. Laptop's moved on to stream-of-consciousness ramblings and I haven't had to answer him for ten minutes because it's like he's talking to himself, the crazy fucker.

Karen's mobile is unobtainable and both kids' phones go to voicemail, so I've left yet another message for each of them but won't hold my breath because they haven't replied to any of the hundred or so I've left in the fortnight since they did a flit. I tried Frank's moby but it was off so I switched to the firearms talkgroup on the in-car set. He's in the sticks again, plotted up at the rear of some detached Walton family farm where John Boy's gone mentalist and holed himself up in an outbuilding with a hunting rifle.

I was angry about Karen and the kids and I'm angrier still about missing out on some action. I've got Mini-me with his motor-mouth sitting in the passenger seat, the city centre is dead but Laptop's going on and on about how he went to Divisional Consultation with Sergeant Baker the other day and, well, it was sooo interesting how they're trying to instigate crucial tactical change to decipher crime trend statistics that determine resource requirements. It's like a high-pitched whine. I'm chewing the crescent of new nail on my left index finger, biting at it, at the calloused skin. I can taste blood and it's enough to make me puke over myself, to stop the panda and walk away with the keys left in the ignition, just walk and keep walking, *anywhere*, because I'm trapped here, really fucking trapped with nowhere to go and I don't think I'm going to last six months of this.

I don't think I'm going to last another six hours.

'You're the most boring person I know,' I say to Laptop, and it aggravates me even more that this boy thinks I'm teasing him all the time now, like we're buddies, because he's grinning at me with shiny eyes. He's become attached, like a talking limpet.

Then, praise Jesus, I get a point-to-point personal call on my radio and it's the front desk clerk at the nick telling me someone's there to see me and no, they won't give their name.

I blue-light it over there with heart hammering, thinking at last my wife or maybe even Rachael's dropped in to see me and this is my chance to clear the air with one of them so my head isn't so cluttered. So I can get to the bottom of why I'm being treated like this. I feel elated as I scream through reds at junctions, Laptop holding on to the Jesus handle above the passenger door, sirens peaking and troughing, speedometer nudging eighty in the thirty limits. Who's going to know anyway? We're just another couple of busies on our way to an emergency.

I drop Laptop off at the side entrance to make a brew, peel around to the front of the nick, can't see Karen's red Mini parked anywhere, take the steps three at a time.

'Someone wants to see me?' I ask the desk clerk and she just nods, tips her head to some dude with an oil-black flat-top and dirty brown leather jacket hovering near the public information board in the foyer.

Not Karen, then. Gutted. I buzz myself out through the security doors.

'You've got an appointment with me?' I ask, and the guy turns around slowly. He's olive skinned, Mediterranean or possibly East European. Early thirties.

He smiles. 'Depends,' he says, calm and measured, voice deep, eyes blacker than his hair. There's no discernible accent and he's a good-looking chap, I'll give him that. Like a young Al Pacino, maybe. I'm struggling to recall if we've met.

'You here to give a statement?' I ask, but can't remember arranging one since being moved here. I've made a point of avoiding too much lengthy paperwork because it takes an age and I have trouble concentrating. 'Or you answering bail?'

Chummy steps towards me then stretches out a hand and I see the expensive-looking Swiss watch buckled to his wrist, the spiky tribal tattoo that looks like a bullet hole surrounded by lightning sparks on the web between his thumb and forefinger. I'm sure I don't know this bloke so leave the hand hovering in mid-air. 'I assume you're PC Jacob Smith?' he says.

'Who's asking?' I say, wondering how he knows my name. For some unaccountable reason I hear *The Godfather* theme in my ears.

He drops the hand. 'Relax,' he says, grinning. Those awful lifeless eyes on me. His teeth are glossy white and even, as if he's had them worked on at great cost. 'We have a mutual friend.'

'I don't have any friends,' I say. 'Perk of the job.'

He nods. 'I've heard you're a funny guy,' he says.

The Godfather score ends abruptly. I feel peculiar, perhaps nervously amused or intrigued, like this isn't real, like I'm a bit-part player in some really poor London gangster flick. I glaze over, can't help myself. 'Funny how?' I say, mimicking Joe Pesci's psycho turn in *Goodfellas*. 'What am I, a fucking comedian?'

His smile dies but he looks positively serene, completely in control, as calm as a cardigan-wearing dad speaking to a garden centre sales assistant. Suddenly I feel foolish. This man is no amateur villain. I see with absolute clarity what he's capable of. The unspeakable acts he's probably carried out in his line of work. I can smell it on him, know it's in his blood, his pores, his soul. I study his features, the crow's feet at the sides of his eyes, the small scar on the point of his stubbled chin, glance down at his meaty hands with their nicks and rough skin around fingernails he's clearly paid to have polished. I picture his face with lips drawn back, that tattooed hand gripping a tyre iron or length of pipe or maybe a nice long machete while he's raining blows on whichever street soldier has been stupid enough to cut the drugs he's been given to sell or skim a few dollar from the proceeds.

And I should be dealing with this, sorting this chump out because I'm the fucking *police,* right; this is my turf, the foyer of my own damn station and what I should really be doing is grabbing this heavy by the spikes of his carefully waxed flat-top and lobbing him down the entrance steps.

But I don't. This is a message from somebody further up the food chain. Way further. My own final warning. And I'm in more trouble than I ever realised.

'I've told Sinclair I'm good for the money,' I say, checking through the segregation window behind me. The desk clerk's head is down and I'm sure she can't hear because my voice is a husky whisper and Young Pacino has that menacing softly spoken thing going on.

He stands there with those black marbles on me, unblinking, breathing slow and shallow. Silently taking me in. He says nothing for so long it's unnerving and I try to convince myself he's ill or perhaps narcoleptic and has slipped into some deep slumber, forgetting to close his eyes.

Then he blinks as if to snap himself out of his fugue state or whatever little ultraviolence daydream he's having where I'm probably the chainsaw victim shackled to a shower curtain rail, reaches out one of those freakily muscular hands and pats me on my left bicep.

'You look in good shape, Jake,' he says.

I feel oddly light-headed. 'Yes.'

'And you have a lovely family.'

'Thank you,' I hear myself rasp.

He winks. 'Let's hope nothing happens to change any of that.'

I swallow, my throat giving a sort of spasm, and I want this fucking guy to leave now please, then I hear my name being called from somewhere behind me, some whiny boy's voice I never thought I'd be glad to hear again. I swivel at the waist to look through the glass to the front desk and it's Laptop holding my mug of tea.

I turn back to face the Pacino lookalike, to tell him it's all in hand, that I've just got to get a grip, talk to my shrink about this, get some help to see me through the next couple of weeks with the disciplinary and the stuff with my family and my parents, but he's gone into the night, the front doors to the station swinging quietly closed behind him.

SEVENTEEN

I slip upstairs to the sixth-floor gym, which I know will be empty at this time of night. I drop my uniform trousers, my boxer shorts, straddle the squat machine, zip open my battered leather carry-case, pull out my works. My last glass vial of Testosterone Propionate, a third of it left. I jam the needle into the rubber cap, draw out some juice, clear like glycerine, pull the hypodermic from the little glass bottle, then hold the syringe skywards and flick it with the gammy nail on my left index finger to clear the air bubbles.

This visit from Young Pacino is a worrying development. I could be heading for a shoeing. Or a kneecapping from the boss, maybe. A blowtorch to my eyelids. Blunt and rusty razor cuts across my torso. Or perhaps they'll skip the entrées and go straight to the main course of testicle removal? They'll be disappointed with their prize if they do because mine have atrophied to shrivelled prunes. Ironic, considering it's their gear that caused it.

I steady myself on the seat, lean to my left, slowly push the needle into the skin below my right hip. Intramuscular jab time. Just east of my glutes. But I'm not concentrating, feel the sharp point go awry and it's like someone scraping my femur as the pin goes too deep but I press the plunger anyway. I know I've nicked something I shouldn't have because when I pull the pin out a fan of thick purple blood spouts from the tiny hole. I see clear fluid bubble out and down the needle-scarred skin of my flank, curse myself for making such an amateur mistake.

I press my palm over the puncture hole for a while. Tidy my kit, pull up my underwear and trousers and then go for it, blast out some sets on the squat machine just because I'm on it, because I'm angry. Then I flip over and off the apparatus and go to the free weights, screw a hundred and twenty kilos onto a barbell, do some incline bench presses while imagining I'm lugging Pacino about and laughing at him while he grizzles and cries like a little pussy and wishes he'd never even contemplated confronting me. I picture my shrink or therapist or whatever that job-imposed hand-wringing busybody is supposed to be called, with her cod-psychology nonsense about the reason for my foot fetish and pathetic efforts to deconstruct me by means of cognitive therapy, of psychoanalysis, her threats to introduce pharmaceutical treatment. Serotonin uptake inhibitors. Dopamine blockers. Drugs that'll fuck up my muscle-building cycle, negate the effects of the steroids. She'll be pushing for the Ludovico Technique before I know it. I shove that bar to failure, creak it upwards and back, do this for ten minutes until I'm spent and flaccid and almost heaving and can't remember why I started. I sit up, rub my hands over my hair, which is getting long now, to be honest. Does it really matter? Does it? In the grand scheme of things? I will beat this. I am pumped. Vascular. Ripped.

I sniff at my damp armpits through the cotton of my white uniform shirt and in all honesty think they're fine so stand and leave the gym to find that gonk Laptop.

I need someone to talk to.

I want to go to the docks.

Oh-three hundred hours. Bang on.

I'm so pleased to see her. She's on a drizzly Radcliffe Street. All the desperate old pros have either picked up paying fuckbuddies or called it quits after being passed over by drunken punters.

Lowri. Walking the street alone. Same red jacket, black skirt, tights, FMBs.

'Leave me alone,' she says, and I'm driving alongside her with the window down. Laptop's in the passenger seat with a mildly appalled look on his face but I ignore him and keep rolling the panda at five miles an hour.

'Just making sure you're okay,' I say.

And I see it in those dark eyes of hers. Know she's tired, bored, sick of this.

Just like me.

'I said, piss off, *ossifer*,' she says, still walking, not looking at me, so I speed up, drive ten feet ahead of her, then park and climb out.

'Oh,' she says, smirking, 'it's you.'

It's raining properly now, pattering on my body armour, fat drops bouncing back from the pavement. Her hair's getting wet. The fur-lined hood of her jacket is already soaked.

'You're going to catch your death out here,' I say.

'Who gives a fuck?' she says, shrugging.

I can't help but chuckle, then I'm serious and think: actually I do give a fuck, more than you probably realise, Lowri, and I know what you're doing isn't good for you, that you should be looking after yourself, and if you can't then I'll make sure I do. You remind me of someone. The girl in the RTC. And this time I could save you.

You could save me.

'Er, hello?' she's saying, and knocking her tiny fist on my chest so I blink, bring myself back, and she's staring at me with narrowed eyes, an amused expression on her delicate, girlish features.

'I can help you,' I say, and think of Tom Cruise in *Jerry*

Maguire. 'Help me to help you. Help *me,*' I place the palm of my hand against my armour, then point at her, 'to help *you.*'

'You're weird,' she says, looking at my fingertip.

I shrug. 'Probably.'

She's grinning and it makes me want to place my arms around her but we've got company. I turn to a mortified Laptop, give him some bullshit story about this girl being my snitch, that I'm after some info, tell him to wait where he is and remember my rules: don't touch anything, don't go anywhere, don't talk to anybody, because you will fuck it up.

'Let's take a walk,' I say to Lowri, and she hesitates for a few seconds, looks from me to the midget sitting in the panda, then around at the buildings of the industrial estate. She's mulling it over so I wait and watch and when she says okay I feel thrilled, recognise this marks a new stage in our relationship.

I am a teenager on his first date. A husband rediscovering his wife after years of numbness. A proud father shepherding his young daughter to her nuptials. A son stepping alongside his beautiful mother.

I feel all these things and more. I'm wet and cold and bone tired yet could not care less. I haven't felt like this for as long as I can remember. Lowri is walking beside me and saying nothing, glancing at me occasionally, a quizzical look on her face, and this is fine. We walk further into the industrial estate, away from the main drag, and I check over my shoulder, know Laptop can't see us any more.

I lean down and take Lowri's hand.

'What're you doing?' she says, and stops. She stares at me then down to my fingers, which are now meshed with hers. I hold tight as she tries to free her hand, checks around the buildings, scans for shadowy figures in the doorways and overhangs.

'Please,' I say. 'There's nobody else here, Lowri.'

I like hearing her name slip from my lips.

'Let go, man,' she says. 'This is out of order. Who the fuck d'you think you are?'

'Please,' I say, and turn to face her. 'It's going to be okay. I'm going to take care of you, *Lowri*. If you're willing to spend time with me I'll make sure I'm always here for you . . .'

She's pulling, looking shocked and confused and not a little unhappy, but I don't care. Other than pummelling people, this is the first physical contact I've had for a long time. I can't let her go.

'Get off me, officer,' she's saying, so I hold tighter, kneel down in front of her, into the puddles of rainwater so I'm looking up at her.

'It's Jake,' I smile.

She frowns, stops wriggling. Her shoulders relax. Our fingers are still intertwined, which pleases me, and I know she's just given up fighting. She knows I'm not going to hurt her, would never hurt her. She flicks her eyes down to my hand, back up to me. She's sodden now; the hook of dark hair has become a limp black rope swinging next to her ear.

'Why?' she asks, and I'm not sure which part of what I've just said she's asking about, but don't care.

I think of Sinclair, of my visitor in the foyer, how much I already owe, how I'm up to my neck in it, but I grin anyway and tell her: 'I'll pay whatever you want.'

'Pay me for what, exactly?' she asks.

It's a good question. I puff out my cheeks and say: 'Your time. For now.'

Lowri studies me for a minute. 'This'd better not be entrapment.'

I shake my head. 'No. I wouldn't do that to you.'

She closes her eyes, tilts her head backwards and to the sky.

I see her breathe in the cold, the drops of rain landing on her upturned face. Thinking. Our future in her hands. Then she looks down, back to me. She nods.

'Okay,' she says quietly.

'Okay,' I say. I am elated.

'But you can't turn up here any more, though,' she says. 'Dressed like that or not.'

'I won't,' I say. 'I'll ring you. I've already got your number.'

'Was that *you* the other night? How'd you get my . . .' And she stops because she knows what I can do. Knows the things I'm capable of.

'Just one thing,' I say.

She knots her eyebrows, stares at me. 'What now? I gotta go . . .'

'What're your feet like?' I ask.

'You're so fuckin' weird, Jake,' she says, but this time there's a gleam in those dark eyes of hers.

I picture us, her standing over me in the rain, me in my plod outfit kneeling like I'm proposing, looking up at her with a goofy grin and my fingers laced between hers. 'You're not wrong there, sweetheart,' I say.

93

Into my station and threaten me I swear Pacino you are going to HAVE IT son I wish I'd checked you out before clocking off but better believe me friendo, I'll be conducting intelligence checks upon return to duty, just going to check that tattoo of yours on the system, find out where you live and RAPE YOUR FUCKING PETS. Would slip in there on days off and check myself but can't trust any of them. None of them. Can I wait four days? Can I? Who is he? Who is he?? Who is he whoishewhoishewhoishe whoishewhoishewhoisheWHOTHEFUCKINGFUCKISHe ??????

Tuesday 26th Mar February

Rest Days.

EIGHTEEN

I'm knocking on Frank's door, a pain behind my eyes like brain freeze, like I've swallowed a gobful of ice cream; my face is twisted, eyes screwed shut and I'm thinking: why can't you sleep, Jake? You really, desperately need to close your eyes and crash for eighteen hours because this is killing you. And I think I might be ill. Possibly something terminal. There's a dull, painful throb in my stomach that just won't go away. I picture a tumour there, a ruinous lump pulsating against the folds of my intestines, microscopic tendrils needling into my stomach lining, my pancreas, my colon.

C'mon, Jake. Peach in. Green out. Like the doc says: positive chi.

My rest days have been a blur. I've achieved nothing. Can't switch off. Last night I lay in bed watching the bedside clock as if my eyelids were stapled open. Worrying about the money I owe. Imagining what Karen was up to. Then Rachael. Then losing track of who was who. I finally clicked off at about oh-six ten hours, dreamed some freaky trip where I was cuffed and stuffed, being led through the ruined city centre, a hybrid of *Children of Men* and Gilliam's *Brazil*, some twisted dystopian cityscape of belching factory fires and bombed-out shopping arcades, Vangelis's *Blade Runner* theme playing while armed quasi-military police baton-charged the scavenging proles into orderly bread queues. Bizarrely, Frankie was running the show, decked out as Hitler and ordering his gun-toting minions about the high street from a raised dais planted in front of Ann Summers. Instead of a megaphone he held a dildo. I was pushed and shoved onwards by barefoot porn actresses in soldier outfits, and everyone was watching. Watching and laughing. They dumped me in a grimy anteroom, a wall of plate glass on one side, and I looked through and saw Karen sitting in a viewing area with Naomi and Ben. Next to them was Rachael. Then Lowri. Then Tommy Hall, Collingwood, the Chinese guy. Ewing. Cooper. Even Mel with her gippy feet. All of them in a neat little row, reading through their programme notes, their little pamphlets with *Jacob Smith: Why Bother?* on the front. At the far end stood Adolf Frankie, waving his Rampant Rabbit about like a crazed conductor. Then I was sitting in the electric chair, wet sponge and copper skullcap wedged on my head, hands and ankles shackled to the wood frame, leather strap between my teeth to stop me gnawing through the tip of my tongue when the inevitable bite reflex kicked in. And I heard the opening bars of a song seep from unseen speakers: the fuckin' Spice Girls. 'Goodbye', I think it's called; the one they released when the Ginger minger quit. So in they came from a side door: Sporty, Posh, Baby, the other one. Linked hands with Karen and the rest of the audience and as one they stood, crooning to me through the window.

Goodbye, my friend . . .

It's eighteen oh-five hours and I'm leaning forward, hand on Frank's door, when it opens and Jessica's standing there in a white vest top and cut-off jeans with bare feet. I'm momentarily lifted.

'Jake,' she says, a little concerned.

'Your dad in?' I ask.

'Yeah . . .' she says, opening the door wider. 'Are you . . . okay?'

I straighten up. Rub a hand over the top of my head. My hair growing out. Longer than it's been for years. 'I'm tickety-boo,' I say, stepping inside.

'You don't look it,' she says.

I'm disappointed to hear this, so implement my breathing plan. Draw in lungfuls of air, of clean energy. Exhale, force out the negatives, the green and poisonous shite that's ruining my karma.

'Well, thanks for that, Lowri,' I say.

'Who?' she asks, but I'm in the hall now, walking towards the lounge, can hear Frankie's voice and really need to speak to him so remind myself to finish this particular conversation later.

He's in his armchair on his mobile and I don't know who he's talking to but he kills the call. 'Jake,' he says, standing. 'You look terrible, mate.'

I *feel* terrible. My guts, they ache like buggery. My eyes are sore, itching.

'Cheers,' I say, and point at his mobile. 'Who you talking to?'

He waves a hand, dismissive. 'Oh, nobody interesting.'

'*Really*,' I say.

He looks at me strangely for a few seconds. 'Yes, Jake,' he says. 'Really.'

'Not Sinclair, then?' I ask. 'Or was it Al Pacino?'

Frank's shaking his head. 'Wha . . . *who*?'

Ah, yes. He doesn't know. That's why I'm here, isn't it? Jessica's feet threw me a tad. And I notice she's walked into the room, is standing behind me and to my right; I can smell that citrus perfume of hers.

Frank is looking from me to his daughter and back. There's silence, as if nobody quite knows what to say. I'm just glad Mel isn't here because I'm sure she would've chipped in by now. Then Frank sighs, asks Jess to put the kettle on for us, so I watch her go, check those slim feet of hers as she paces out, toes scrunching through carpet fibres, and I'm trying to work out just when it was I last had sex, when I had any form of intimate contact with a woman other than holding hands with Lowri, and as hard as I might I really can't recall. Weeks. Months, maybe? And Frank's saying something to me but it's distant, muffled like his head's in a bucket, so I tune back in and he's asking me what's been going on, how am I, what's the news with Karen? So I lie and tell him everything's good, there's nothing going on, just sector work and catching up with *myself*, y'know, just a little *me time* like the doc told me so I can figure things out before Karen comes home. Frank's saying, *Yeah, how's that going, the therapy thing?* and I want to tell him it's a crock of shit but at least it's keeping Professional Standards off my back, but I don't because it's not why I'm here.

I breathe through my mouth. Peach in. Exhale through the nose. Green out.

'Can you lend me six thousand pounds, please?' I ask.

Frank says nothing. I'm not sure if he's totting up his current bank balance.

And I explain to him about the money, the visit from Young Pacino, that li'l Mexican standoff in the foyer, but I don't need to elaborate because Frank's not stupid; he inhabits the same strange and cruel world I do. He gapes at me for a minute or so before sinking into his chair, placing his head in his hands.

'My God, Jake,' he says at last, fingers still covering his eyes.

'I take it that's a no, then,' I say, and wonder if a packet of Tums might get rid of this belly ache I've got. Some Gaviscon, perhaps. I've heard Gaviscon is good. I make a mental note to drop into a chemist on the way home. 'I need help here, mate,' I say. 'My credit cards are pretty much maxed out. I'm desperate.'

Frankie looks at me. Just looks. Then he gets up from his chair, walks past me to the lounge door, and I'm starting to think he's going to tell me to leave but he's got his mobile in his hand and he pauses in the hall, turns to me, and I swear I feel myself welling up when he says: 'I've got to ring Mel. Discuss what we're going to do to . . . help you.' He jabs the phone in the direction of the kitchen. 'Stay here. It could take a while.'

He looks miserable as he says this and I'm torn between hugging him and feeling ashamed, so do nothing. I just watch him disappear, hear footsteps on the stairs. I drop to the settee as Jessica reappears.

'Thank you, sweetheart,' I say, taking the mug of tea.

She stands over me. 'Where's Dad?'

'Important phone call,' I say. 'He told me to tell you you've got to entertain me.'

She doesn't move for a moment. Just eyes me, those thick black lashes of hers static beneath her shaped eyebrows. 'Did he, now?' she asks.

Is she teasing me again? Peach in. Green out. Where's your balls, Jake? Shrivelled, yes. Removed? No. 'Thought we could finish off the conversation we had the other week?' I say before talking myself *out* of saying it. I look from her face to her chest, her midriff with its pierced belly button, to the three-quarter-length jeans, her feet.

'Really?' she says, her eyes narrowed, hands balled and on her hips. 'Which part would that be?'

'Where you couldn't stay downstairs with me to watch *Platoon*,' I say. 'Because if you did . . .' I let the sentence hang there, just as she did.

Jessica blinks, lets out a sigh. She checks the doorway. We can hear Frank's voice from the room above: it's high and strained, like he's arguing.

'I was pretty drunk that night,' Jessica says finally. 'I can't really remember coming home, never mind what I said. What's my dad doing?'

I don't want her to get sidetracked so just take the plunge. 'Your feet are so beautiful.'

I'm not sure what her reaction is. Shock? With a side order of disgust? Then she says: 'How can you call feet beautiful? That's sick.'

I'm having one of those moments when I wish I could erase the last few minutes, delete them from the DVD hard drive and start afresh and damn, my tumour hurts so much.

'Ha, yes,' I smile, feeling like vomiting. 'It's, y'know, a line from a film.'

And she kind of laughs, like it's a big weird joke she doesn't quite understand, but that's all right it's good old Uncle Jake messing about again so she drops into a chair, switches on the television, mentally dismisses me. I shake my head, try the breathing plan but can't get my diaphragm to operate and I've had enough of people telling me things like this, I'm sick of people telling me I'm sick, that I need help, that there's something wrong with me. I sense that wave start to build again, hear the white noise in my ears, and I don't want to explode here, not now.

She's staring at the soap on TV and it's like I'm not here. One foot dangles from the edge of the chair. I listen to Frank's muffled voice, think how I should just tell Jessica everything. Maybe she'll listen. *I was paying you a compliment, Jess. You do have wonderful feet. You're so lucky.* Explain to her how the doc says I'm a podophile, that it's not sick, that I could list other peccadilloes people have which *would* give her reason to freak out: creepy shit like wanting to fuck lactating pregnant women, acrotomophilia where I could only get it up if she were a multiple amputee. There's some crazy stuff out there I could tell her about, stuff I've discussed in therapy and checked on the 'net. What I've got is a form of paraphilia, brought on by an intensely traumatic experience as a teenager. That should tug at her heartstrings, right?

But as I'm thinking this I'm staring at that foot hanging off the edge of the settee, imagining myself dropping to all fours, crawling across to it, licking the arch, the heel, shrimping those toes. And Jess will writhe on the cushions, arch her back, moan softly as she closes her eyes, *yes, Jake*, she'll say, *that's right*, as one of her hands slips down the front of her cut-offs, as she places her other foot on my groin, grinds her heel against it, tramples my balls . . .

I blink. I have my biggest hard-on in years. It's colossal. Throbbing at the front of my jeans. Visible, like a thick tube beneath the denim. And Frank's stopped talking upstairs. He's finished the call. Shit.

'Erm,' I say, 'I have to go.' And I do. Now. This boner ain't going anywhere. I could hold my breath for an hour and it wouldn't deflate. Not with Jessica here. If Frank sees it I can forget about any help with the money. He'll know. And now I can hear him moving about up there.

'Oh,' Jessica says, turning to me. 'Aren't you going to drink your tea?'

I let the mug hover over the bulge. 'I forgot an important . . . thing.'

'What shall I tell my Dad?'

'I'll ring. Yes. I will.'

She stares at me, head cocked to one side. 'Ooo-kay . . .'

So I stand, mug still placed strategically. Jessica rolls her eyes and shrugs, swivels her head back to the TV. That foot, those painted toenails, still dangling there.

I know in her mind I'm already gone from this house. She's not even looking in my direction. I pace into the hallway, feel that wretched clawing sensation in the bottom of my guts and wish I could just hug her, simply place my arms around her frame. Nothing sexual. No perversions or erotic transgressions.

I step out of the front door into drizzle and think: I just need someone to hold on to.

I lay out my supplies on the lounge coffee table.

The dregs of a Testosterone Propionate vial. Two Trenbolone Acetate. No Arimidex at all, but my nipples aren't tender so I can deal with that. Some old Equipoise, barely a hypo's worth. An almost-empty blister pack of Clenbuterol. That's it. Nothing else. I don't know where I'm going to get a top-up.

I check the fridge for beer, the shelves for spirits, and there's none, so slump into the settee. Getting dark outside. I switch on corner lamps, uplighters. Channel-hop through property programmes, chat shows, twenty-four-hour-misery news. Think about firing up the PlayStation but the prospect of repeating the same level while trying to conserve ammunition for the big boss fight at the end is unbearable.

No ammo. No steroids or booze. No wife or kids. Nothing. Four empty days. I ring Frank, get no answer on either phone. Walk the downstairs rooms, brush my fingers over favourite cups, photo frames, ornaments; find myself staring into the kitchen sink with the tap running and can't recall getting there. I climb the stairs, see posters and jewellery and unwanted music CDs Ben and Naomi left behind. In the master bedroom I open Karen's wardrobe, touch the few items of clothing hanging there. Find the red halter top I bought her on my birthday, raise it to my face: it's been washed but I can smell her perfume, the faint floral scent. I bury my face in it. Breathe it in. Where are you, Karen?

It's nineteen fifteen hours. I don't know how long I've been awake.

I stagger into the bathroom, turn on the shower, strip off. Then I remember about my hair, what a mess it is now, how unprofessional it must look while I'm patrolling. I dig out my clippers from the drawer in Karen's bedside table, plug them in, turn them on, adjust the blade then sit in front of the mirror. Strike a pose. Flex. Tense my pecs, my delts. Rock up my abs. I think I'm losing weight. Is something eating me from within? Is it over thirty-six hours since I slept properly? Forty-five minutes this morning, does that count, especially when it involved the Spice Girls and my best friend poking the air with a sex toy?

I walk downstairs, ignore the fact I'm stark bollock-naked and the blinds are still up, check my mobile for messages. Nothing from Frank. Maybe I could ring Lowri. Have a nice chat, right? I drop to the settee, rolling that lovely name around my mouth again, thinking maybe this'll calm me down a little before I shave my head, before I wash away the day. I speed-dial her number and I'm saying *LowriLowriLowri* and she answers after one ring, knew it was me because she's added my name to her contacts list and that pleases me. It makes me happy. I am Lowri's friend.

'Hey, Jake,' she says and I know she's smiling from the tone of her voice.

I grin, push myself back into the cushions, stretch my bare legs out. This is strangely erotic.

'Hi,' I say. 'It's so good to hear you, d'you know that?'

She laughs; it's deep and throaty. A dirty laugh. I like it. 'You saw me a few days ago,' she says, and I think about that for a moment and really can't remember if I did or not.

'Just talk to me, *Lowri*.'

She giggles again. 'You're mad,' she says, and on this occasion I forgive her for saying it because now I'm relaxed. Naked. Phone in my left hand. My limp cock and shrunken scrotum in the other.

'Just talk to me,' I say again, and she hesitates, asks if I mean dirty and if it does it'll cost me so I tell her yes, if you like, and yes, I'll pay whatever you want just put it on the tab and fuck knows where I'm going to find the money but then off she goes and it's all premium-rate sex-line stuff so I smile, I'm nodding, rubbing myself and there's nothing happening there, nothing at all, which is a disappointment, but my eyes are blinking slowly, I'm listening to that earthy voice of hers, those words in my ear, the breathiness, the obscenities and descriptions of what she's doing to me, what she's going to do to me when she sees me next and I sink further into the cushions, hand falling away from my groin to the settee, I can hear the shower running upstairs, remember the clippers are still on and shaving nothing but air and I really should lower those blinds, drop them now before we go any further and I will but just need to close my eyes for a second and listen, breathe in the peach, blow out the green, breathe in, breathe out, breathe.

thought about what I'll do to this lot if they kick me out of the job, I've thought about it long and ~~bread~~ hard because, let's face it, what else have I had to do these last few days? Really? What have I had to do to occupy myself? So if those fuckers in Professional Standards do my legs I'm going to ——

1) Set fire to all the Gatso speed cameras in the county ——

2) Get hold of a few cheapy mobiles, not register any of them, then make false 999 calls every day for a month ——

3) Jam potatoes into the exhausts of every traffic patrol car in the city

4) Send anonymous letters to the press detailing how inept this organisation is

5) Deliver pizzas/curries/taxis/gravel to Chief Officers' home addresses

6) Pay some girl (maybe Lowri?) to leave dirty messages on the bosses' home telephones — see what their wives think of that ——

7) Take a shit in one of the drawers of Collingwood's old desk — a gift for Ginge. (maybe I should leave a dead fish while she's away for the weekend? — they could DNA-test the stool and trace me...) ——

8) Post the door security entry codes for every station in the force area on the 'net ——

That'll learn 'em.

NINETEEN

Laptop volunteered us to ops room before I could grab his dwarf hand, stop his stumpy fingers transmitting, and now I'm here in this hovel, this stinking one-bedroom ground-floor council maisonette with its kitchen-stroke-diner, its sink full of scummy water and festering dishes.

There's kiddies' TV playing on the battered set in one corner. The girl on the sagging settee is five, maybe six, a hollow-eyed angel with black hair in untidy bunches, staring vacantly at the television with her mouth full of cornflakes. She's in a school uniform of some sort, a red and white gingham dress, knee socks grey where they haven't been washed properly, once-patent leather shoes scuffed and losing their stitching. Her mouth works at the cereal, eyes on the gigantic purple dinosaur prancing across the screen to some inane ditty. I'm not sure if she's desperately trying to avoid watching the commotion around her, or is so inured to it she hasn't even noticed. Like it's the norm. But then I suppose if you live in shit long enough you don't smell it any more.

The girl stops chewing for a second, looks up at me, at Laptop.

'Is she getting better?' she asks, but there's no emotion there. Her voice is flat, listless. World-weary before she's old enough to know what the phrase means. I glance across the room.

Two paramedics, a blur of green jumpsuits, they're working on her mother where she lies on the floor near the other chair. The woman looks about thirty-five, thirty-six, but I'm probably well off the mark because the heroin's aged her prematurely. Her works are laid out on the glass-topped coffee table. Dirty needles. Couple of hypodermics. A bent spoon, blackened where she's cooked up. She's all grey-green skin and dark hair matted with vomit. Pulse fading. No breathing there. *C'mon*, they're saying to her, rummaging through their bright orange kitbags for adrenalin shots, saline, more needles. *C'mon, love, stay with us*. I watch the dinosaur dance across the screen.

They'll be lucky to find a good vein on her. Old track-marks, telltale mini-bruises and scab lines, they're dotted from her wrists to what's left of her biceps. When we put the front door in she was comatose on the settee, jeans around her ankles, half-full syringe of brown shit hanging out of her groin. A nice straight femoral scag injection.

I look at the little girl, this pretty thing with black crescents beneath her eyes, her alabaster skin, and try to imagine the things she's seen. The life she's had with this junkie mother. And I look back to this woman wasting the time and effort and equipment of the paramedics and my fists clench.

'Your mum's going to be okay,' says Laptop, and he's probably right; they'll bring her back around and she'll take it easy for a while, for a couple of weeks perhaps, and then the memory of what she's put her daughter through will fade. Then some other plod, some other ambulance crew, will be standing here doing it all over again.

So I wait and watch, wishing I was someplace else, and the woman's suddenly awake, sucking in a chest full of air, sitting up against the settee and looking around at us with dried puke on her chin.

'Wha' the fuck you lot doin' 'ere?' she shrieks, and she's yanking at her jeans, rolling onto her knees with her bony arse hanging out for all to see; pushes past the two guys who've just saved her life and shuffles across the room to her daughter. She hugs her, knocks the cereal bowl with one scabby elbow. Milk spills onto the little girl's lap. Her eyes never leave the television.

'Get out,' the mother hisses, so I look to Laptop, to the paramedics.

'You're a disgrace,' I say to her, really not caring any more.

This scrawny woman, she snaps her head around, draws back her top lip. Her teeth are brown, stunted and rotted from the gear. She looks feral. An animal. 'You can't talk to me like that,' she says. 'I pays your fuckin' wages . . .'

So I step over to this smackhead, feel Laptop's tiny hand on my arm, shove it off. I lean down to the woman, take her skeletal, grubby hand in mine, and while she's looking up at me all saucer-eyed and fearful I shake it. And then I can't let go. I'm squeezing, can hear a faint *click-click-click*, realise it's her knuckles popping, her carpals and metacarpals cracking, and I tell her *thank you, I've always wanted to know just who it was that paid that money into my bank account every month and I should be grateful, shouldn't I, I mean how hard must you find it, paying all that cash to me so I can do my job, especially when you're the* victim *here, isn't that right you're just so unlucky in life and you never had a choice and really you need all the money you can get for your habit because sticking a needle in a major artery in front of your daughter is your only means of escape*, and my hand squeezes, she's crying now, big whiny sobs tearing out of her and the daughter's crying too, then Laptop's pulling my arm and the paramedics are at it as well so I let go. Just stand over her, breathing hard.

'You fuckin' *pigs*,' she screams.

'You fuckin' junkies,' I say back.

'Jake . . .' says Laptop, staring at me. The paramedics are standing in front of the television doing the same. I can hear music, some nursery rhyme, the mother's hugging her child and they're sobbing together so I turn to the medics and tell them to move, they're upsetting the little girl because she can't see her programme, so they shuffle out of the way, confused, still watching me. I place my hand on the kid's skinny shoulder.

'Be good,' is all I can say to her but it seems hollow and pointless so I walk towards the door, swipe a handful of the paramedics' sterilised hypodermic syringes from the top of the coffee table, think how I'll need them for my juice later today, and leave the flat. Leave Laptop to fill in the forms, to ask ops room to ring Social Services.

I sit in the panda car, engine running, counting as the wipers chug across the windscreen and I don't know how long I'm there but hear more vehicles arrive, the junkie woman screeching and screaming, the unmistakable sound of van doors slamming shut as she's locked in the rear cage. I hear the soft and vacuous words of a male social worker, picture him with his goatee and brown corduroys, ushering the girl in the gingham dress to his car so he can dump her with the nearest foster family.

Laptop climbs into his seat, bringing a burst of rain and cold air with him. 'All sorted,' he says.

I don't look at him. 'I need a drink.'

He waits a beat. The wipers judder. Then: 'We didn't think you'd be interested so nobody's mentioned it,' he says. 'But the shift is out tonight. Hitting the town to blow off some steam. Seven pee-em at Anzac's. You're welcome to come.'

I weigh it up: standing around some city-centre bar with kindergarten cops I have nothing in common with, or sitting in an empty house in my boxer shorts trying to get it up while Lowri whispers filthy nothings down the phone. It's a tough call.

'I haven't been to Anzac's since I was your age,' I say.

'The licensee owes our Inspector a few favours,' says Laptop. 'Drinks are free for the first two hours.'

I turn to him. 'Sold.'

The parade room's deserted so I log on to a terminal, thinking maybe I should fill in some online forms or check through my deliberately slender workload, but end up snooping about to see if there's been any incidents involving Karen or the kids so I can trace them that way.

I'm digging through the calls that came in on my days off when my mobile rings. The number's withheld. Lowri, calling from a landline somewhere? Frank?

'Jake?'

Male. Cheery. I vaguely recognise the voice.

'Er . . . yeah?' I say, clicking through reams of shitty domestics.

There's a pause. Then: 'I want my fucking money, Jacob.'

My mobile suddenly feels very heavy in my hand. Hot against my ear.

'*Pacino*,' I croak.

'Who?'

'How . . . how did you get my number?'

Another pause. 'I'm very resourceful, buddy. Tenacious, you might say.'

'You can't do this to me,' I say. 'I'm the bloody poli—'

'That's of no relevance to me,' Pacino says, still sounding affable and really rather buoyant. 'Six thousand. From you or Sinclair, it makes no difference.'

'It's all in hand,' I say.

'Please don't let me take this to the next level, Jake,' he says, and cuts me off.

I stare at my mobile. Look around. Thank fuck there's

nobody here. I throw the phone in the nearest bin. Stare at it. Retrieve it. What if Karen tries to get in touch? If Naomi or Ben call? If Frank rings to tell me the money's sorted? And this is the only number Lowri's got.

I have an unshakable image in my head. My genitals in a vice, the handle being turned by a smiling drug warlord.

I kill the computer, stand, kick back the chair. My vision is blurred. I'm stumbling out of the parade room, down the corridor, feeling with my hands, trying to remember where the damn toilets are and I bump into somebody and I think it's Baker and I mumble *sorry, Sarge* and know he's looking at me oddly but can't stop and then I'm in the gents leaning over the toilet and up comes my breakfast. Porridge. Two bananas. A rice cake. All pink and sugary from the strawberry protein shake I washed them down with. My first decent meal since God-knows-when.

I slump down the toilet wall, sit on my haunches. I don't even realise I'm wailing until there's a knock on the cubicle door.

'Jake? You okay?'

It's Baker.

I don't answer. Place a hand over my sticky lips. If I stay here long enough, stay quiet enough, maybe he'll just go away.

I spend three hours getting ready. Iron the clothes I bought on the way home. Iron them again. Hang them in the spare bedroom to maintain the creases. Polish my shoes, bull them to a parade-ground shine. Shave my hair. Shower for a whole hour.

I eat in the lounge, sitting with no clothes on again, fill my empty stomach, line it with the last tin of tuna from the kitchen cupboard, two plain chicken fillets with rice and broccoli. Slug a pint of milk mixed with six egg whites. Pop the last two Clenbuterol tablets, use one of the clean needles the paramedics gave me, or I took from them, I can't remember which. I draw out the last of the Testosterone Propionate, stretch the skin below my left hip, use my thumb and forefinger to pull it taut, stick the needle in and press the plunger. Almost weep as the Testosterone disappears into my body. Pull out the needle. Sit back.

I wonder if Young Pacino knows where I live. That's a fucking worry. And I can't get hold of Sinclair for gear nor money. I need to speak to him. Urgently. I hope Frank comes through. I hope he's talked Mel around, explained how serious the situation is.

I check the time on the DVD player. Eighteen ten hours. Too early to drive into the city centre. So I wait. And wait. Sit naked and alone in silence. Can hear my stomach bubble and whine as the food settles. Rachael. Don't think about her, Jake. *Don't*. But I wonder if she'll be there tonight? Maybe that's why I've put in all this effort to get ready. To make her see what she's missing. I lean forward, flex my pecs, my delts, curl my hands into fists to pump my forearms. What we had was good, wasn't it? Brief but beautiful. A beautiful mistake.

And I know I shouldn't but I'm running scenarios through my head, how I'll react if she shows at the Anzac bar tonight; then I'm pacing the lounge, naked, talking aloud, losing myself. Smiling, trying casual and indifferent. Frowning and doing angry, humiliated. Weeping, all hurt and heartbroken. The DVD clock shows eighteen fifty. Running late. Maybe this is for the best. Maybe I should hold these thoughts for later. Because if Rachael's there . . .

No, Jake. Stop it.

I climb the stairs to get dressed.

My belly's full of lager, warm and bloated.

An hour and a half without moving from my seat. Laptop's making my head spin, shooting back and forth to the bar to get them in before our two hours of *gratis* drinking are up, *woot*ing and doing some odd little dance to the Eighties synth music with a goofy smile on his face. I'm necking everything he places in front of me and secretly considering changing his nickname to Lapdog.

I've plotted up so I can watch the door. Watch everyone coming in. Scanning for Sinclair. Young Pacino. Rach. Karen. Sitting here at this trestle table pocked with old fag burns, rows of dim red bulbs hanging from the ceiling beams. Surrounded by people, alone. I think about slipping out to spark up a cigar, perhaps slipping away full stop because none of them would notice. But I don't. I'm still hanging on to the hope that Rachael will turn up.

I swivel my head, look out the window, to the arcade outside, the line of pissed-up cops queuing to flash the badge at the squat little hardnut at the door. *Do you take warrant card? That'll do nicely, sir.* And in you come for free. All the men dressed in the regulation off-duty jeans, Timberland boots and surfing shirt combo. The women with their hair down, war paint on, still stiff and alert despite half a dozen Bacardi Breezers. A new generation coming through Anzac's front doors; half the city's plods in here and barely a civvy in sight because they know Old Bill have taken over.

Baker's sitting opposite me, flanked by his kiddie cop shift.

I can't seem to stop catching his eye. He nods at me again so I lift my pint, take a swig, nod back.

'You okay, Jake?' he asks, leaning forward and shouting over the music.

'I'm wonderful,' I say. 'Can't you tell?'

Baker scoots his chair closer to the table. 'I thought . . . you know . . .' he stutters, glancing around furtively. 'The thing in the toilets today? Was it the incident with the mother and her kid?'

Jesus. I don't need this. This boy, sergeant or not, asking *me* if I'm okay. Like he can help somehow. Like he can empathise, use his vast life experience, all twenty-five years of it at most, of nothing but school and drinking his way to a uni degree and accelerated promotion. So I tell him yeah, it was a shocker but I'll manage, then turn away, eye the queue again. Get up for the first time since I arrived, neck the rest of my pint, step over to the bar for another freebie, find my legs aren't working properly, but I've missed the slot and now they're charging, the bastards.

Then Laptop's next to me, pissed, elbows on the bar counter and swaying, sleeves of his shirt mopping up the spillages. 'All right there, Tee?' he says, like we're fast friends, buddy cops, Butch and Sundance except nowhere near as cool.

'Whas' this "Tee" thing, pigmy?' I ask him, and marvel at how pissed I actually am now. My mouth feels Novocained.

Laptop laughs uproariously, throwing his head back. Everybody looks. He overbalances, stumbles against the bar. Watching him makes me feel sober, so while he chuckles away I order another pint, just the one, no going in rounds with these muppets now they're charging and I down it in one, slam the empty pint back on the counter, signal for another.

Laptop's arm is suddenly around my shoulder, hanging at an awkward angle because he can't reach properly. I freeze.

Can't bring myself to look at him. 'S'our nickname f'you, big guy,' he shouts in my ear. He must be on tiptoes. 'Y'know . . . T Rex? Get it?'

But Baker's pulling him away before I can reply, sitting the gonk down next to him and having a quiet word. T Rex? Huge, frightening, powerful? Is this what they call me when I'm not about? I pick up the new pint of lager, have lost count of how many I've sunk since arriving here, my guts are sloshing about, my six-pack morphing into a keg. My head's starting to feel a little loose on my neck.

T Rex. Big, strong meat-eater. The nasty fucker in *Jurassic Park*. I *like* it.

I step back to the table, surprised how heavy my feet feel.

'My round,' I say, feeling a little strange, that this could be a turning point, a watershed moment where I finally become part of this shift. Where I become part of something again. 'Time for ol' T Rex to gerrem in!'

Everyone laughs. Laughs *with* me, I'm sure of it. Laptop's off again: *heeyaaargh-argh-aaaargh!* BMX is rocking back and forth, slapping her surprisingly dainty hands on her thighs. Her nicely toned thighs in their tight jeans. Even that taciturn golden boy Baker, he's shaking his head and grinning.

And I actually start enjoying myself. The drinks are still coming and I don't know if it's me that's paying or Laptop fishing out twenties and I don't care because these faces are all around me now. Gravity, Chi-Chi, Three Amp. My shift. These wild and crazy guys who've gifted me this awesome nickname, who've *embraced* the man I am, accepted me into their little clique, and the music's playing and it's classics like Depeche Mode's bouncy 'Just Can't Get Enough', Soft Cell's seminal 'Tainted Love', Duran Duran's New Romantic masterpiece 'Rio', and those red lights pulse in the rafters.

I see BMX and Roid watching me from one corner, know

now that Rachael's a no-show and it kills me but you've gotta have a fallback, gotta have a Plan B, and this girl, this easy ride, she's pretty hot in a plumpish kind of way, chunky but funky, she's eyeing me now as I head towards her, my shoes still not quite gripping the floor of the bar.

'Wanna dance?' I say to BMX, tensing my pecs.

I can smell her perfume; it reminds me of Jessica's. Citrusy, delicate. Her hair's a dark brown Louise Brooks bob. Her feet are short and stumpy, but the toenails are glossed and most importantly they look clean. Not too shabby . . .

'With you?' she asks, smiling.

That sour-faced munter Roid, she's glowering at me but I ignore it. 'Yeah,' I say, grinning, knowing I'm on to a winner. 'C'mon. Dance with T Rex.'

'Ooo, I'd be honoured,' BMX says, looking down at my feet. ''Specially since you made the effort to dress up.'

And they walk away laughing. I'm confused because it's not play-along laughter, it's mocking and spiteful, so I check down, wonder what she's on about, see I've worn my tactical boots to the bar, completely forgot about the shoes I spent half an hour polishing. I watch the girls go and I'm getting angry here because BMX was my Plan B, my fail-safe, some stocky little no-mark I'd never give a second glance under normal circumstances but here she is taking the piss with her poisonous little redhead friend and I'm walking after them, desperately trying to carry out my breathing exercises, my chest tight, can't inhale never mind exhale and they're still laughing, I'm closing the gap and if I get my hands on them . . .

Then I hear Roid: 'Dickhead. As *if*. Who does he think he is?'

And BMX: 'Yeah. T Rex. Smelly old fuckin' dinosaur . . .'

I stop walking, stand at the edge of the dance floor, pick up the nearest pint glass, push away hands that try to grab it back, smash the glass on the floor, then I can't hear anything because my head's full of static, it's rocked back and I think I'm screaming. My throat straining. Eyes on the shitty little bare red bulbs. And I know if I look back down I'll drown under the weight of everybody's gaze because they'll all be watching now. Watching; saying nothing in that judgemental squeaky-clean new-breed-of-copper way. So I close my eyes, wait for the hiss in my ears to fade, wait for the music to wash in and then it does, it's Culture Club and I can't remember the song title but it doesn't matter because I won't hear it finish.

I keep my eyes on the floor, push through whoever gets in the way and leave.

Code 45 Code 45 Code 45 Code 45 Code 45 Code 45 Code 45 Code 45 Code 45

I'M NOT GOING TO TALK ABOUT IT

I wake, cold, eyes gummed shut with sleep-gunk. Can feel a warm, heavy weight on my chest. Can't move. Don't know where I am. It's freezing, the hairs prickling on my forearms. I know I'm still drunk, know I'm lying on my back. There's a tapping noise above and behind me, an incessant hollow knock – *tonk tonk tonk tonk tonk* – and my swimming head throbs, amplifies the sound until it's the beat of a bass drum between my ears and I'm fighting the urge to be sick. My God, Young Pacino's burying me alive, isn't he? That noise, it's him hammering in the last few nails . . .

Open my eyes quickly, squinting. Murky grey light. Grey everywhere. Look down, see dark hair. Somebody's head on my chest, my jacket hiding the face. Still the knocking, so I force my head backwards, tilt it so I'm looking upwards, ignore the twinge of my muscles where I've slept awkwardly and see a face pressed up to a window.

Some guy, forty-something, pasty faced, wearing a beanie hat. Unshaven. Not Pacino, thankfully. He looks half puzzled, half amused. His spindly fingers are curled into a fist and hovering against the glass. I see nicotine stains around the fingernails.

'Thought you two were dead,' he shouts, mouthing it as well, as if I may be deaf or just plain fucking stupid.

You two. I shift my head, look down the length of my body. See the black hair splayed under my jacket. I push the jacket to one side, see the red coat underneath and then she moves, lifts her face, eyes all puffy, blinking at me.

'Mornin',' Lowri says, croaking a puff of breath into the cold air.

I quickly look around, neck burning. We're in the back seat of my truck.

'Get up,' I tell her, pushing her off me, away from me, feeling a mild sense of panic. I hoist myself up on an elbow, shuffle backwards, sit upright. There're empty bottles of Stella in each footwell. The dash clock shows oh-six fifty-three hours.

Lowri sighs, looking miserable and tired. She has bed hair. She pulls at her coat, covers herself against the cold, shifts across to the far side of the seat.

Beanie hat is still gurning at the window. I look past him, see lit streetlights, low redbrick buildings, roller-shutter doors. An industrial estate someplace. Not Radcliffe Street. I have no idea where I am. 'Take a picture, mate,' I say to him. 'It'll last longer.'

His hand is still resting against the window of my wagon. His face falters, the cheeky little smile vanishing, and then he's a tad put out that he can't watch any more, that I haven't thanked him for waking me up like this, so he twists his hand at the wrist, raises his middle finger and flips me the bird before walking away.

'He likes you,' says Lowri.

I check my clothes: still buckled and buttoned. 'Did we . . .?' I ask her, not sure how to finish.

'No,' she says, shaking her head patiently. 'We just talked. Or rather you did.'

'Good,' I say, closing my eyes. I think I'm relieved.

'*Good*?' she says, and starts to pull on her coat. 'Thanks very much.'

'I didn't mean it like that,' I say, but I'm not quite sure what I meant.

'Whatever,' she says, and pulls open the door. 'Ring me when you want to bore me about your parents again.'

'Lowri, wait . . .'

'Fuck off, Jake,' she shouts.

Then she's climbing out and I'm reaching after her with one hand, reaching across the back seat to the open door because I don't want her to go like this. I can't remember what we talked about last night but I must've needed it, must've known she'd listen. I want to tell her more, to explain how I feel about her, to work out what she means to me while I'm doing it.

But the door slams shut and she's gone, her jacket a fading red smudge through the condensation on the truck windows.

and he's not saying anything, just sitting there not saying a damn word why don't you just TALK you sulky stunted spawn of the devil, just say something because I'm sick of this, I'm sick of these pointless calls I have to attend with you riding shotgun, even the drunks, these muppets here who think it's funny to call me ossifer, to call me five-oh, piggy, fascist, scuffer, filth, who think I've never fucking heard it all before, they're better company than you, do you know that? Do you? They're better than you. I wonder if anyone would notice if I just strangled you, buried you in a shallow grave somewhere? Get out of my panda car, Satan's lovechild. Get out! The power of Christ compels you! But these drunks, I can't let 'em get away with it. I call in the van, set the TSG on 'em, watch the Ugly Bus boys go to work on the pissheads. What a giggle.

2320 I can smell roast pork, which is a very bad sign indeed. She's gone, man. I can tell, sitting here with the devil's imp, that stink in the air. That stench of burnt gammon steak wafting around this cluster of bungalows. Old gripper probably dropped her Superking into her lap when she dozed off. Or maybe a clutcher? You know, dodgy ticker giving out and she falls into the log fire or something? Poor old bugger. Such a shame. But I'll be fucked if I'm sticking around to do any of the paperwork. Fuck that for a game of soldiers!! Let the detective knobs

TWENTY

Lapdog's strangely subdued.

No annoying laugh, no stream-of-consciousness ramblings, he's not even volunteered us for anything tonight. It's like I've gone deaf. We do a couple of drunk nuisance incidents, turn over a car full of shit, and they're clearly on the rob but we find nothing so I consider winding them up for a public order arrest but remember the paperwork involved. Cut across the city to help out at a domestic when, predictably, the wife who rang us for help started attacking the bobbies who were arresting her husband for chinning her. Turn up at some OAP complex, find our Inspector there with Baker and Gravity, Trumptons swarming about playing with their hoses, hear it's a genuine, that some old dear's turned herself into a crispy critter so disappear sharpish before the CID rock up and collar us to take twenty-seven-page statements. Boring, monotonous sector stuff. Pondlife and drunks, mongoloids and druggies. People not knowing how to look after themselves.

The calls dry up at oh-one hundred, so I just drive. Drive anywhere and everywhere, like I used to with Frank, when we were the firearms night crew with the whole force area to cherry-pick. Except I'm not with Frank, I'm with this sulky, catatonic midget and there's six hours to kill. Six long hours of silence, of atmosphere. I don't know who's done what, who's the bad guy here. Who's supposed to be angry with who. Maybe Baker tore a strip off him last night for the nickname thing. Perhaps he thinks I'm pissed off about it, want to lay into him a little and am waiting for the right moment. What he doesn't know is I really have more important things to be worrying about. That I miss my family. That I'm so tired I feel the ache in my bones.

It's a shame. The gonk was starting to worm his way into my affections. Like an over-enthusiastic puppy you can't be bothered to kick any more.

I give it an hour, do a last loop of the centre, the panda puttering along in first past the Duke Road shops, the castle, the dead pubs and clubs on the high street; through the pall of greasy air and river of chicken curry cartons on takeaway alley. It's cold and late, there's nobody around, like the city's taking a breather. Lapdog's quiet throughout. I reverse the car into the entrance to one of the arcades, deep enough so the civvy camera operator at the nick can't pick us up, lower my window and turn off the engine.

'So,' I say, turning to Lapdog. 'What's up with you, drama queen?'

There's nowhere for him to look, nothing for him to pretend he's interested in. Just a shop wall. His head kind of vibrates, like he's struggling not to turn my way. Then he gives up and looks at me with his wide boyish eyes, those weirdly long lashes of his fluttering beneath furry eyebrows, and I know he's nervous but there's something wrong, something wrong here *again*, a problem in work and I'm not sure if it's of my doing but want to know.

And then he says: 'I can't say.'

Jesus. 'No, actually you can.'

Lapdog looks upwards, glances at me, gives a nervous smile, teeth stringy with bubbles of saliva. 'Gossip . . . you know.'

'Obviously I don't know,' I say to him, calmly as I can. 'Because if I did I wouldn't be asking, would I?'

And I'm beginning to wonder what Baker's cooking up

behind the scenes, what contact he has with Ewing at Professional Standards, whether he's been tasked with keeping a watchful eye and promised he'll progress his career if he finally kills my own, and I'm mulling all this over, breathing hard and gritting my teeth; but then I'm thrown, lose my train of thought because Lapdog does the strangest thing: he begins to cry. Right there in the passenger seat with my face pressed up to his, an inch apart, seatbelt straining at my shoulder. My top lip drawn back, bottom lip wet, spittle gathering in the corners. His baby fingers covering his eyes. My spittle on his fingers. I feel his warm breath on my face, puffing out the sides of his hands as he sobs and hitches his chest.

'Hey, come on,' I say, moving away from him a little, settling back into my seat. How embarrassing. I'm checking around, making sure there's no public about, no passing drunk to see me leaning over this midget with calming hands raised as he blubs and drips snot onto his utility belt. 'C'mon, fella. I was just asking.'

'It's just rumours . . .' he snuffles. His voice is thick, churning words. He's sucking in tiny gasps. 'About you and . . . stuff you did with someone. Someone who's a friend of a friend. I . . . I just don't want to get you in any trouble.'

Christ on a crutch. I can't be doing with this so fuck the consequences. I pull out my cigars, light one. Pull on it as hard as I can, fill my airbags with good, dirty smoke. Exhale. Blow out the green. Or on this occasion the blue-grey, but whatever: I feel instantly better.

'You can't smoke in police vehicles,' Lapdog says and I swing my head to him, shrug. His cheeks damp and pitiful. His eyes cracked with red, mournful.

'Have one,' I say, offering the tin. 'You know you want it.'

'I don't smoke,' he sniffs, all prissy again.

'Yes you do, Ben,' I say.

One of those bushy brows of his arcs in the middle. 'Ben? My name's Ma—'

'Shut up,' I shout.

I hear a familiar petrol engine whining. Screaming almost. See a flash of red pass across the front of the panda. Chili red? *Karen* . . . It's Karen's Mini Cooper. Got to be. I turn the key in the ignition, ditch the cheroot, push down on the throttle.

'What're you doing?' Lapdog yells, eyes wide, head darting about.

'The car,' I say. 'Got to check that car.'

'I didn't see anything,' he says, holding on to the Jesus handle as I peel out of the arcade entrance. I ignore him, accelerate in Karen's direction, see brake lights flash in the darkness a hundred yards ahead. It swings left past the Euro Arena. She's really motoring. Crimson lights flashing on and off as she cadence brakes around bends at speed.

'Shall I call it in?' Lapdog's asking, fingers on his radio, eyes glittering now, adrenalised, excited, thrilled to be part of a follow. No more blubbing and snot runners hanging from his conk.

'Leave it,' I say. 'Ops room'll just stand us down.'

The car judders as it takes a right at the next set of traffic lights, straight through a red, must be nudging fifty by my reckoning. I'm closing the gap.

'It's two up,' Lapdog says oh-so-helpfully and I say nothing, just straighten my right leg, push my boot onto the accelerator pedal. I can see, boy. I have eyes. A driver and a passenger. Karen and Naomi, maybe. Or Ben. Or . . . wait. Her new beau? Some guy she's already shacked up with, who the kids are already calling Daddy? Oh, dear. How I wish you weren't here, Lapdog. How I wish I was on solo patrol, behind this car, behind Karen, fingertips hovering near the dashboard control panel, just one click away from illuminating the blue strobes, the wailers. From making her stop so I can see who she's with. So I can deal with it. With *him*.

Then we're taking a left fork at about forty, more streetlights here, the roadway more illuminated, and as we enter Vichy Boulevard my heart hangs heavy when I see it's just some Corsa, a red kiddie car with body kit, twin chrome exhausts, tinted windows. Souped up, Max-Powered to the hilt. Not a Mini. Not Karen after all. Just some boy racer out for a spin.

I flick the strobes on anyway because Lapdog's looking like he's about to wee his pants and will start crying again if I drive off without him getting the chance to have a word. The Corsa runs for a little, the driver contemplating whether to stop. Possibly pissed. It's done a half-dozen moving traffic offences anyway, but I couldn't care less. I'm trying to recall why the dwarf was crying.

Halfway down the Boulevard, the Corsa pulls over and I ease in behind it, see the silhouettes, the dark shadows of the guys inside gesturing and waving their hands about, short sharp movements like they're arguing.

'All yours, mate,' I say to the midget, and he's out of the panda car with his booklet of Fixed Penalties before I can finish the sentence.

So I sit, let my pulse settle, watch Lapdog talk through the front passenger window. To some hulking brute, by the looks of things. Shoulders filling one side of the car. Neck thick as the headrest. The driver's bent over to one side, looking past his companion at the stunted police child at his window. Whoever it is, he's an agitated fucker. Jerking his arms about, slapping the steering wheel. Pointing and jabbing his fist at li'l Lapdog.

I sigh. Climb out of the panda. I don't want any aggravation tonight or any night from now on, thanks very much, so step towards the Corsa, preparing myself to defuse the situation, to spare Lapdog a mauling at the hands of these two clowns, just as long as it negates any paperwork, as long as I don't have to stand in court again for a case I don't give a shit about. Too much going on, Jake. Too much . . .

The passenger door opens, Lapdog steps back a-ways and the big guy unfolds himself from the Corsa.

It's Sinclair.

'Well, well,' I say, and he's checking from the midget to me, back and forth. Like a tennis spectator. But there's something not right. For a monster of a man he looks pretty fucking perturbed. Twitchy. In the background the driver's gobbing off, still in his seat, telling me we've only stopped them 'cos they is black, innit? As if I can see through tinted glass from sixty yards away at fifty miles an hour at night, the cock.

'Shut the fuck up,' Sinclair yells at his companion, then looks at me, eyes still nervous, still shifty. 'Jake,' he says. 'Thank God it's you.'

I'm confused. I thought he'd be asking me for money. Not looking desperately relieved to see me here. I quickly check the driver: some black kid in his late teens. Not Young Pacino from the station lobby. I breathe a sigh of relief of my own.

'I'd like to speak to the driver alone,' squeaks Lapdog.

I'm just watching Sinclair. Never seen him like this. Not in all the years I've known him. The guy's normally an animal. Something's definitely rotten in Denmark.

'It's my nephew, Jake,' Sinclair says, waving a hand at the driver. 'Family, you know?'

'I know all about your family, bra,' I say to him. 'That your brother who came to visit me the other night while I was in work? I can see the resemblance.'

'I'd *like* to speak to the *driver* alone,' whines Lapdog. I can't see him but picture him stamping a foot on the road.

My eyes are on Sinclair. Studying him. Reading him. He gives the slightest of shrugs, a microscopic widening of the eyes. Silently pleads.

'Put the driver in our vehicle then,' I say to Lapdog, and step towards Sinclair. 'I'll deal with this guy here.' I take him by the arm, by his forearm which is almost thicker than my thigh, lead him back to the passenger seat, sit him in it. He closes the door as I walk around the Corsa, climb into the driver's seat.

'Before you start, I'm good for the money,' I say, not looking at him. He's rifling around in the glove compartment.

And then he says: 'Fuck the money, bra. You gotta help me out here.'

I snap my head towards him. 'Help you? You want me to help *you*? They've got my mobile number. They probably know where I *live*.'

'Please, Jake.'

And it's then I see the package in his hands. A brown paper bag with the top rolled closed, lying on his upturned palms like an offering to the gods.

'What is it?' I ask, looking at the indistinct shape within the bag. I can smell something familiar. And I can smell sweat, smell fear coming from the man in the passenger seat next to me.

'You gotta help me out here,' he says again. 'My nephew . . . he ain't got no licence to drive, man. No insurance, nothing. I know your buddy back there's going to find that out pretty soon and you'll have his wheels towed. And once he sees my boy's got form for dealing he's gonna be crawling all over the car with a fine-toothed, y'know?'

And he's right. I can hear Lapdog running checks with ops room right now. The registration plate on the Corsa I'm sitting in. The name of the kid driving it. Then he's asking for a drugs dog to RV for a sniff, gets Baker to authorise a garage call-out, to seize the vehicle for scrapping because Sinclair's nephew probably can't even spell *drive legally*.

Sinclair hears the transmissions.

'When they take the car they'll find this,' Sinclair says. He shifts the paper bag towards me. 'And then he'll, both of us, we'll be in a world of shit, Jake . . .'

'I'm not taking anything from you,' I say to him, shaking my head. 'You've got me into enough trouble.'

'They're looking for me too, bro,' he says.

'My heart bleeds.'

'I'll get your debt written off,' he says then. 'Gone, baby. All gone.'

I stare at him. Look down at the bag. See dark stains on its surface. Smell that annoyingly familiar aroma. It looks light. Inconsequential. Like there's air trapped inside the paper. This crumpled gift horse. This six-grand golden handshake. 'What?' I ask him.

'Do this for me, Jake,' Sinclair hisses, thrusting the package closer. It's nudging my ribs now. 'Do it and I'll see the money you owe becomes a big fat zero. I swear.'

I look down at his shovel hands. Glance behind me, through the windscreen of the panda car, see Lapdog's soft little face flashing blue and white beneath the strobes. This is my out, here. I can sense it. I can walk away clean. One strand of the fuck-up that is my life at the moment sorted out.

'What is it?' I ask Sinclair again. I take it from his hands. Feel the weight, guess it's in the ounces. Feel damp on my fingers. The aroma tickling my nostrils. I bounce it once, twice. This is our agreement, then. I will take it from him, whatever it is. He will square everything with his business partners. We are gentlemen. We have each other's word.

'Thank you, brother,' Sinclair's saying, but I'm not really

listening. I'm calculating just how costly this favour is likely to be.

So I unfold the top of the bag, pull it open, it's got to be drugs, got to be gear of some sort and I reach in thinking what the hell I'm going to do with a big chunk of base amphet, a bar of cannabis resin, but at least I'm going to be free of debt so does it matter? and please, please, *please* let it be juice instead, let it be some vials of Propionate. I feel my heartbeat pick up speed, begin to sweat like Sinclair, hear the *whumpwhumpwhump* of blood in my ears, am vaguely aware of Sinclair opening the car door, squeezing himself out into the night, trudging over to his nephew. Of Lapdog finishing his checks over the radio. Of flashing blue lights on roadside foliage.

I pull out the contents of the bag. It's a rag. A folded piece of dirty cloth. Something solid inside. I carefully open each corner, tug at the frayed edges, then my breath catches and I know what that smell is now, it's oil; so I transmit to Lapdog, tell him to let Sinclair and his nephew go. That the Corsa is clean. We'll just tow it away to teach 'em a lesson.

I look down. Look down for what feels like a long time. The rag is open on my lap, splayed like the petals of a filthy flower.

Well, well. *Say hello to my li'l frien'.*

It's a Kahr PM9 nine-millimetre ultra-compact in black polymer. Matt-blackened stainless-steel slide. Three-inch barrel. The ultimate concealed weapon.

A mouse gun.

Nice.

	my prayers were answered. Resolution in sight. Keep chugging along, Jake. Yeah.
1045	For a moment there I thought it was them. The goons, for their money. All
	that hemm hammering on the door, but lo and behold, who was it but good old

★

I end the call, drop my mobile to the bedside table. Laugh.

I've had just three hours' sleep after the night turn – blissful, dreamless sleep – and ordinarily I'd be rather upset to be woken this early, but now I'm absorbing what Ewing's just told me, his gutted and begrudging tone, and it's enough to make me push that to one side and savour the moment. Feast on it. Revel in it.

Because I'm in the clear. Ready to rock 'n' roll again.

Good old Frankie. Stood tall when it was required. Backed me up over the Oriental guy with his ganja factory and the gun. With that sorry-looking chav on New Year's Eve. Corroboration, that's the key. Complaints dropped. No further action. NFA. Yeah, I've got to play the nodding dog about giving Rachael grief, most likely have those matters informally resolved, but I'll sign whatever paperwork they want so it's all filed away and forgotten about. It's a small price to pay.

I told Ewing I considered being removed – *temporarily*, I stressed – from the firearms unit punishment enough. All quite upsetting, I said. Humiliating, even. He stammered and stuttered, desperate to get off the phone, but this was my moment, my time, *me* time, so he coughed and cleared his throat and told me my ballistic kit, all the hard-earned tactical gear they swiped for examination after that incident up the sticks, had been released by Forensics and I could collect it from HQ whenever I liked. Office hours, of course.

I lie on my bed for a while. Stare at the ceiling. Whoever's up there, I thank you. No more complaints. No wife and kids, sure. No firearms work . . . yet. And I'm hoping Sinclair's done the decent thing and called off the heavies. But the worm has definitely turned!

I ease myself up on one elbow, pull open the drawer on the bedside table. Push aside my unofficial pocket notebook. The oil-stained rag rests among the household crap. I lift it out, marvelling once again how light it is. Drop it on the surface of the quilt, unfold the corners. Look at the mouse gun. A dark and beautiful piece of craftsmanship, a nine-millimetre pocket rocket.

I stroke the snub-nosed barrel lightly, delicately, with the pad of my forefinger.

'Aren't you a pretty little thing?' I say. I lift it, wrap my hand around the grip, wave it about, *bang-bang-bang*, I hear myself say, and if there was a mirror in this shitty spare bedroom I'd do the Travis Bickle thing from *Taxi Driver*. I slip a finger into the trigger-guard. Pull on the slide, yank it back, amazed at how effortless it is. How easy. Like wielding a toy. I check the mag, drop it from the grip, count four rounds plus the one I've just chambered.

Good job things are getting better. Improving. Just think, Jake. Just think what could've happened if you'd had this thing at the nick when that heavy turned up. Or in Collingwood's office with Ginge leering at you. Or perhaps while you stalked the corridors of power at HQ after being bullied and tortured by Ewing.

I'm folding the rag back around the PM9 when I hear a knock on the front door. I freeze. Look about quickly. I'm not expecting anybody. Do they know I've got an illegal firearm in here? A drug dealer's shooter? Is this a raid? Who can it be? I've just been picturing popping a cap in Young Pacino's face; is it him? Here to collect the cash I owe? Or maybe to tell me I'm free and clear, that Sinclair's put the word in, that he thought he'd drop by and tell me in person because it's the proper thing to do. No hard feelings, eh?

I scoop up my mobile, tuck the mouse gun in the waist of my boxer shorts at the base of my spine. Jog to the top of the stairs. 'Hello?' I call.

No answer. My right hand reaches around to my lower

back, fingertips brushing against the pistol grip. I take the stairs slowly, holding my breath, bare feet soft and soundless on the carpet. Do a tactical sweep. Flatten myself against the wall; small steps, quiet steps down the hallway, up to the front door.

I slide to one side, press my ear up to the door. I'm picturing Pacino out there right now and know it's all gone tits up, Sinclair couldn't pull it off, couldn't help me out; in fact his business associates, those guys at the top of the food chain, they were *outraged* at his suggestion that my debts be wiped and now he's in pieces in a suitcase on the side of a road somewhere, Pacino's at my door with a Samurai sword, blowtorch and quite possibly a rocket launcher and all I have is somebody else's cap gun that I'm not even sure works.

'Identify yourself,' I call, and hate the sound of my voice. High, tremulous. A schoolgirl on helium. I'm about to vomit. My hand is squeezing the mouse-gun grip. My other hand grasps the mobile, ready to dial three nines.

'Open up, you fuckin' donut,' shouts Frank. 'It's me.'

I could weep. I'm starting to well up as I tuck the shooter back into my pants and unlock the front door, so glad my buddy's turned up because now we can celebrate, I can thank him for everything, can hug him and punch him on the arm, laugh and joke about everything that was once wrong but is now starting to go right.

Frankie stares at me, eyes flicking up and down behind his glasses. 'Sexy look, Jake.'

I have no clue what he means so check myself, rub the back of a hand over my chin and feel growth, look down, see there's the odd questionable stain on the front of my boxers, see the definition on my abs has softened, my fingernails are gunky and blackened, the skin on the edges of my right fore- and index fingers are mustard brown from the cigars. I examine my nails again. Sniff them. They reek of oil.

The gun. It's still tucked into my boxers.

'Frank!' I say, a little too loudly, and he flinches. I step backwards, push myself flat against the wall, feel cold paintwork on my shoulder blades, my latissimus dorsi. Keeping the shooter out of sight as I usher him in.

So he steps past me, eyeing me as he goes, walks towards the lounge and I check outside. All clear. Close the front door, follow him, making sure I'm behind him all the way, hiding the mouse gun. He flops into one settee, winks, congratulates me about Yeh and Cooper, about the complaints from the gook and the chav being NFA'd and the rest just swept under the carpet, so I ask him how he knew and he gives a mini-shrug, says *you know what it's like, mate, word gets around*, so I nod and grin, wait in the doorway, silently pleading for him not to ask me to get him something from the kitchen because I'll have to explain why I'm walking backwards out of the lounge.

Then I panic when he gestures for me to take a seat, the copper in him coming out, that commanding presence thing Frank does so well, so I shuffle forwards with the cheeks of my arse clenched, pushing out my gut so it tightens the waistband, so the PM9 doesn't drop to the floor. I scoot to the two-seater nearest the door, ease myself down gently with my mobile in one hand, place it on the arm of the chair, breathe an audible sigh of relief when I'm on the cushion, my pants still in place and the handgun invisible, pressing into the small of my back.

'You got piles or something?' he asks and I nod, pull a face, a yeah-I'm-guilty-of-overdoing-the-rich-food dismal expression, as if Karen leaving has turned me into a takeaway king.

'Anyway,' he says, and I'm fidgeting in my seat, wondering if I'm about to shoot myself in a kidney because I'm not sure if I clicked the safety on the mouse gun, can't remember if it actually *has* a safety, and Frank's obviously dismissed my faffing about on the cushion as a side-effect of my arsegrapes so takes a breath, reaches into his trouser pocket and pulls out a thick envelope.

'Here,' he says, leaning forward, gently holding the envelope between outstretched fingers, face pale and serious, so I stretch my arm out, careful not to move my upper body too much, mindful that I could take out a large portion of my spinal cord if the cushion I'm resting against catches on the trigger.

I take it. Open it. It's stuffed with banknotes. Fifties. Bundles of cutter, wrapped tightly with strips of white paper across the centre of each package. I flick through one of them. Count the bundles. Do the maths. Twelve of them at five hundred quid a pop equals six grand.

'I guessed Sinclair's people wouldn't take a cheque,' he smiles.

And I'm numb. I gaze at the cash in wonder, muse how today has been a day of receiving unexpected gifts, of tiny things with great power, of how Frank – despite his best intentions, despite his answer to my calling – may just be too damn late.

But I'm thanking him anyway, telling him *wow, you really didn't have to do this*, and he's speaking slowly, patiently, telling me how he's gone through murder with Mel to talk her round so he can give me the money but it's what friends are for and *this is how we're going to play it, this is how we're going to clear your debt with Sinclair, okay, buddy? And then you're going to pay us back every month, starting next month, interest free, matey, of course, no strings, just get yourself sorted so you can work on Karen and the kids coming back,* and blahblahblahblahblah I'm not listening. The gun barrel's gouging at a strip of skin where I've shifted position, digging away at the meaty part around my hip as I push back into the cushion to keep it in place.

It's going to go off. I know it.

I'm breaking into a sweat, feeling hot and cold flushes, suffering here, wallowing in misery, in torturous white-hot agony. I try to maintain the smile. This loaded pistol, one edge of its muzzle now half a centimetre into my flesh. Please get out, Frank. Please leave immediately. Please.

'I know you're suffering so I won't drag it out,' he says at last, and pushes himself up from the settee. 'I'd better make a move.'

'Oh, thank you,' I'm saying, the envelope clasped in my hands in front of my slick chest, my chin raised, eyeballs bugging. 'Thank you, thank you, thank you.'

'No need, Jake,' he says, slapping me on my shoulder as he walks towards the lounge door. 'It's times like this that you need your friends to pull around you. I'm sure you'd do the same for me.'

I nod. Just keep nodding, Jake.

'Don't get up,' he says. 'Those haemorrhoids are a bitch. Take it easy.'

He's leaving. 'Thank you,' is all I can say. I'm rigid in my seat. I'm not sure if it's warm sweat or blood I can feel trickling down the crack of my arse. I want him gone. Out of here. Nothing personal. It's not you, it's me, honey.

'By the way . . .' he says, stopping at the lounge door. Christ. Jesus. God all-fuckin'-mighty. Won't you please *go*? And then he tells me about some party he's arranged, some *getting away with it* bash at his place later this week when we're next on matching rest days, *y'know, a few drinks with some of the firearms lads to celebrate Professional Standards dropping the complaints, Mel doing some buffet food 'n' that 'cos she knows what you've been going through,* and I'm just ducking my nut here, nodding like a nodding machine, and I tell him *yeah, Frankie that'll be great, that'll be a blast, all the old crew around*

again, lemme give you a ring and hey, thanks for everything, mate,
you're a real trooper, you really are . . .

And then he's gone and I'm just a curled-up ball of greasy
sweat on the chair. Doubled over. Muttering *praise be* to
whoever. Frank's cash still clutched between my thumb and
forefinger, smudged with the oil from my fingernails.

I reach around, pull the muzzle out of the skin to the right
of my spine. It pops, a watery sucking sound, and I feel faint.
Sparks in your eyesight time. I sit back, taking it carefully, *ow-
ow-ow*ing as I lower myself into the cushion. Check the PM9,
see blood and tissue around the muzzle. Wipe it on my boxer
shorts, add to the stains.

I lift the envelope to my face, squint the flashing dots away,
see the bundles and bundles of cash that I may not even need
any more.

'Good ol' Frankie,' I say.

And then my mobile rings and Lowri's number's on screen.
I haven't spoken to her since she stormed out of my truck.

'Hey, darling,' I say. 'Sorry about the other morning.'

There's silence on the other end of the phone. I look at the
money. Think about my tab with her. The walking and
talking, the holding hands. All those wanna-fuck-me-stud
telephone marathons. Those times when I know she's
charging me to sit listening with my limp cock in my hand.
Those times I didn't have any cash to give her.

I drop the envelope to my lap, run my fingers across the
flank of the mouse gun.

'Want some fun together?' I ask, and shudder as she giggles
in my ear.

TWENTY-ONE

drunk into the cage. Five of them! Five tiny clone plods who couldn't handle a lone sixty-odd-year-old scabies-ridden weakling tramp when he started cutting up rough outside the bookies (N.B. can I call him a tramp? What's the wanky PC term for them now? 'Homeless Person'? 'Outdoor Outcast'? 'Stinky Fucker'? I must check.) But an assistance shout? For one drunk? I came screaming down with Lapdog, found the envy shoppers were watching, the mid-morning traffic at a standstill. An embarrassment. A mess. All grappling hands and prolonged scuffling nonsense, frightened to be too robust with the smelly old bastard and I couldn't bear it so in I went, got the cuffs on him ay-sap and Roid, she was in the thick of it and no use at all but at least she was wearing rubber gloves for her personal Health and Safety, just getting in the way, bumping against my left hip and telling me I hadn't gone through the Conflict management model, wasn't using Home Office-approved restraint techniques, someone's going to complain. And when you're in the middle of a street fight with someone, when you're clearing up the chaos your colleagues have created, when you've turned up to assist them in their time of need that's just what you want to hear. It's all that really matters, isn't it? It's the most important thing. You stupid, irritating fucking muppets. You

Shit.

Baker climbs into the passenger seat. Didn't see him coming. I quickly close my notebook, tuck it into the pocket of my body armour. Try to remain calm, twist my hands around the steering wheel as he shuts the door on the pissing-down rain.

'You're keen, doing your notes already,' he says with a matey grin. 'Great to see.'

I say nothing. Why are you in this car with me, Baker? Where's Lapdog? I feel safe with Lapdog.

'The old fella was a bit of a handful, wasn't he?' Baker says.

I'm staring straight ahead. 'Not really.'

'Oh,' he says. He's quiet for a moment. I sense he's struggling to remain cheery, to mask the real reason he's taken it upon himself to ride shotgun. I've got you pegged, Baker. Sussed. You're Ewing's bagman. Professional Standards' lackey. Their snitch.

'Shall we go for a spin then?' he asks.

'If you like,' I say, not liking the idea at all.

I can see he's nodding to himself, see his neat hair, his perfect career-climbing unaffected-by-the-weather hair, moving back and forth out the corner of my eye.

'Be nice to have a chat,' Baker says. 'I haven't really had the chance since you were moved . . . since you transferred on to the relief.'

I start the engine. Watch as the uniformed Oompa-Loompas close the van door on the tramp. Lapdog's standing in the murk, eyes on the panda car, on me and Baker, as the city centre gets back to what it was doing before this brief carnival sideshow began. I wish I'd remembered to speak to him. About the gossip. About why he couldn't say anything to me. But I got a little sidetracked. With Sinclair and the money and the gun. With everything else again. So maybe this is where I find out.

So I drive, touring the pedestrianised shopping streets, down to the Bay where Baker waves at the tourists stupid enough to come here in this weather, back up to the industrial estates where I think about Lowri, wonder what her feet look like, imagine coming over her toes, her small and clean and slender toes with nails varnished in purple – yeah, I think she'd probably choose purple – and I'm not listening to my companion at all. Grunting and *yeah*ing where I consider it appropriate, where there seem to be pauses in his conversation, as if he's seeking acknowledgement or for me to concur with whatever jobspeak nonsense he's banging on about. We're husband and wife and I'm trying to watch the football while she yaps about her mother's gout problem alongside me on the settee.

I'm chewing the inside of my mouth, this chump's voice needling at my ear. This leader of chumps. Can't wait until tonight. Frank's house. The party. All the guys, all the real police from the firearms teams. A few ales to celebrate not losing my job. To see Jessica again. It's the only thing that's getting me through today.

Then Baker's touching my arm, his fingers tugging at the sleeve of my jacket, so I flinch and he's saying to me, 'Pull over here, Jake.'

I look at him for the first time since he got in the car.

'We need to talk,' he says.

So I pull over, engine idling, find I've driven back to Radcliffe Street without thinking; that we're next to some plumbing depot, the rain's heavier now, hammering down, a metallic drumming on the roof of the panda car, and here we go, this is it, this is where Baker admits he's watching me, that Ewing's assigned him to dig the dirt, to bury me if he can, to finish the job Professional Standards couldn't.

Except he says nothing of the sort, just asks me how I am, how things are, tells me he knows it's been tough and he's been through tough times himself, and I have to stop myself from laughing, from giggling at his cack-handed touchy-feely nonsense, and he feels more uncomfortable than I do now, but then you wanted the stripes, kiddo, so you get to deal with this sort of crap. His face is drawn, nervous. He keeps talking, even brings one knee up onto the seat as he faces me, trying for casual, but he's pale and his throat is working as he swallows, tripping over his words and reaching for the right things to say. This twenty-something singleton still wet behind the ears, who's been in the job a strawberry season, dispensing words of advice to *me*.

'And I know things got a bit out of hand the other night at Anzac's, with the nickname thing, but I've had a word with the shift and it won't happen again,' he's saying, and I chuckle to myself because I can barely remember. It seems so long ago.

It's painful, sitting here listening to Baker, and I've had enough, so I just wave a hand and tell him: 'It's all good, Sarge.' Because it is, really. Everything's starting to work itself out.

He lets out a long breath. Relieved, probably. 'Anyway,' he says. 'We're out again tonight if you're interested. Take two, as they say. Booked out one of the restaurants down the Bay.'

'The Tidal?' I ask. Karen's favourite.

'Yeah. Nice, right? You fancy it?'

'No can do,' I say. 'Got plans.'

So Baker nods and tells me it's a shame but if I'm busy, he understands, just thought it would be nice to come along and show some support, one of the girls from the other side of the city just passed her exams, has got her ticket to sergeant, and I'm mentally rolling my eyes at the thought of yet another copper with no service strutting around telling people like me what to do but then he's talking about who it is, the girl who's being promoted, and my guts, my aching guts, they do a little somersault and my chest suddenly feels like it's being crushed.

It's Rachael.

'Don't really know her myself,' Baker's saying, but I'm staring out into torrential rain and my head feels frozen, deadened. 'You know what it's like, all these faces across the city,' he's saying from somewhere in the panda car. 'But

Laptop joined the job with her other half, Clive, I think his name is, you know him? Anyway Laptop's been invited then he sort of asked us along and . . .'

I've tuned him out. I'm here but I'm not here. I'm working things out. Calculating. Making a mental itinerary. Seeing if I can do both. Frank's. Rachael's. Rachael and Clive. *Cliff.* All this stuff cluttering my head. All these things to resolve. All these people abandoning me. Whenever I'm getting on the front foot something always knocks me back.

After work I take the hour-long return trip to pick up my kit at HQ, ignore Ewing while I'm there, mock the chicken-necked receptionist, then drive home at ninety miles an hour.

At home I press my clothes, remember to put my tactical boots away so I don't wear them again. Shower, do the whole beauty thing, exfoliate, scrub those shitty boils clustered around my shoulders and collarline. Ring Sinclair but get no answer, rant down the phone at him because I'm still getting funny fucking phone calls from Young Pacino and it's obvious he's squared *nothing* away yet. Do two hundred crunches, flip and press-up to failure, until my upper back and pectorals feel nice and warm. I sit on the edge of the bed, reach down next to the bedside table without looking, lift up one of the dumbers and start working my arms, do set after set of reps, swapping hands, controlling my breathing, the peach and green. This is easy. Oh so easy.

Imagine the faces if I *did* walk in The Tidal. Not that I would. But imagine Rachael sitting there, mid-whisper with Cliff, the whole place going quiet like that scene in the country pub at the start of *An American Werewolf in London.* I'm working my arms and picturing it, me breezing in on the rain, doors swinging shut behind me, the music and conversation dying. Cliff soiling himself. Right in front of the entire police division. *Sorry,* he'll say, an apology for everything. For all he's ever done or will do. For being him.

And Rachael will realise her mistake, excuse herself from the table, rush over to me and we'll embrace, right there in front of Baker and Lapdog and all the other tools I have to work with. And the music will start up again because normal service will have resumed. Order will return to the galaxy. And I won't have to do anything, because I'm on a roll now and this is how it will be.

I stop lifting because I'm getting carried away, I'm thinking about things I shouldn't, and anyway the dumb-bell feels odd and misshapen in my left hand. Way, way too light.

I look down and realise I've been holding the mouse gun all along.

| 1935 | RV @ Frankie's – real man's party. Interview several persons present re. my wife and children. No updates. Ignore discussion of firearms incidents as, to be frank (ha.!), I'm jealous. I'm even jealous of Tommy, which is a first. But this could turn out to be a pretty bloody good night despite Mel, because guess who's in the |

It feels so good to be back among the fold.

Frank's house is all banter and Sixties sounds. Joplin, Hendrix, The Doors. Bottles of Jack Daniel's. Stella kegs. Cigars on the patio in the cold. Political incorrectness. Real war stories from seasoned grunts. Genuine laughter. Most of it at the expense of Ginge, the new Inspector. Nearly twenty of us here and not a midget cop or FNG in sight. Frankie, Thrombo, the rest of the crew. I can *smell* testosterone. There's Tommy Hall, of course, but you can't have everything. The Sarge's avoided me since I arrived, deployed himself in the kitchen with fat hands permanently hovering over the weird finger-food things Mel clearly sweated over when she had to slide pre-packed Tesco trays into the oven for ten minutes until done.

But . . . all this for me. I've felt the odd twinge since the tales got going, since they've been discussing incidents I've missed after being shipped back to sector. But we've all got our weapons somewhere. I'm still part of the firearms team.

I'm in the lounge, arm draped around Frank's shoulder, the Kahr PM9 tucked snugly into my sock, notebook in the pocket of my jacket hanging off the end of the hall banister. The booze, it's eating at my guts. Warmth spreading to my chest. The minuscule pigs in blankets burnt by Mel aren't soaking any of it up. Got to be careful. Got to conserve some energy, stay sharp if I decide to take a trip down the Bay.

'I owe you, bra . . .' I'm telling Frank, because I feel like I should be saying something, should be showing a smidgeon of gratitude for this bunfight, for the money.

'Is no problem,' he says, head wobbling about, one eye closed behind his glasses, and tells me he knows I'd do the same for him. And I'm not sure that I would. I'm not sure about anything at the moment because Jessica's eight feet away and sitting on one settee with her friend. Some pissed-up mousy-haired thing, a Plain Jane I've never seen before. Both of them dolled up to the eyeballs. Denim hotpants, halter tops. Pure jailbait. Whispering to each other.

And then Frank asks me about the cash, if I've settled everything with Sinclair, Jagger's roaring out 'Paint It, Black', and I nod, lying, tell him *yeah, mate, all sorted*, because I can't really get into this now as Jessica's legs are crossed at the knee, a three-quarters empty highball glass of Jack nestled between her naked thighs, her right foot raised in the air and completely bare. She's wiggling her painted toes, rotating her foot at the ankle. Showing it off as she gossips with Plain Jane.

I down my drink, grimace. Make for the kitchen, find a sober, sour-faced Mel there, apologise again for ruining her kitchen door, thank her for everything, gesture at the food, sigh as she huffs and tells me there would have been more but she didn't have the money, *know what I mean, Jake?* and Tommy's beside her, arms folded, nodding slowly to himself with his plump little lips pressed together. I snatch up a couple of pathetic vol-au-vents, shove them in my mouth, tell them *oooh, I'm stuffed*, then pour myself a tripler, a Greek measure, a big old hit of Jack with a Coke afterthought. I neck it. In one. Slam the glass down on the worktop.

'Yaaaaarrrgh!' I growl, striking a pose. Bent over slightly at the waist. Arms curled, knuckles of each fist touching in front of my midriff. Classic Schwarzenegger. Mr Olympia time.

'I don't care what you've been through,' says Mel. 'You're a dick.'

Yes, but Jessica's toenails are a glorious bright red tonight. Strumpet red. I refill my glass, omit the Coke. Back into the lounge, find Frankie's crashed and burned in one corner, head on chest, glasses hanging off one ear. What a wuss. It's only twenty-one twenty hours. People are still dancing, throwing moves, cutting some rug around him and over him.

I slip in between Jessica and Jane. Shuffle them apart, ignore their blatantly fake protests. I will take control of this situation before I lose control. Before the drink hits me. I am on a roll.

'My life can only get bett-aaaaah!' I sing.

'It's *things*,' says Jessica, rolling her eyes. '*Things* can only get better . . .'

'It's the twelve-inch remix,' I say, lying. 'Haven't you heard it?'

'Whassa twelve . . . twelve-inch?' asks Jane, and I see she's looking up at me in a peculiar way, the way Lapdog sometimes does, eyes wide and shiny. I ignore her.

'Nice display earlier,' I say to Jessica. I'm close enough to smell her, feel the heat of her body against mine. The shampoo scent of her hair. The JD on her breath, strong and bitter. She's well oiled here. I'm willing myself not to look down the front of her tight white halter top but it's a struggle. I wonder if she'd notice?

'Meaning?' she asks, eyebrow raised.

Oh, you know what I mean. You know exactly where I'm coming from, you foot-twirling little minx. 'Very impressive stuff,' I say, winking.

Jessica checks around, at people waving hands in the air as Free's 'All Right Now' chugs from the speakers, at the slumped form of her lightweight father, over to the kitchen door where her mother's probably still griping about me while she counts out ready-made ham and cheese spirals. She checks her watch, lifts her right foot; I see it's been slipped back into a matt-black leather pump.

'Is this a film quote thing again, Jake?' she sighs.

You teenaged temptress. You've got me in the palm of your hand. Or is it the arch of your foot? Ah, who cares? I can't breathe, can feel her rubbing the side of her shoe against my leg as she taps her foot to the music. Just the briefest of touches, a gentle sweep up and down the outside of my left calf. I'm starting to feel pissed. Intoxicated. With the alcohol, the situation. And my stomach isn't hurting for the first time in so long. Instead I feel a wave of small shivers through my lower guts, my groin. Thank Christ the lights are dimmed because I'm sitting on Frank's settee with his daughter and nothing but the three-millimetre-thick cloth of my trousers separates her from my hard-on.

'Gotta go toilet,' I say to Jess. I need to. Five minutes, that's all. Got to piss. Catch my breath. Stop my head spinning. Time to adjust. I have to adjust to what's going on. And I really have to adjust my underwear. 'We'll finish this conversation shortly,' I say, standing and holding her gaze for a few seconds, and she just stares right back and I know now that I'm *in* here. I'm on a gold-plated promise. I can't fucking believe it.

So I take the stairs four at a time, hand covering my crotch-tent, see Frank still dozing next to the speakers, Jessica laughing with the other girl, probably laughing at how brazen she's been with me, how she's so dirty and dangerous and full of life and really, really crazy to be doing it but she's going to *do it* with her dad's hunky best friend, tonight. She's finally decided to give herself to me. To *me*. Possibly with her mate tagging along for the ride. I could manage that. A little bit of charity never hurt.

I can't believe how I've managed to turn things around in such a short period. Is there no end to your upward trajectory, Jacob Smith?

I lock the bathroom door, try peeing in the toilet but everything's standing to attention so give up and piss in the sink. Check my face in the mirror. Rearrange myself, zip and button myself back up. Pull up my right sock, ensure the mouse gun's secure. Throw a few poses, my casual shirt bulging in all the right places. Check the front of my trousers, chuckle to myself. Throw my head back and laugh out loud.

I walk downstairs, trying for casual, as casual as can be with shaky knees after more than three-quarters of a bottle of JD, with a nine-millimetre concealed weapon rubbing the skin of my ankle. I can't see Jessica. Nor her desperate drunken friend. Did they follow me up and I missed them? No worries. Head for the kitchen, keep myself in the driving seat, grab another drink. There's just Mel, Tommy, and what's left of the food. I'm confused now. A little concerned. I step out onto the patio; maybe they like a crafty fag and they've slipped out to have a snout.

There's nobody there.

'Where she gone, woman?' I ask Mel in the kitchen.

'What?' she asks. Tommy's pretending not to notice, like he's discovered an extremely interesting prawn wrapped in filo pastry. 'Who the hell d'you think you're talking to?' Mel almost shrieks, and I'm glad the music in the lounge is loud enough for nobody else to hear.

'I . . . Jess?' I say. 'I was . . . We were talking 'bout something and hadn't, y'know, she hadn't finished. Jessica.'

Mel just glares at me, cheeks burning, and I wonder if she's overdone it in front of the oven. 'She's gone,' she says.

What the fuck? 'What d'you mean she's gone?'

'*Out*, Jake,' Mel says, and I feel that sickening, roiling sensation explode in my belly again. 'Clubbing, probably. How should I know? Nobody tells me what's going on around here any more. And why do you care?'

'But . . .' I say. 'We were talking about . . . stuff.'

'Well boo-bloody-hoo,' she says, and it takes all the strength I can muster not to reach down to my sock. 'It's what they *do*, Jake,' she's saying. 'Why on earth d'you think Jess would want to spend the whole night here with us oldies? Her and Izzy just took the free drinks and food then cleared off to meet their mates. And to be honest,' she looks me up and down, then at Tommy, 'I can't blame them.'

No, no, no, no, no. *No*. This is simply not right. I was on a promise. I have an *erection* here, for God's sake. Jessica's still in the house. I know it. She's just teasing. Yanking my chain again. I'll search upstairs. Play her game of hide and seek if that's what it takes.

I pour another tumbler of bourbon, neck it, leave the kitchen. Step over Frank's feet, dart into the hall, stumble up the stairs. Legs shaky. Too much Jack again. Can feel it muddying everything. That tingle in my arms, my throat. That heat on my tongue, my breath.

I'm swaying as I check the upstairs rooms, flinging open doors as if to catch her by surprise. Bathroom, cloakroom, spare bedroom. Nobody there. No Jessica. Hide and seek, is it, baby? I'll play along. I've all the time in the world here.

Never been this far along the landing, seen inside these rooms, in all the years I've known my best friend. New territory. Strange, exciting times. I get to the master bedroom door, really into this now, my hard-on back to full strength. Locked and loaded. I reach in through the doorframe, feel along the wall for the light switch, flick it on, jump into the room with the tent in my trousers on full view, arms raised and fingers waggling, *ta-daaah!*, and see her lying there on her parents' bed, lying there spread-eagled and waiting, but then I focus and it's just a pile of coats. And she's not in the wardrobes, under the bed. Where are you?

I push open the last door on the landing, push it open slowly, savouring this pause for breath, this feeling of impending nirvana. Delaying the final pleasure for just a few seconds more. I will remember this moment. The muffled voices and laughter downstairs. Music pounding through the floorboards, Jim Morrison wailing, 'Don't You Love Her Madly . . .' My heart keeping time with the bass line. The giddy swirl of my head. Lips tacky from the whisky.

'Respect the cock!' I shout, and turn on the light in Jessica's bedroom.

There's nobody here. Rock posters, desktop computer, clutch of oversized teddy bears on the single bed, clothing strewn about the carpet. And me. With my pointless erection.

I dig my fists into my eyes. Push against the lids until it hurts. You fool, Jake. You stupid fucking idiot. She's gone. She *knew*. Even got her homely friend to play along. 'You scheming little pricktease!' I shout, then hunch over, finger to my lips. Shhh. Got to keep it down, bra. Got to be quiet while you're in this room. Gather your thoughts. There's still Plan B. Still the restaurant and Rachael. I need to get my head straight. Need to sound this out with someone. Too drunk, man. Too drunk to make a decision here.

I pull out my mobile, dial Lowri. 'Hey, J,' she says. 'What's up?'

I'm so relieved to hear her. So pleased there's someone in my life who'll listen without judgement. Who won't dangle herself in front of me then whip everything away just for a fucking giggle. So what if it costs me? Doesn't everything cost you something somewhere along the line?

'I'm stuck,' I say to her, breathing heavily down the phone. 'I need help.'

'Oh, I'm sure I can sort you out, honey,' she says, then she's off and I'm trying to stop her, saying no, wait Lowri, that's not what I mean, but she's talking in my ear in that breathy, gravelly voice of hers, that smoky voice I love so much. I'm standing here in Jessica's bedroom with a boner in my trousers, it's all so surreal, such a bizarre situation, and Jessica, no Lowri, it's Lowri, she's going for it, telling me how she's gonna ride me like a pony next time she sees me, clamber on top and grind it, Jake, yeah I'm really gonna grind it, and the phone's digging into my ear now, I'm pressing hard enough to make pain shoot down my jawline, pacing about the room with this voice coming out of my mobile while I pick up a pillow from the bed and sniff it, smell that familiar citrus scent, drop it back to the bed. I'm so horny I could scream. So pissed I can barely stand. So lonely. So alone.

And I'm rubbing at my crotch while she whispers that smut, the brilliant filth, and I pull open a wardrobe and oh, be still my beating heart. It's the black diamanté high-heeled mule sandals. I think of the night Jessica started all this. Wearing them when she came home.

'You know you want to, Jake,' she's rasping in my ear. 'Do me,' she's saying, and my left hand cramps as it squeezes the phone. My breathing is shallow, quick. My other hand is frantically undoing my trousers. Belt. Button. Zip. I drop them around my ankles. Lower my boxer shorts. Feel the material gather slightly around the bulge of the mouse gun. Stand in front of the open wardrobe, in front of the sandals.

This is so wrong. But such blessed relief.

My hand gets to work. Those sandals are beautiful.

'Do me now,' the voice says, and I picture her, see Frank's daughter naked, feet circling the air, which is a lovely surprise, isn't it? Very pleasant. 'Take me anyway you want,' she's saying. 'Take me *every* way you want. Treat me like the slut I am. D'you wanna fuck me, baby?'

'Yeah. Yes I do . . . Jessica.'

I'm so lonely.

'Then fuck me, Jake.'

'I am. I am. I am . . .'

I am so alone.

'Harder . . .'

'Yeah . . .' Somebody please help me. 'Yeah . . . yeah . . . yeah . . .'

'Harder, Jake . . .'

'Help me, Jessica.'

'What the *fuck* d'you think you're *doing*, bra?'

I turn, see Frank in the doorway. He's pale. Shaking. Sucking lungfuls of air through his nose. Snorting almost, like a bull about to charge. I wonder how long he's been standing there. Long enough, I suspect. I look down, see my hand still gripping my penis. Softening now, as you'd expect given the rather awkward circumstances.

'Frank . . .' I say, but I have no time to say anything more because he's on me, always so quick over short distances, one hand against my throat and barrelling me backwards into the wardrobe. He's squeezing. Hard. My eyes are closed. He reeks of booze. *Sorry*, I'm trying to say. *Sorry, Frankie. Sorry sorry sorry* . . . but I can't get any words out. He's strangling me here. My phone's in my hand, the hand I'm using to try and push Frankie away. Can hear Lowri, bless her, she's still talking dirty, her voice tinny and faint. And then I'm being pulled forwards by the collar of my shirt, so quick I can't see anything but a blur of teddies and indie pop stars when I open my eyes, my legs waddling inside the tangle of my bunched trousers, Frank's hands on me, slapping me, thumping me a few good ones on the face and neck and perhaps I need this, maybe this is *right*, this beating, this pounding I'm getting. So I let myself go with it, allow Frank to do whatever he sees fit, then I'm onto the landing, can hear him screeching something but it's unintelligible, he's too drunk to make sense, I'm too drunk to understand, then there's more pushing and I'm on my way down the stairs with my limp dick bouncing about in the fresh air, falling, tumbling over, the carpet burning the skin of my arse, my thighs, my knees, the music's still blasting and nobody in the lounge even knows what's going on.

And then I'm sitting on the cold wet driveway, one leg of my trousers completely off, rainwater freezing my shrunken nuts and the slamming of Frank's front door reverberating around my skull. My jacket lies in a puddle, thrown out after me. The business end of the mouse gun is peeping out of my sodden sock and pointing at my face.

'Jake?' I hear, a voice seemingly from far away. 'Jake? What's happening?'

I glance down at my hand in my grazed and chafed lap and

after all that's just happened find the mobile curled between my fingers.

Lowri's still on the line.

Code Red – urgent assistance required. Code Red. Code Red. Code Red. Red. Red. Red. Red Rum. Red Rum. Redrum. Red Riding Hood? Red Riding Hood. Am I the Big Bad Wolf? Code Red Riding Hood. Where's that slut Lowri???????

I NEED ~~HELP~~ LOWRI

TWENTY-TWO

I'm home, in bed, there's sunlight in the room and I can't remember getting here but feel like I've been run over. Or I've got polio. Does it happen that quickly? One minute you're a walking talking human being, then you go to sleep and the sneaky fucker creeps over you, spreads through you, and when you wake your central nervous system is shot?

Am I paralysed? Is that what this is?

I'm trying to wiggle my fingers, my toes, groaning under the quilt when nothing happens and silently cursing Mel because this is probably her fault with those undercooked mini sausage rolls. Then I remember Jessica's bedroom, Frank turfing me out and . . . I think I'm going to puke.

I strain every muscle in my upper body, will them to work so I can roll over. Don't want to drown in my own vomit lying on my back, can feel it rising upwards already so over I go, onto my side, dog tags tinkling. I piece together what I can from the abortion that was last night, those memory flashbulbs going off in my chronically aching skull as I'm dry heaving towards the bedroom carpet.

'Frank . . .' I moan, and it turns into a coughing fit. 'I'm sorry, brother . . .'

Then I hear someone coming up the stairs.

I'm on my side, frozen, staring at the bedside table where my unofficial pocket notebook sits alongside a pen and the pistol, the footsteps are louder, whoever's in my house is nearing the top of the stairs. I'm hoping it's Frank and last night was a bad dream, a sweaty vol-au-vent-induced hallucinatory nightmare, that he's here to do the wakey-wakey eggs 'n' bakey routine before wheeling me into the shower then we'll head for the gym so I can blow it off, our *new* gym which is miles better than The Elite could ever hope to be. But no matter how hard I try to kid myself, I know it won't be him. Not this morning. Maybe not ever again.

I reach out towards the mouse gun, one stiff trembling arm across a gap of maybe two feet that feels like a mile. I grasp for the pistol grip, miss it, grab for it again. See fresh cuts and nicks on the skin around my knuckles. Take hold of the PM9, ease it under the quilt as the person approaches the bedroom door. Maybe it's Karen, then. Karen and Naomi and Ben. *Surprise!* they'll yell as they burst into the room. Carrying gifts, of course. Yeah, Jake. Right.

What about Rachael? Here to kiss 'n' make up. To tell me she's made a horrendous mistake. That Cliff is gay. That he's really a transsexual. That he's actually a gay transsexual eunuch married to a lesbian. Called Ginge.

I hold my breath, peer over the edge of the quilt as the bedroom door slowly opens, and when I see Lowri there holding a mug I don't know whether to laugh or cry or tell her to get the fuck out of my house, you filthy whore. I drop my head back to the pillow, breathe. Eyes on the ceiling. I'm so tired.

The mattress rocks a little as she sits on the edge of the bed. 'Are you . . .?'

'Awake?' I grunt, not looking at her. 'Unfortunately.'

'Are you okay? I made you some tea. Didn't know if you take sug—'

I flip the top of the quilt down with my fingers. 'What are you doing in my house?'

She rolls her eyes, places the mug next to my pocket notebook. 'You asked me to come back here with you, remember?'

I shake my head. Feel pain down the back of my neck.

'Thought not,' she says. 'But then you were fuckin' smashed.'

I'm sore all over. 'Did we . . .?' I ask, and steel myself for another tongue-lashing, but she just smiles and shakes her head, tells me *no, no we didn't do anything and your settee is really comfortable to sleep on*, and for a moment I'm surprised at how understanding she is. But then you can buy a lot of patience when you wave six grand under somebody's nose.

I'm watching her, this stranger in my house, this teenager who reminds me of a dead girl in a Clio, this sad and fragile-looking thing who's probably tougher than any man I know. So pretty. Such a dirty, pretty thing. I think about Karen again, what I'd say if she came home right now, found me lying in bed with an eighteen-year-old tea-making hooker and a gun in one hand.

Lowri's glancing about the bedroom, quiet now. Her face has softened; there's something in her eyes I've not seen before. She looks happy. Relaxed, even.

'You've got a nice place here,' she says eventually.

I nod. A nice, empty place. 'Why d'you do the things you do, Lowri?'

'Why do you do the things *you* do, Jake?'

'I can get you out of your . . . line of work. Help you, y'know.'

She chuckles, waves a hand around at the room. 'You already are.'

'You can't stay here forever,' I say. 'I had . . . have a family.'

'So you've told me.'

I can't recall this. 'What about your parents? Aren't they worried about you?'

'What about yours?' she asks, her face hardening for a

second. Then she reaches across to the bedside table. 'Cool!' she says. 'Is this your, like, police booklet?'

My shoulder screams as I snatch my pocket notebook out of her hands. 'Don't,' I tell her. 'It's official police, er . . . stuff. For work.'

I tuck it under the quilt, slide it next to the mouse gun. Can't remember writing in it last night, but must have done. Must've come back here and completed my notes after what happened at Frank's.

'What's with all the cuts and grazes?' she's asking, eyeing my hands and forearms from beneath the dark whorl of her fringe.

I'm too ill to explain. To conjure some lie. I sink back onto the pillow again, feel sick just from the smell of the tea she's made. 'I used to call you Little Red Riding Hood, you know,' I say, draping an arm across my eyes to block out the sunlight. 'To my friends. My friend. When I had one.'

She doesn't reply. There's silence and I sense she's watching me. Then I feel her shift off the bed, hear her softly padding across the carpet to the door. I wonder if she's barefoot?

'Because of my coat,' she says. 'I know, you've said. C'mon, you'd better get up. You're a late today, apparently.'

'What?'

'You told me to tell you. You're a late. In work.'

Shit. Work. I'm on afternoons. A bloody late turn, feeling like this. Looking like this. I check my watch. An hour before I have to leave.

'How about I rustle you up some breakfast?' she asks.

I swallow. Headache kicking in now. Mouth arid, lips gluey. 'Bloody make yourself at home, why don't you?' I croak, and it's only teasing really, just needling her slightly because that's what we do, isn't it? Me and Lowri, that's what we're like together. We're Richard Gere and Julia Roberts in *Pretty Woman*.

Except she's quiet for a few seconds.

'It's just nice to have a home for a little while,' she says then, stepping out of the bedroom, and I wish I could take it back.

I'm feeling sick and miserable when I walk into the parade room and it's obviously going to be one of those days because the kiddie cops are sitting about with long faces. Silence but for the burble of radio traffic. Everybody motionless, staring into space. Like a wake or something.

I keep my scabbed hands in my pockets, wait for anyone to speak, but get nothing so shrug and go prepare a brew. Dial Frankie's phones for the hundredth time but his house rings out and his mobile's off. Lose count of the sugars I spoon into my mug, stop caring, slurp it as I walk back into the parade room and gag because it's sweet as a milkshake.

I take my seat next to Lapdog, dump my paperwork on the tabletop. 'What's happertaining, *paizan?*' I ask. 'Somebody died?'

Lapdog looks at me with those oh-so-emotional fawn's eyes. His staring makes me feel uncomfortable.

'What?' I ask, and check around the table. All of them – Roid, BMX, Three Amp, the rest – wretched expressions on their faces. Sergeant Baker's got some serious anger going on, too.

'Haven't you heard?' Baker asks.

'Heard what?'

Baker gives a small shake of his head and juts out his bottom jaw, showing a predictably perfect set of white teeth. 'We've got one of our own in hospital,' he says. 'And he's in a bad way.'

Ah. Injury on duty time. Always gets the blood flowing across division. Some poor plod's had a shoeing at a call, I bet. Knife pulled on him, maybe. Or in the wrong place at the wrong time against the wrong crackhead burglar who just wouldn't take telling when he began sticking a screwdriver in the copper's neck. And now everyone's thinking about revenge. About their own vulnerability. It could've been me, they're thinking. There but for the grace of God . . .

'Shit,' I say, not really caring that much at all because I'm a little preoccupied with my own problems right now, but I try for a despondent look to match everyone else's. 'Wow. That's bad luck. How'd it happen?'

'Got jumped,' says Lapdog from beside me. 'At a cashpoint.'

BMX bangs the table with a hand, love her. Ooh, the emotion. 'Some fucking *coward* attacked him when he popped out from the restaurant last night,' she shouts.

What?

'Okay, calm down,' Baker says but there's that sudden whooshing in my ears. I can't hear him properly. Everything's off-kilter. I'm looking at him but it's another face I see.

'Hang on . . .' I'm saying. My voice seems distant, like I'm going under a general anaesthetic. Just slipping away and the doc's asking me to count to ten . . . 'He wasn't . . . wasn't on duty? Who we talking about here?'

'Clive Turner,' says Lapdog, and I feel his eyes on me. 'From Clinton Street nick.'

'Oh,' I hear myself say. Look down at my hands beneath the table. See the cuts and raised lumps around my knuckles. Did I come straight home with Lowri? After Frank's? Where did you go, Jake? Where have you gone?

And Baker's shushing the kids, telling them not to worry, the CID are on it big time. I can't sit here any more. I stand and steady myself, make sure my legs are going to work when I walk to the tea room, tell them in sombre tones I'm gonna make another brew, make a nice cup of tea for us all as we bond over this traumatic incident. I walk to the kitchenette, switch on the kettle and grip the edge of the worktop. Bent over. Head lowered. Breathing deeply.

And then I giggle my fucking head off. Giggle so hard my shoulders are juddering, my cheeks wet with tears. Then I stop. Check the doorway. Hear them in the parade room, the raised voices, Baker calming them all down as they piss and moan about their banged-up buddy. Oh, thank you, whoever you are up there. Thank you for this gift, for doing this job for me. I lift up my hands, see the grazes, know I got them at Frank's. I know it wasn't me who gave Cliff a tuning. Too drunk, bra. Too damn drunk to do much of anything as far as I can remember.

So I make the tea, wipe my damp eyes, get my poker face ready and go back into the parade room.

It's gone deathly quiet again.

'Tea's up,' I say, standing there with the tray.

Everyone's staring at me.

And I see Baker's holding my work pocket notebook, my official one. Good for you, son. Check it over. Sign it off like you do every week, make sure it's all in order for those muppets up at Professional Standards.

But he's holding it up between finger and thumb like it's a piece of shit he's discovered, like it's some poisonous lump that'll infect him in some way. He swivels his head towards me, swallowing. The blood's drained from his face.

'Laptop . . .' he says, eyes wide and on me. 'Laptop wanted your notes from the tramp arrest yesterday morning . . .'

'Yeah,' I say. 'And?'

He lifts my notebook up further, dangles it in mid-air. 'He found . . . What have you written here, Jake?'

Oh, for fuck's sake. I step over, dump the tea tray on the table. Take my notebook from him. Check the page he's been looking at. Read what I've written there. The frantic, jagged handwriting. My private, drunken thoughts. The description of what I've done. What I did. To Cliff. To Clive. Because it was me after all.

And I wrote about it in the wrong notebook.

I can't move. Can't look up. Perhaps if I stay like this they'll just ignore me and go away. Leave me alone. Understand what I'm going through at the moment. That I need help. But I hear the sound of chairs being pushed back from the table, of protection equipment rattling on utility belts, of footsteps advancing towards me.

When I raise my head I'm surrounded by the shift. Encircled. All of them. Looking up at me, fury and disgust and astonishment in their eyes. Lapdog's right in front, the point man with Kwik-Cuffs out of their pouch and poised in the Home Office-approved application position.

'I thought it might've been you,' he says, his voice queerly menacing. 'Clive told me . . . told me everything about you and Rachael and . . . I didn't . . . didn't want to believe him.'

'C'mon, Lapdog,' I say, shrugging.

'My name's *Martin*,' he growls. 'And I should've said something . . . done something before you got to Clive . . .'

I never liked working here anyway.

'You'll never take me alive, fuckers,' I say to them, and smile.

Then they're upon me.

TWENTY-THREE

I'm at home but completely lost.

Everything I've ever clung to has gone. I'm just a man sitting in his pants staring at a widescreen television I haven't finished paying for. In a house where I can no longer afford the mortgage. Trapped by the hire-purchases of comfortable suburban life. With unanswered texts and voicemail messages from Young Pacino on my mobile, telling me the jig's up and I've forced his hand, that pretty soon he'll have something to really grab my attention. And my very own teenage ho preparing lunch in the kitchen. I'm mulling over going upstairs, wrapping my lips around the muzzle of the PM9 and pulling the trigger while she's pottering about. This busy little streetwalking bee, making nice and homely. Getting her feet – which I still haven't clapped eyes on – under the table while I sit here not caring.

'Talking to yourself again?' she asks, and I turn to see her slinking into the lounge carrying a tray. Her movements are relaxed, languid. She glides, almost. Not like an awkward teenager. Two deep bowls rest on the tray, braids of steam twirling upwards in front of her face. She pauses as if waiting for me to speak, looks mildly irritated. 'Fine,' she says when I don't answer, and sets the tray on the coffee table. 'Talk away. Just don't call me a ho, all right?'

I can't be bothered defending myself. Just thinking out loud, baby. I swivel my head back to the telly.

'What you watching?' Lowri asks, sinking into the settee beside me. She curls her legs beneath her, socked feet towards my bare thigh. Coiled. Catlike.

I say nothing because I have no clue. It's talking heads. Could be the news. A 'Nam documentary, perhaps. Maybe even hardcore porn, some weird shit with hairy dwarves or something. Who knows?

Lowri's digging quietly at her microwaved spud. I can see her out the corner of one eye. See her glancing at me every few seconds.

'You've got to eat,' she says.

'I will,' I say, but probably won't. Not today. My stomach . . .

She reaches across; the skin on the palm of her hand is soft and dry on my forearm. It makes me catch my breath. I look at her looking at me.

'Those are some good cuts there, J,' she says, squinting at my wrist.

The cuff marks. Lapdog stuck them on good and proper. Locked, rigid. By the time they'd pinned me to the floor and got them on me I was exhausted. Nine of them to bring me down. Takes it out of a man, wrestling with so many people, child cops or not. And then for good measure they gave me a blast of CS spray, which was a tad uncalled for in my opinion.

'I'll survive,' I say, but I'm really not sure about that any more. Been doing a lot of thinking these last few days. Had a lot of time on my hands. Plenty of long, drawn-out seconds that've ticked into minutes then bled into hours and I don't think I've slept since they booted me out of the cells with a charge sheet gripped in my hand. GBH, guys. Serious stuff. Bailed to court in two weeks with conditions I don't enter the city centre. That I don't enter any police station within the force area. That I leave Cliff and Rachael and pretty much anybody connected with them well alone.

They made me hand in the uniform I was wearing. My friction-lock baton, cuffs, CS spray, too. And the old warrant card. Suspended good and proper. On full pay, but it'll just be a matter of time. Just be a matter of potting me in court for shoeing Clive and then it's *adios*, Jacob. Goodbye and thanks for all the fish. It's been emotional.

Worst thing is, they took my official and unofficial pocket notebooks. Right there in the custody suite after they locked me up. Bagged and tagged. Huzzah for them. But what am I going to write in now? What about *my* evidence?

'Fuckin' pigs, man,' Lowri says.

'Yeah,' I say. 'Ain't they?'

And I could go over the wall for what I did to Cliff. Couple of years at Her Majesty's pleasure, most likely. Three hots and a cot with an hour of exercise each day.

Lowri finishes eating, gets up, asks me if I want any of the food and I don't reply so she tuts, gathers up the tray and sashays out of the lounge, so comfortable in my house now. So at home. My surrogate wife. My proxy partner. My replacement child. This beck-and-call girl who's all things to this man.

I hear her cleaning up in the kitchen, running the tap, loading the dishwasher, opening cupboards, spraying and wiping and humming to herself. Happy. Relaxed. I watch her come back into the lounge, skinny hips rocking gently from side to side in her jeans, toes curling upwards in her socks as she pads across the floor. She has an easy look about her. Contented.

In the fingers of her right hand she holds a joint. A thick fuckin' doobie. Five Rizla papers long, at least. A *Withnail and I* Camberwell Carrot.

She flops back onto the settee. 'D'you mind?' she asks, flicking the spliff skywards with a look that suggests she couldn't give a toss if I minded or not.

'Drugs,' I say.

'Yes,' she says. 'Well spotted.'

'Illegal drugs,' I say.

'Yes, they are,' she says with a lopsided smile. 'Very naughty.'

'And I'm a police officer,' I say to her. 'Aren't I?'

Lowri places that soft hand on my forearm again. Looks into my eyes. 'You really need to chill out a bit, Jake,' she says.

And she relaxes back into the cushions, sparks up the joint. Draws on it, takes a big chest full of smoke, removes it and closes her mouth, holds her breath, puffs out her cheeks and glances at me. I watch, mentally timing her, counting silently. Then she's bobbing her head because I'm counting out loud, bobbing down then up in little jerks as I'm counting *forty-four, forty-five, forty-six* to see how long she keeps it in. And suddenly this is funny. This is *fun*.

While she's sitting there gurning with her bulging, amused eyes, I sit forward, look around for my Café Crèmes, can't find them, take my ashtray from the coffee table and place it on the settee between us. Then she faces me, jerks her eyebrows up, leans over and exhales. Blows the smoke in my face. It billows around me and I gasp, breathing it in.

'Give it to me,' I say, taking it from her. Bollocks to the job. I stick it between my lips, take a good, long hit. Fill my lungs with *ganja, man*. Hold my breath. Hold it and stare at Lowri, see her laugh as she counts for me now, start bobbing my head as she's saying *eighty-one, eighty-two, eighty-three* with widening eyes and then I open my mouth and let the smoke drift out, thick grey plumes rising up and over my face.

'Nice,' I say, nodding, and she chuckles. That deep, rough sound of her voice.

So we sit and pass the spliff back and forth in silence, my little hoochgirl and me, my partner in crime. When it's done and my head is reeling she skins up, a masterful display of roll-up creation, a long and tight joint packed nicely with blow. It's awesome. Wow, I hear myself gasp. Out the window I see the sun hanging low in the sky. No cloud. Warm orange light falling through the windows onto my naked midriff. A beautiful day at last.

Lowri's drawing on the end of the second spliff, eyelids heavier, cuddling a pillow in front of her, legs tucked up on the settee. Such a pretty girl. Lush dark hair plunging down to her shoulders. Her tiny frame, her small, compact breasts, that slim, delicate neck. And those eyes, those huge black eyes with their long spiked lashes.

I would, Lowri. I would but for the things you've done. Why have you ruined what we could've had? If only I'd gotten to you sooner. If only I'd taken you away from it all; if I'd saved you before you immersed yourself in that world of filth. But I still would, you know. I think I really would . . .

'What?' she asks, puzzled. She outs the joint in the ashtray. 'You would what?'

I look away. Place a hand over the front of my boxer shorts to hide the bulge that's formed there. 'I . . . Do you . . .?'

She shifts position, moves closer. I feel her fingertips on my chin, those long nails of hers. She gently pulls my face around, back in her direction, and now there's barely three inches between us and I can feel her warm breath on my cheeks, smell smoke and cannabis resin. Her eyes are huge. So close. They fill my vision.

'Do I what, Jake?' she asks softly. Her fingertips are caressing my jaw, my throat. Her other hand cups my left hip. Our legs touching. Electricity there. My hairs standing on end.

'Do you want to . . .?' I stammer, the tickle of her nails making my breathing rapid, my heart race. I push down on my boxer shorts. Push it away.

'Want to what?' she's whispering in my ear now, hot breath on my flesh, fingers rubbing against my neck then my delts, my pecs, and down my abdominals towards my groin. And she knows what I mean. She knows what I want.

And I would, Lowri. But all those faceless, nameless strangers. Those paying punters you've sucked and fucked. The things you've done . . . My grubby angel. My polluted princess. You foul feast for the eyes. You sexy slattern. You're nothing but an achingly gorgeous filthy flatback. Too late, Jake. Much too late again, like that night with the Clio. Like the night with my mother and father . . .

And suddenly it clicks. I know where I've been going wrong.

'D'you want . . . to double up on the PlayStation?' I ask.

She jerks her head back, hands falling away from me. 'Erm . . . what?' she asks, but she's grinning and shaking her head. Completely stoned. Totally nonplussed. Mouth loosely open. Face flushed. I wonder if I look the same. I don't feel that different but I'm having difficulty blinking. Like invisible fingers are pulling up my eyelids.

I stand, switch on the PlayStation, grab the controllers. The lounge judders, like I'm viewing a film that's jumped its sprockets on the cinema projector. Had to be skunk we were smoking. Potent. Lowri watches me, tongue pushed into the side of her mouth. Amused. Annoyed. *Vietnam Encounter II* loads, the title screen flashing onto the television. I sit down again, can't stop smiling. Can't seem to blink and my eyes are drying out.

'You want me to play a shooting game with you?' Lowri asks, staring at the widescreen. 'Come on, Jake. Wouldn't you rather—'

'It's 'Nam, baby,' I grin, handing her a controller. 'The fuckin' *'Nam*. Now light up that spliff and let's play, hoochgirl. I got some cleaning up to do.'

She hesitates for a moment, eyes narrowed, mouthing

hoochgirl? as she shakes her head, but I don't mind because after tonight it's the start of everything. I watch her spark up the doobie, think how I'm going to enjoy this last blast because I know what I have to do now and what it's going to take. I've gotta be quicker. Gotta get in there sooner. Gotta work from the bottom up. Begin the clean up. Alone. First at home, with this game. Clean the goddam VC out of the ville. Then move on. Move out. 'Cos those gooks are running riot out there and the sun may be shining but this is still a desperate, desperate land we live in.

And I don't want to be too late to deal with anything any more.

So we work the tunnels first, busting caps in tandem, our strange little relationship transposed to the screen. Mowing down VC, fragging ammo dumps, pausing to high-five. Lowri's shouting, screaming with laughter and I'm ordering her to tell me *love you long time, GI, you Number One, me wan' sucky fucky,* and I'm laughing too, taking more hits on the spliff, hitting that marijuana, that *Mary Jane,* then Lowri's on a rampage, her grunt going berserk, she's got the red mist, is wiping out wave after wave of Charlie and basically kicking my arse with her score.

'You're bloody *rubbish,*' she snorts at me, falling back into the cushions as she kills the last Big Boss to complete the game, and normally I'd turn the fucking PlayStation off for that, maybe even write her out a Fixed Penalty, but I don't because she's right. This girl who has nothing, who's so happy in spite of it, happy because of what I've done for her and who's shown me what I have to do to make things even better, she's right.

So I keep on laughing and I think it's because I'm frightened to stop.

TWENTY-FOUR

Today's outfit:

An old pair of Lava Combat GTX boots I've used for gardening; standard-issue police cargo trousers, ironed with military precision; Damascus Imperial neoprene knee pads; a limp and frayed leather belt I found in the bottom of a wardrobe and which I haven't worn for a decade; empty CS pouch; Fobus cuff-case, also empty; neoprene friction-lock baton sleeve with no baton; miniature paperwork holder with pens, paper, Post-it notes and some ancient, invalid Fixed Penalty chitties; no new pocket notebook yet but that'll be resolved imminently; Blackhawk Hellstorm Light Operations gloves; white shirt, also ironed with a nice hit of starch; epaulette on each shoulder, one of the numbers askew because the damn fastener is missing; Web-Tex Cross-Draw Vest with no Personal Protection Equipment whatsoever; clip-on polyester tie, shiny with age, with all the times it's been yanked off by whichever scrote fancied their chances; and an old helmet, my first-ever tit with the force crest on it, the crest which has changed three times since I joined. I'm standing by the window now, in the early morning sunlight, reading the scribbled comments inside my old lid, the graffiti, the handwriting of all those colleagues whose names I can't remember, the old sweats from my first station whose job it was to wind up the probationer, to tease and taunt you mercilessly, to make sure you shut up and made the fuckin' brew, boy, clean the bastard panda out before I sit in it, kiddo, no you do that sudden death, I'm too long in the tooth for all that mess, FNG. Because it's character building, isn't it? That's why they did it. What doesn't kill you makes you stronger.

In fifteen-year-old ink I read *JACOB YOU FAGGOT*. Turn the helmet around, check another section of the cream lining, see *YOU SOFT FUCKING SHANDY DRINKER*. Then *THIS HELMET BELONGS TO PC 754 JACOB 'MENTAL HEALTH ACT' SMITH*. Underneath the sweat-stained brown leather of the forehead-guard is a childlike drawing of a knife, the words *SON OF SCROTE* alongside. Ah, those funny guys. Those cheeky little tinkers. Those happy days.

I've been up for two hours, showered, run the clippers through my hair again, shaved and moisturised, deodorised and eau-de-toiletted myself. I still look like a sack of shit, but it'll suffice. I'm just glad I never throw anything away. Not deliberately, anyway.

It's early, oh-six thirty hours, and Lowri's watching me dress from her side of the bed, from her side of the king-size in the master bedroom we've now moved into, her head on the pillow, hair all over the shop. She's wrapped in the single quilt I gave her last night so she could sleep next to me. No touching, intimacy, contamination. But at least she was there. I slept like I haven't done for months.

One eye closed, she watches me sleepily. 'Where you going?' she asks, yawning.

'Work,' I say, snapping on my glossy tie.

She eases herself up on an elbow, blows a stray clump of hair out of her eyes. 'But—'

I hold up a hand. Stop, in the name of the law. 'I've got work to do,' I say.

'Jake . . .' she's saying, but I'm walking towards the bedroom door now, helmet tucked under one arm, thinking how today is going to be a good day. It's time to get down and dirty. No more tardiness. No more torpor. I will make this world a better place and thereby make myself a better man.

'Are you doing anything tonight?' I ask her at the door.

'Um . . .' she says, shrugging. 'I wasn't planning on going anywh—'

'I'll be in touch,' I interrupt. 'We'll RV after my shift. Be ready.'

She narrows her eyes, awake now. 'For what?'

I don't answer, leave the bedroom. Grab my Café Crèmes in the lounge, my lighter, my wallet, an unsmoked spliff because we were so toasted last night we couldn't even lift it from the coffee table. Wedge them all into the thigh pocket of my cargos next to the mouse gun. Check the bundle of cash in the other pocket, drop a couple of fifties onto the table for Lowri. Check my watch. Oh-six forty-three. Right on time. I step into the hallway, examine myself in the mirror. Dig my mobile out of the other cargo pocket, slide it into the radio pouch on the Cross-Draw vest, plug the lone MP3 earphone I found in Ben's bedside drawer into my left ear, then jam the jack into the top of the phone.

And I'm cooking on gas. Let's make a difference, Jake. Let's get out there and show this world what you can do. What things could really be like for them if everyone just did what you're about to do and cleaned up around the damn place.

So I open the front door, step out into the cold sunny morning for my first shift on solo patrol. From somewhere behind me I hear Lowri's pained voice, calling from the top of my stairs, telling me *Jake, no, don't go*. But I have to.

I close the front door and walk away quickly. Because I have to.

on with my routine patrol. I can't let the fact that the public are too bloody stupid to take care of themselves ~~does~~ distract me from the job at hand. Why don't they get it? Do they not realise if it wasn't for me, for the thin blue line, there'd be anarchy? Maybe we should strike. Just for a week. They'd be begging us to come back to work. Weeping at our feet, at the steps of police stations. Throwing themselves at me, pleading for me to don the outfit once more so their lives would be bearable again. It's only when something you've taken for granted for so long disappears that you realise just what you had. I mean, look at me! What a cockhead. Karen, where the fuck are you? Naomi. Ben. Please. Please.

0817	Verbal warnings re. disorderly appearance, Thompson Street. Youths spoken to and advised. No further action required. Now that's discretion!! No forms, no ~~fuckiss~~ bits of paper for statistics!! Good ol'-fashioned police work. Well done, Jakey! I'm Dixon of Dock Green, me. And ain't that what the public always wants us to be??
0843	Multiple cautions issued for Vehicle Excise Licence offences — see below for summary
0920	Code 50 — refreshment break, man 🌀 HAHA
0945	Criminal damage, Capitol Road — Fixed Penalty Notices issued x 3 !!!! Woosh. Brownie points for me or what? I am on fire here. ~~Falmi~~ Flamin'!!
1110	CODE RED. DISRUPTION OF MAJOR TERRORIST PLOT. AM IN DANGER NOW. CS INCAPACITANT SPRAY DISCHARGED. FULL NOTES TO FOLLOW.
1207	Have changed mind re. Dixon of Dock Green. Didn't someone shoot the old fucker?

'Good morning, madam,' I say.

The woman beside the till has the early morning pallor of someone who hasn't slept properly before getting up at ridiculous o'clock to meet the newspaper deliveries. Bent over, plump backside in the air, sweating as she cuts plastic ties from bundles of red-top rags. She jerks upright at the sound of my voice, startled. Relaxes when she sees the uniform.

'Oh,' she says, primping her greying hair with one hand. She gives a relieved laugh, like a whinny. 'You made me jump, officer. Lordy!'

'God always falls asleep on the job,' I tell her, smiling faintly underneath the brim of my helmet. Warm but firm, that's the way to do it. Reassuring, professional. She looks momentarily puzzled. 'But I don't,' I say. 'Just doing the rounds.'

The woman hesitates then shrugs. She's holding scissors so I keep my distance because you can never be too careful out here. 'Well, everything's fine. Just opening up for the day.'

'Hmm,' I say. 'But I snuck in here without you noticing, didn't I? Eh? Right up behind you. Didn't even hear me, did you?'

'Um . . . no,' she says, blinking up at me.

'You should be more careful,' I tell her, wagging a finger. 'More *aware*. Old dear like you, on her own at this time of the morning. Anyone could do you over, snatch the takings. Know what I mean?'

'But this is a village shop,' she protests. 'We've never had any problems here . . . And who are you calling an old dear? What's your name again?'

I tilt my head to one side, hold up the finger I was just wagging at her, give her a shushing gesture. Is that ops room transmitting? Can I hear them via the MP3 earpiece? I believe I can. 'Roger that,' I say to nobody, fingers pressing the side of my mobile phone, mouth up to the tiny blank LCD screen. 'I'll be clear from my current call in around . . .' quick check of the watch, '. . . ten minutes.'

The woman waits for me to finish radio procedure, watching me with sullen eyes. I let go of the phone, shake my head. 'Yet another incident they want me to deal with!' I say with a dramatic sigh. 'Can't stay too long. Kettle on?'

'Look,' she says, waving a hand around. The scissors flash under the fluorescents so I take a step back. 'I'm really rather busy.'

'We're all busy,' I say. 'But there's always time for a brew.'

'I'm grateful you popped in,' she says. 'But honestly, I don't have time for anything at the moment.'

'I'm here to help *you*, madam. Put the kettle on please.'

She's moved behind the counter now. My eyes are on the scissors. 'The owner'll be in any minute,' she's saying, looking at the door. 'I have so much to do. I'm awfully sorry, officer. Maybe next time?'

Fine. I glance about the store, this shop sitting half a mile from home and which I've never been into before. Could've made a nice little tea stop on the patch. Then I check the tobacco display, do the litmus test. Can't see any Café Crèmes on the racks, know I'll never shop here for anything as a result.

'You have failed, madam,' I tell her. 'Not a decent smoke in the whole building.'

She screws up her face. 'What?'

I walk to the door, see the rotary display stand next to it. It's filled with stationery. I select a red notepad. A Ryman Europa Midi Pocket Notebook, as a matter of fact. *With margin.* Nice . . .

'Call me if you need anything,' I say, and slip the notebook into my shirt pocket.

We are back in business.

'I . . . I will,' she says, then asks me my name and number but ops room are transmitting to me and of course I have to listen. My other finger is upright again. Quiet, woman. Official police business. She's open-mouthed, staring at me now, free hand feeling about for the cordless phone I can see leaning against the Chupa Chups lolly display.

'All noted; show me en route,' I say into the mobile and leave.

I've got the Bee Gees' 'Stayin' Alive' in my head as I pace down the sloping main drag towards the city's student area and I'm annoyed because the music is inappropriate for serious police foot patrol. I stop walking to make the music go away. Smile at the groups of kids traipsing to the local school. 'Morning,' I nod. 'Morning . . . morning . . . morning . . .'

Most don't answer. Just glower at me from under their fringes. These scruffy little iPod zombies. These spotty walking hormone sacks. How sloppy they all look! Nike trainers, ill-fitting blouses, tatty trousers hanging off arses to show their bundies. This isn't right. I may not be the best-dressed officer in town, but it's for a reason. At least I *want* to make more effort.

'Oy you.' I point at a clump of shuffling fifteen-year-olds. I stand in front of them, block their path. 'What on earth d'you think you're doing?'

They stop. Swap glances. I hear a snigger. One of them, a chunky fellow with Neanderthal features who's as wide as he's tall, he looks up at me. 'Wha'?' he mumbles.

'Look at you,' I say. 'Just. Look. At. *You*.'

Cro-Magnon boy, he sniffs. 'We ain't done nuffin', officer.'

'What's with the pants then?' I demand. 'Eh?'

Five pairs of eyes looking at me. Clueless.

'Our . . . pants?' says Chunky. He looks down at his trousers.

'Deary, deary me,' I say, shaking my head. 'Call that a uniform? You're just adding to the problems, aren't you? Don't you think the world is in enough of a mess as it is, without you lot walking around like you've shit yourselves? Eh?'

'Thought the police weren't supposed to swear,' says Chunky.

'I'll fucking well do what I like, tubs,' I tell him, moving closer. The mouths on these kids today. The complete lack of respect. 'And what I'm telling you lot to do is pull your bloody pants up! Literally and metaphorically!'

I wait, watch as they yank at their clothing. Tidy themselves up. Other children rubberneck as they pass by.

Chunky's starting to get upset. I think he's about to start grizzling. I bend forward slightly, place my arm on his shoulder. His deltoid is flabby, no definition at all.

'I'm not one for losing my temper,' I tell him, staring into his weepy eyes. 'But I'd rather catch you now before it's too late. Before it's too late for *me*, know what I mean?'

He nods and I'm not sure if he's grasped it but it'll do so I pat his bulbous upper arm, wince as the flesh jiggles beneath his shirt. 'Good lad,' I say to him. 'You're all going to be good lads, I can tell. Now on your way.'

So off they skulk, Chunky with his head down, his companions slapping him on the back and glaring at me. I'm waving them off thinking job well done, see one of them flipping open his mobile phone, skinny fingers punching the keypad three times.

I walk quickly down the hill, take the first turning I come across, some posh tree-lined avenue. I'm thinking about Chunky's mate and his undoubtedly grateful phone call to the station. It's clear my work in this location is complete so I speed up, take my lid off, carry it. Decide to jog a little. Then run. If any of the residents sees me I'm just a local plod chasing down some crims. A bobby legging it to a house alarm. Nothing to see here, sir! Go about your business. Let me handle it . . .

I follow the avenue as it curves left, dart through a gulley onto a dirt track at the back of these mansion houses. Stop, squat on my haunches against a wooden garden fence. My chest wheezing from the cigars and last night's weed. Check the PM9, my tin of smokes, the reefer. All there. Everything good.

I smoke a couple of miniatures. Do half the joint. Toke and listen to the ebb and flow of a siren, a siren that comes mightily close to where I'm sitting and smoking before falling away again, wailing into nothingness. Out the spliff by pinching the ash off the end, stick the rest of it in my cigar tin.

Back on the main drag I head downhill, follow the pavement south, head feeling a little muggy. I go a mile, maybe two, without passing a soul. I'm bored with nobody around to provide advice to, so start examining the windscreens of parked cars. Clocking the tax discs. I'm appalled to find one in five out of date. Out of date! In this day and age, when you can order your bloody Vehicle Excise Licence over the Internet. When you don't even have to get off your backside!

It's a nuisance not possessing any proper caution forms to affix to the windscreens so the Post-it notes have to suffice. I use nearly a whole pad of luminous yellow squares by the time I'm nearing the student area, leave a long line of bright pieces of paper warning each and every car owner they need to get a grip. They're handwritten and not particularly professional but they'll do. It's small-time stuff police-wise, but Baker will be proud of me when he finds out. All those quick hits for the duty register. Sixty-four cars booked up for no tax! That'll bump up the figures for this month's Home Office bean-counter report . . .

I keep walking. On the front foot at last. Up and at 'em. I'm on the fringes of what I think is Rachael's sector, pootling along nicely, feeling pretty mellow now, stopping to exchange pleasantries with some of the old grippers out shopping for condensed milk and cat litter. *What's the time, officer?* they ask over and over until I'm telling them – nicely, of course, got to stay a pro – to buy a bloody watch.

It's all mundane stuff. Stuff I can do without thinking, which is helpful as the reefer has made me forget where I'm going and what I'm supposed to be doing. I know I've got to be quick about it, though. There's a sense of urgency I can't shake. A sense that time is running out and only I can do what's necessary . . .

I'm a hundred yards further down the road, feeling a little tired now, like I need to stop a while and gather myself because I haven't done such a lengthy foot patrol for years; my feet are on fire and I'm holding on to a lamppost as traffic goes by, mulling over where to go next. I know once this shift is done it's back to Lowri. Sort her out good and proper. Then Frank. Karen and the kids. My job. Possibly even Rachael and Cliff. My 'making amends' list. Rebuild the bridges and rebuild your life, Jake. Stay on the road to somewhere. But I have a vague idea that right now I may be getting too close to something, to a place I shouldn't be, but as I'm trying to remember what that's all about I see three kids loitering in an alleyway to my right.

Three teenagers, seventeen at the most, all sports clothes and shaved hair. Skater trainers, Chucks or Vans, thick coloured laces that aren't done up properly. One of them has a Halfords carrier bag. They haven't seen me, are too engrossed in whatever the one kid has in the bag, are huddled together while they fish around in it and then, oh dear, out come the aerosol cans, one each, and I can't believe it when they begin spraying the whitewashed wall. Hands jerking about, quick movements as they squiggle in bright spray paint, laughing and gesturing, and if that wasn't bad enough one of them pulls a piece of paper out of his pocket, they study it for a few seconds then work on the wall again. Working as a team. I stare, shaking my head as I realise what they're doing. They're starting to spray a *mural*. A mural! Not thirty feet from the main road. Unbelievable.

'Stop right there!' I shout, and it takes some considerable effort to make my legs move. I'm running, thinking how I could be home with Lowri now, that this is quite tiresome, all this plodding about, when I could have my feet up on the coffee table while she beats me on the PlayStation.

They freeze. Gaping at me as I sprint towards them. The one with the carrier bag does a strange kind of shimmy as if he's about to give it toes but then decides not to bother. I'm too quick. Right on top of them before they can get going on the mural. They drop the aerosols, swap brief glances, look about as if to say *nope, officer, weren't us. Don't know nuffink about spraying nuffink.*

'D'you think I'm stupid?' I ask them, breathing heavily. 'Do you?'

Silence. They're studying the tarmac floor of the alleyway.

'You're in for it now,' I tell them, looking at the graffiti on the wall. 'What the hell's all this supposed to be?'

'Street art,' one of them says quietly.

'Art?' I laugh. 'It's just luminous scribbles, boy.'

'We was jus' taggin' our names, mate,' another one says.

'I'm not your bloody mate,' I tell him. Gesture to the wall. 'And look at it! It's just . . . mess! Nothing but a dirty mess for other people to have to endure.

'They don't have to look at it,' Carrier Bag boy says.

'You're not getting away with this,' I shout. 'Don't you know that low-level crime increases the public's fear of crime overall?'

'Eh?' asks Carrier Bag.

Idiot. 'What you've done here is just the start,' I say, moving closer. 'It's just a few small steps to a life of crime, boy. Possibly worse. You could end up as a threat to the security of this country. It's lucky I got to you so quickly. To nip it in the bud.'

'It's just spraying a wall . . .' one of them mutters, eyeing me with an odd expression.

'Right,' I say. 'You've asked for it.' I whip out the old Fixed

Penalties, ask their names, addresses, dates of birth. The boxes on the pro forma aren't big enough for all the details but I write them down anyway. Fill in three of them as best I can. Rip the top copy off each, hand one to each of the *artistes*.

'What's this for?' Carrier Bag asks, looking at the chitty with a mystified expression.

'A fine,' I tell them. 'For criminal damage.'

'But it's a parking ticket,' he says, wrinkling his nose.

'Don't be clever with me!' I yell, then clench my jaw as they look at each other, look at me. Start giggling. Cheeky little bastards.

'Come on,' Carrier Bag says to his chums. 'Let's chip. This dude's a freak.'

My fingers toy with the mouse gun through the fabric of my cargos. I feel the muzzle, the trigger-guard. The handle with its magazine of five nine-millie bullets. 'Laugh all you want, boys,' I tell them as they shuffle towards the main drag. 'You won't be laughing when you've got to find eighty quid each for those fines, yeah? Ha! Yeah? Are you listening to me?'

They disappear around the corner. I hear screams of laughter. Bend down, grab one of the aerosol cans. See green paint on the nozzle. Slide it into my CS pouch. Take a deep breath, try to relax after the confrontation. Another job well done. Another small incident taken care of for the greater good. I pull out my cigar tin, select the half-smoked reefer, light it and take a long drag. I hold my breath, lean against the wall. Exhale. Nice. Very, very nice. Just chill and smoke and work out what you need to do next, Jake. I finish the spliff, amble out of the alleyway.

My face hurts and it takes a moment for me to realise I'm grinning uncontrollably. I really can't relax my cheeks or lips. Not to worry. Adds to the agreeable air. The smiling, helpful policeman. I nod at a couple more pensioners. Wave back at a bus full of primary school children, forget to stop waving even after the bus has driven off and it's just me shuffling down the street with my arm in the air. I lower it. See bemused drivers watching me. Decide to take a detour so duck into the first store I come across.

A basement Internet café, some dimly lit oh-so-trendy gaff like the coffee shop out of *Friends*. Heads turn as I walk through the door. Funny looks. No friends here, then. But that's cool, man. I'm here to do a job, aren't I? This is what I get paid for. To be unpopular. I can hear static from the banks of computer flatscreens, a loud buzz in my ears. I ignore the soap-dodging students who whisper and mutter as I prowl the workstations checking over their shoulders for any dodgy goings-on. Bank fraud, maybe. Online gambling. Illicit paedo stuff. They're hunching over their screens so I can't see anything.

This is proving far too difficult. 'Any online fraudsters in here?' I ask instead.

Faces swing towards me. Huge eyes everywhere. Nobody says a word. Hmm.

'Any kiddie fiddlers, then?' I shout. 'Put your hands up if you are, it'll save a lot of bother in the long run.'

'Haven't you got anything better to do?' I hear from behind me.

Someone in here's got a bit of front, have they? I turn in the direction of the voice, see an Asian lad. Late teens, glasses and weirdly shaped sideburns that start at his hairline then thin out as they swoop along his jaw. Staring at me over the top of his specs.

'Why?' I say, glancing around. Everyone's stopped what they're doing. 'Am I making you nervous?' I walk over to his terminal. 'You got something to hide, friend?'

The guy leans, blocks the monitor with one shoulder. 'This is private,' he says.

'Not on my patch it ain't, sonny,' I tell him, and take hold of his upper arm, push him to one side. He's on a wheeled swivel chair so slides about five feet to my left, protesting as he goes. The website he was looking at shows schematics, building specs. Architectural blueprints. I click through his recent history. One of them is of the new Euro Arena, not two miles from here. I spin around to look at him.

'Why are you looking at building plans?' I ask.

'S' for my degree,' the kid's saying angrily. 'Okay?'

I look him up and down. 'Checking for structural weak spots, eh? Points of entry? Places to maximise casualties?'

'What?'

'You know *exactly* what I mean,' I say to him.

'No, actually, I *don't*,' he says, but I'm not convinced. There's something wrong here. Something not quite right. It's then that I see the rucksack on the floor underneath his workstation.

My breath catches. I look from the rucksack to the Asian kid. I step over to him, take his arm again.

'You're going to have to come with me,' I say, but have no clue where we'd go if he did. 'I'm arresting you for being Muslim without due care and attention.'

'What you on about, mate?' he squeals, flapping his arm to shake me off.

'The rucksack,' I growl at him. '*Your* rucksack. I caught you checking out building plans. Caught you early, before you could start. Before you could be radicalised, yeah? What's in the bag, kiddo?'

I sense another person at my side. Won't be any form of backup, not at the moment. This is solo patrol time. I quickly check, see a woman decked out in business duds, dark suit with blonde hair wrenched back into a ponytail. It's too tight, has pulled the skin on her forehead as well, so now she has this strange, permanently surprised expression.

'What's the problem here . . . officer?' she asks me. She appears baffled, looking from the struggling kid to my Web-Tex vest.

'Police business,' I say to her, holding up my free hand in front of her face. 'Back away please, madam. We might have to evacuate.'

She turns to the kid I've got hold of. 'Is everything all right here, Rakesh?'

'Get this copper off me,' he shouts, still flapping about on his wheelie chair. 'He's making out I'm fuckin' al-Qaeda or somethin'!'

The woman's still swivelling her head back and forth, from the kid to my vest. Then she asks me: 'Why are you covered in green paint?'

'What?' I ask.

'You've got paint all over you,' she says, pointing. 'I work as a Special, you know. Your uniform doesn't look . . . Are you really a police officer?'

'Of course I'm a bloody police officer,' I tell her, cursing those kids in the alleyway. Cursing myself for leaning against the wall while I had a sneaky toke. 'A *real* police officer, too, not some stupid hobby bobby like you. Now please back the fuck off!'

She takes a step or two away from us. But this is getting out of hand. I can see other people rising from their chairs, advancing towards our testy *ménage à trois*. The woman's pointing at the kid I've got hold of, shouting something about honours student and research, but I'm losing control of this situation so press a button on my radio – not my radio, my mobile – and say to nobody, say to ops room – loud enough for this kid and the woman and everybody else in here so they won't mess with me any further – that I need a van, maybe assistance at the location, nod quickly and say *yeah, immediately please, you're thirty seconds away? That's all noted, just hurry it up please* and then I see the business woman speaking on her own mobile phone, saying *I don't know who he is, I don't think he really is a police officer, you'd better send a unit down here straight away because he's causing all sorts of problems, I think he's not quite right. You've been looking for him all morning? Well, he's here right now . . .*

And then I'm surrounded, like a wagon train by Injuns. Hands on me, pulling and jostling. Raised voices, static from the flatscreens, sirens in the distance but getting louder. The kid breaks free from my grasp and nobody's listening as I explain, no one wants to hear what I've got to say even when I tell them there's a bomb in the building, so I decide enough is enough, I'm trying to do my job here but everyone's being rather obstructive, these people are not assisting me *at all* and it's a sorry sign of the times when an officer of the law can't rely on the public he serves.

I'm under attack. Could end up seriously injured. I reach down, wrestle my right hand through the clump of arms gripping onto my vest, try for the mouse gun but can't get to it. Grab the next best thing. The less lethal option.

I take hold of my CS canister, pull it from its pouch, smash my arm upwards to force whoever's holding me away so I've got a clear shot.

'Spray!' I shout, loud enough to warn anybody within the vicinity that I'm about to discharge a Section One firearm in the building; that there could be cross-contamination and they might be affected.

I depress the nozzle, flinch when a big puff of luminous green paint explodes outwards. Not what I was expecting. Not exactly CS incapacitant, but it does the trick. I keep my finger on the nozzle, pressing, arcing the aerosol around the room.

The kid gets a face full, flaps his mouth like a landed tuna, paws at his eyes. Business woman, her suit's ruined, blonde hair now a punky green, she's going round in little circles, *oh oh oh*ing with eyes closed, the outline of her mobile on her cheek where the spray paint missed. Everybody else backs off.

I look around. Shocked faces. Green faces. Hear sirens. My backup. Nearly here but too late anyway. I've dealt with this situation. The matter has been resolved to the satisfaction of all parties. I stare at the kid, at the paint covering his face and hair and clothes.

'That's a beautiful colour, man,' I tell him. 'Really quite vibrant.'

And I thank everyone for their assistance, quickly walk out through a rear fire door.

Maybe I won't go home today. Not after all this hard work. Not after this.

1905	RV with Lowri Horton @ Executive Suite, Chambers Manor Hotel. Full tactical
	sweep and clear of suite, balcony, outer corridor, lift and main lobby. Nothing
	untoward located. And the suite, man! It's well posh. Even got a proper ~~fridge~~
	fridge instead of one of them dwarf mini-bar things that Lapdog probably has
	as his normal fridge at home. But four hundred quid a night? I just thank Frank
	for the cash, and the fact it's only one night I'll need this place for. And thank
	Christ it was available. I needed somewhere to plot up for a while, let the dust settle after

TWENTY-FIVE

I tell Lowri to take her time, enjoy a long soak. Stick some music on the little stereo system they've built into the vanity unit – whale sounds or something. Light the candles I bought. Relax, girl. Pretty yourself up. Style your hair. Moisturise every inch of skin. Perfume all those delicate places, use whatever's in there. Varnish every single nail. I'm so pleased you brought the clothes I told you about over the phone. I've laid them out for you on the bed. On our bed. Make sure you're wearing them when you come out in ninety minutes, not before. Make the effort. It's a special night.

She gives me a knowing smile, a look which says *at last, at last we're going to do what I'm paid to do*, then I hand her the large glass of white which she downs in one and I'm thinking Christ, that's Pouilly, thirty bloody quid a pop here, but say nothing because there's bottles of the stuff and I've barely dented the cash Frankie lent me so top her up again. She skips up the half-dozen steps, disappears into the bedroom. Moments later, water's running from the en-suite bath taps.

I pick up the welcome book, check the laminated menu, dial room service. Order half a dozen overly complicated arty-farty dishes, replace the receiver, forget what I've ordered because I'm not concentrating but it doesn't matter anyway, I'm not hungry. Pour another tumbler of Jack at the bar, look around the hotel suite again. It's enormous. An opulent split-level palace. Lounge area with deep, plush sofas. Dining section with table and eight chairs that dwarfs mine at home. Separate – and huge – bedroom. Top spec Bose music system.

Widescreen on the wall that's got to be a sixty-incher. The place is bigger than my house.

I open the French doors, step out onto the balcony, out into early evening rain. Balance my drink on the railing. Light up one of the joints that Lowri rolled earlier, look down at the traffic, at people going about their business, oblivious to the uniformed policeman toking on a spliff and watching them from above. I pick at my fingers, at the brilliant green paint seemingly tattooed onto the tips after this morning's terrorist incident.

Wish I'd asked Lowri to bring me a change of clothes when I rang her and gave her the address. Stupid, really. Bit awkward when I was checking in, trying to cover everything with my fleece. Not thinking straight again. I pick up the Jack, breathe in the sour, malty aroma. Toss it over the railing again. Stay lucid, Jake. Stay on the page. I take a few hits on the joint to keep me as chilled as the wine in the fridge.

After an hour I hear her walking around in the bedroom. I hop up the steps with the last of the Pouilly, rap on the door, open it a few inches and slip the bottle through the gap. Smile faintly as she thanks me.

There're three knocks on the main door so I bark at them to leave it outside, slide a fifty under the gap. Wait, wait some more, open the door and wheel in the service cart. They've provided everything. White linen. Polished cutlery. Fine crockery. The food in silver-service dishes. There're even bloody napkin rings. I set the table. Light candles. Dim lights. Flip through the handful of CDs I took out of the truck when I arrived. Put soft music on the stereo. *Movie Adagios*, some multi-CD thing I picked up last year from Tesco or Smith's or possibly on a rare visit to Chavsda. Pure romantic class. I check my watch, grab another Jack, pick up the half-empty bottle. Sit at one end of the table, place the Jack Daniel's bottle and tumbler in front of me and look around at what I've done here. Use these last few minutes to mentally run through what I've got to do tonight.

Lowri appears as I'm picking on a granary roll. Perfect timing: Mascagni's *Cavalleria rusticana* from *Raging Bull* is soaring from the speakers, the violins reaching their peak.

'How do I look?' she asks, giving me a twirl. She staggers a little.

I whistle. Smile, nod approvingly. She certainly scrubs up well. Hair dark and silky. Fingernails and lips a deep scarlet. Eyelashes thick, curled upwards. She smells fantastic. I'm disappointed she didn't bother with the skirt and strappy sandals I told her to bring from home; has opted for her jeans and the ever-present Fuck-Me Boots. At least she's got the top on. The red halter top I bought for Karen all those weeks ago.

'Aren't you gonna change too?' she asks.

'Does the uniform make you nervous?'

'Not really,' she says. 'It's just a bit . . . odd.'

I shrug. Who cares?

I've already opened another bottle of wine. Lowri takes a seat opposite me. 'Fine, a meal with PC Plod it is. May I?' she giggles, pointing at the ice bucket.

'Fill your boots,' I say pointedly.

She glances down. 'Sorry. Sandals didn't quite fit.'

I watch as she pours herself another glass, fills it to the brim. Takes two large gulps. Sways her head to the music, to Pachelbel's *Canon* from *Ordinary People*, even though she has no clue who it is. The candles, they're barely throwing any light around. It's almost gloomy in here. Lowri, sitting there with her dark hair and that halter top. If I squint, girl . . .

'That colour suits you though,' I tell her.

'Y'know me,' she says, pinching at the top. 'Li'l Red Riding Hood.'

'I suppose that makes me the big bad wolf?'

She studies me for a few seconds, one eye closed, one side of her mouth twisted upwards as if deliberating. Then: 'Nah. You're just a gentle giant. With a few personal issues.' And she laughs, necks the rest of the wine.

I say nothing. Just smile, cradling the tumbler in my green-tipped fingers. This is going to be easier than I thought. She's filling her glass again, spilling some of it over the table with an *oops, sorry!* And I ask her if she's hungry, if she's ready to eat.

'I'm ravenous,' she says, eyeing the domed silver lids. 'Wha' we got? Smells great.'

'A Last Supper,' I tell her, standing up with the tumbler in my hand. I fake a stumble, roll my eyes as Lowri chuckles at me, point at the half-empty bottle of JD.

She's still cackling as she asks, 'Last supper? What's one of those?'

'It's what we're having,' I say, and start removing the lids. She's right: the food smells great. Looks fabulous, too, even though I have no clue what any of it is. 'The best meal you could imagine, the last thing you'd want to eat before the end.'

She stares at me for a moment, head wobbling, eyes heavy. 'Cool,' she says then, slumped in her seat now. What I've said hasn't even registered. She drains her glass, refills it. Pulls the two-thirds-empty bottle out of the bucket, waggles it at me. Ice water flies all over the tabletop but she doesn't apologise this time.

'Y'might wanna gerranother, J,' she smiles dopily. 'This stuff is fuckin' lush.'

I dish up, open more wine, light the reefer, pull on it. Those breathing exercises, so useful. Peach and green time. Bollocks to the no-smoking rules. I drift off a little, the music filling my head, then Lowri's telling me not to bum the whole spliff, to eat some food while she has a toke. And I don't have a problem with that at all because it'll tip her right over the edge.

'Wow, tastes good, Jake,' she says after a while, but she's picking at the food. Too drunk now, past being hungry. Dropping her fork, slurring. Drawing in the wine like a machine sump. Stopping every now and then to puff on the joint.

I watch her performance. Eat. Clean my plate. Gaze at her as she slouches first one way then the other in the chair. 'I was thinking,' I say. 'Nobody knows you're here, do they?'

Lowri blinks, stretches those pitch-black eyes of hers, rocks her head back and forth as if to clear the haziness. 'Erm . . . M'pimp knows I'm goin' with you,' she says. 'But doesn't know I'm 'ere. He don' care anyway. Jus' long as you pays me and I gives him his cut end of the week, he's a happy camper.'

Such good news. I think it may be time to move things along a little. 'Are you *going with me* then, Lowri?' I ask, smiling thinly at her. My fingers are rubbing the rim of the tumbler. 'We haven't really had a go at anything . . . yet.'

She rests her chin on the palm of her hand, elbow almost missing the edge of the table. Looks at me in what I assume is supposed to be a sultry, come-on expression but her face is slack, her eyes can't seem to fix on me. 'We can 'ave a go now,' she says. 'If y'like.'

I change the music, slip a Doors CD into the drive. Turn up the volume. 'Break On Through' kicks off. Time to break through, Lowri. To push on through to the other side, to leave behind everything you've ever believed in. *Who's this?* she asks, and I tell her it doesn't matter. I grab the wine bottle, Lowri's glass. Take her hand, marvel at how small it feels, look down as she glances up and grins her lopsided grin. Lead her across to the lounge area. To a sofa that's bigger than my bed. She sits, pulls at her boots clumsily, wrestles them off. Sinks back into the cushions with a sigh, curls her socked feet under her. Lowri the cat. She'd purr if she was able.

So I tell her to sit tight, wait while I freshen up, all that food and smoking has made me want to clean up a little and she nods, eyelids heavy, says *I'll be waiting for you, Jake. I've waited this long I can wait five minutes more, baby, I'll be right here.*

And I climb the steps to the bedroom thinking: I'm sure you will but what an odd thing to say, what a peculiar thing to come out with, but it's probably the wine. I'm in too much of a rush now to mull it over. In the en suite I throw cold water over my face, stare at my pale reflection in the mirror. Get everything straight in my head. Put on my fleece, zip it up to the neck so it covers everything. Check I've got the truck keys, the last three reefers. My new pocket notebook. The mouse gun.

Lowri hasn't touched any more of the wine. The bottle sits where I placed it on the coffee table. She's stretched out now, has plumped a cushion, placed it under her head. The Doors are still rocking from the speakers. 'LA Woman'. One of her feet taps along to the music, out of sync with the bass line. I stand over her, fingering my dog tags through my clothes.

'Hey, Jake,' she mutters, not looking up at me. 'Y'ready?'

I'm ready, Lowri. But are you? My little hoochgirl. My grubbily gorgeous companion. Are you ready for what's in store?

'J?' she sighs, eyes closed now.

I sit on the edge of the sofa. Place a hand on the silky skin of her arm. The track finishes playing. Silence for a moment. 'I'm still here,' I whisper.

'S' good,' she says quietly. Lips barely moving. 'I'm glad.'

I hear a slinky, haunting guitar riff come from the speakers.

Fingerpicking. Like a sitar. The rattlesnake shake of a tambourine. The beginning of 'The End'. I run my fingers across her skinny bicep, up towards her shoulder. Hold my breath. Squint. Touch the red halter top, feel the fabric against the pads of my fingertips. She stirs, rolls her eyes around beneath the lids. Her chest rising and falling slowly, breathing deeply.

'Thank you, Jake,' she mumbles, my fingers wrapped in that ebony hair of hers. 'Jus' wanna thank you for everything.'

I lean into her. Breathe in that intoxicating mixture of cannabis and wine. Of her young skin. 'Shh,' I say softly.

'But I love it here . . .' Lowri's muttering, my face millimetres from hers. My fingers ploughing through the hair above her ear. 'I love wha' you've done f'me . . . I love being with you . . .' and I can barely hear her now, hardly make out the words. I rest my hand against the side of her face, my mouth hovering over hers, so close I feel the warmth of her skin, her hot breath on me, the faintest tickle of her lips against mine.

'An' I think . . .' she's murmuring. 'I woulda done this f'nothing 'cos I think . . . y'know . . . I think I might be . . . might be kind of . . . y'know . . .'

I kiss her. Gently clasp her hair. My other hand, it grips the red halter top. I breathe through my nose, breathe in her perfume. She doesn't respond, doesn't open her mouth or probe with her tongue and this is fine, this is how it should be, this is just me making amends and rebuilding bridges and putting things right. It was never going to be an easy process.

She's asleep before I pull away. I raise my head, my hands still holding the halter top, her hair. My eyes narrowed, blurring everything.

'I'm a good man now, Karen,' I say to her. 'I'm not my father.'

And I place my arms around her slender frame. Hold her. Close my eyes and hold her for a few minutes. Then I stand. Watch her unconscious form, let my eyes roam over her. I take a last good look. Because it's time to clean up, Lowri. Time to restore order. And you're just the beginning.

There's one more thing to do here. One more hurdle. Her socks. I reach down, a flutter in my gut. Pull them off. See her feet for the first and last time. And I can't help but smile. I knew I'd be right. I knew it all along. So I just stare, not moving. Look but don't touch. Remember this moment, Jake. This feeling that you've moved on. That you're over this part of your life now.

So I work the socks back on, nodding my head to the rolling drums, to the hypnotic rhythm of the almost flamenco-style guitar. Do the boots, zip them back up the side of her calves, lift her from the sofa.

The song finishes. Lowri is asleep in my arms.

My watch shows twenty-one forty-four hours. Should do it in plenty of time.

2145	Immediate response re disposal of teenage hooker. Flick on the blues. Why are they not working on this bloody firearms truck? Why are they flashing orange? Must remember to submit a defect form to HQ Fleet Management when I call in there on

I head north in the darkness.

Take the back roads out of the city, the wipers on intermittent. The pitter-patter of rain on the windscreen, the squawk of rubber across glass. The radio's off. The satnav screen radiates a blue glow. I'm cruising at just under the limit. Not many cars on the road, the odd pair of headlights coming up behind me and overtaking. Some flying south on the opposite carriageway, towards the capital.

I've a vague idea of where I'm heading. Where we're heading. Lowri's comatose on the back seat, one arm hanging into the footwell. Hair lying across her face, snoring quietly, so faint I can barely hear it over the rumble of the diesel engine. I've tilted the rear-view mirror so I can watch her sleeping in the pale light of the satnav. Keep an eye on her. She's drunk so much. She's so drunk. Don't want her to choke on her own vomit. Don't want anything to happen to her until we get to where I'm going. Until I've done what I've got to do.

It's just me and the rain and the hypnotic sweep of the windscreen wipers. An open road ahead. I consider keeping my foot on the accelerator. Just drive until you can't drive any further, Jake, until nobody – including you – knows where you are. Would anyone notice if I disappeared? I wonder. Or Lowri? I know it keeps going, this thing. This dual carriageway. Just winds its way north until you hit the sea and then it's stop and figure out where next or keep going and do a *Thelma and Louise* over the nearest cliff.

But I'm not on the road to nowhere any more. I've got things to do. Things to put right. And this is just the start.

The dash clock shows twenty-two ten exactly. Making good time. I take the offslip for the sticks. When I see the direction sign for Canningtown, I wince and accelerate past the turnoff.

It takes another twenty minutes through sinuous thirty-mile-an-hour zones flanked by the shadows of mountains, through rows of isolated, weary terraces, past long-dead collieries and fenced-off, rusted, coal-storage depots. I drop down from the bypass, head into a town, another place full of narrow one-way streets and lines of ten-year-old cars parked at the kerb. I see nobody. Not a soul. Just drizzle speckling the amber glow of the streetlights.

I follow the perimeter road in a huge loop, cut across a stone bridge, past an empty pub. The road drops away on one

side, drops away so steeply I'm looking over fencing but c
see a thing. It's just blackness.

I glance out through the window to get my bearings. Thi
must be it. I think it's time. My heart has picked up the pace
a little. Can feel the mouse gun in my cargo pocket. My nine-
mil security blanket. Lowri hasn't stirred once during the
journey.

I climb out of the truck, take off my fleece, dump it on the
driver's seat. Feel chilly rain on my forearms, my bare
forearms sticking out of the short sleeves of my shirt. Raise
my hands, straighten my epaulettes, check the epaulette on
my left shoulder, make sure that bloody loose number's still
there. Tug on my shiny tie, check it's clipped on properly.

I open the rear door, lift Lowri off the seat. She gives a
whimper. I hoist her upwards, carry her in front of me. Kick
the truck door closed.

'It's time,' I say to her, but her eyes are closed, head lolling
backwards, mouth open and catching rainwater. I walk
around the truck, around to the fencing and the blackness and
that sheer drop with the squall of wind whipping upwards,
like a cold hand on my face. I think of what this girl means to
me. I think about it for a long while, standing there with my
shirt getting soaked, the raw and biting blasts of air driving
wet strands of Lowri's hair into my eyes, making them sting.
Making them water.

And she means everything and nothing. She's the end and
the beginning. A means to an end. Something I have to do to
move forward.

'It really hurts me to set you free, Lowri,' I whisper into her
ear. 'But you can't follow me.'

Thank you, Jim Morrison.

And I turn away from the precipice, carry her around the
front of the truck, across the road. Check the numbers on

the houses, the column of narrow two-up two-downs, hope I've remembered the right address from my old unofficial notebook. See muted light through curtains in the front window. I shift Lowri's weight to one arm, hammer on the front door. Carry her properly again. Wait.

The man who opens the door is a tired-looking forty-something in a sensible grey jumper and grotty slippers. Old before his time. Thinning comb-over, pudgy white face above a short, small body. The air of someone who's given up expecting anything good to happen to him. One of those handbag-sized dogs is yapping at his feet in the narrow passageway.

'Oh no, mun,' he blurts, hand going up to his forehead. Eyes darting about pathetically. Panicking. No idea what for. If Plod calls at your house this time of night, got to be bad news, right? Bad news whatever time of day, come to think. But he's wrong.

'Mr Horton?' I ask patiently. Still in the fucking rain.

'Yep, that's . . .' he says nervously, then his eyes drop from mine and he trails off.

It takes a second for him to register that I have his daughter in my arms.

'Oh my God,' he rasps, staggering. He places a hand to the wall to steady himself.

'This is for you,' I tell him, and step forward. Lift Lowri over the threshold. Out of the drizzle. Out of my life.

'We thought . . .' He's stuttering, spitting everywhere. 'We thought she was . . . Oh, my baby . . .' He lurches forward, arms outstretched.

A dumpy, big-breasted heffer of a woman appears behind him. 'Jeff? Jeffrey?' she's squealing, arms raised. They're saggy and baggy. Dinner-lady arms. 'What on earth's going on?' And then she sees, places her hands up to her mouth, flaps those bingo-wing triceps against her chest and the squeal becomes a screech. She's screeching her daughter's name over and over, cheeks wet with tears.

The stupid Paris Hilton dog is still going for it. Lowri's father sinks at the waist a little when I hand her over, his face turning a shade of crimson. She instinctively folds herself into him; I feel an ache in my chest. Take the strain, fella. Hold on and never let her go again, no matter how hard it becomes.

'Is she ill?' he asks, cuddling Lowri to him. He's got her at an awkward angle, like a child clutching a ragdoll; one of her FMBs scuffs against the carpet. The woman is fussing her hair, hugging her and her husband at the same time. Laughing and crying at the same time. I'm watching, eyes flicking between this man and woman and wondering how on earth they managed to produce such a beautiful daughter. Maybe it was an adoption job.

'No,' I say. 'Just very drunk.'

'She's so headstrong,' says her mother. 'Always was. I don't know why she ever left here but, y'know, officer, there's not much in the way of excitement up here, innit? You know what it's like around these parts. We haven't had much to shout about for so long but we always tried to provide for her, me working down the Top Club and Jeff here—'

'Well, she did it and that's that,' I say, cutting her off and wondering why on earth these members of the public insist on telling me their miserable life stories.

'Yes,' she says. 'She probably thought it was a good idea at the time.'

'Like asbestos,' I say.

'We haven't seen her for so long . . .' the father says. 'Didn't know what she was doing. We'd almost given up . . .'

'Where did you find her, officer?' the mother asks.

I shake my head. Back out of the passageway, into the rain.

'It doesn't matter,' I say, and jab my finger at them. 'Just don't make me come back here. And don't give up on her. Ever. She needs you. People need their parents.'

They're nodding solemnly, Lowri hanging in her father's arms, the mother biting at a nail on one of her fingers. I don't know if their daughter will still be here this time tomorrow. She could wake in her old bed, realise what I've done, walk out all over again. I'm not convinced these walking stiffs will fight to get her back on track. But I've done what I can here. I've shown them you don't have to give up hope. I've shown myself I'm capable of fixing something.

'Thank you, officer,' the father says, moving to close the front door.

'Yes,' says the mother. 'Thank you so much. You must give us your name.'

I stare at Lowri, glance up into the night sky, the drizzle like pins and needles on the skin of my face. I'm struggling to remember ever feeling so good about being a police officer. 'It's MacReady,' I say, looking downwards. 'PC Frank MacReady. And wait . . .'

The father stops closing the door. I step into the hallway. The mother's watching me intently, still chewing on that nail.

'Wait a minute,' I say to him. Then I kiss Lowri's forehead. Softly. Breathe in her scent one last time. Smell the damp of her hair, her hotel perfume. The weed and wine. I touch her face with my hand, stare at those closed eyes.

'Goodbye my little hoochgirl,' I say, and smile.

'Oh,' the mother says.

'Officer?' the father asks, turning slightly to move Lowri away from me.

'It's all right,' I say. 'I'm better than my old man. I've just proved that, haven't I?'

They're still standing in the doorway holding Lowri as I

drive away. Just goggling after me, probably thinking *what the fuck?* I don't look back. Light up a cigar. Lower the window as I puff on it. Puff on it with rain blowing in, thinking about what I've achieved here. What this will mean to those people back in that house. What else I've got to do, because this has shown me what it means to reconnect with your parents. Even after years have passed.

I get about half a mile down the road. Pull over, engine idling, wipers flopping back and forth. I'm drawing on the cigar, taking deep breaths while I suck on the end of the cheroot, then I'm coughing, spluttering all over the steering wheel as I think about what Lowri said to me tonight, that she might . . . *might be kind of . . . y'know . . .* and the coughing fit won't go away and, before I know it, it's morphed into something else entirely.

I begin to cry. Sob like a big pussy. Like a toddler, all snot and hitching breath and juddering sighs. But that's okay. I feel like I need to. So I just let it go. Let it all come out. I roll that name around in my mouth again, curl my tongue around that L while I weep and laugh at all the times we've had, at all those things we've done. *LowriLowriLowri . . .* And then I stop saying her name. Swear to myself I'll never say it again. Resume sobbing, which is fine.

This is just the beginning. There'll be more tears before it's over.

2245	Code 20 – at scene. Mister Lowri Horton returned. Goodbye my dirty angel.
–	my wonderful whore. My fingers are crossed for you. My fingers are crossed for
	me, too. I have my list, you see. We didn't talk about it, but it's there. In my head.
	Stuff I've got to do. The right stuff. Now I can cross you off. And next on the list is

TWENTY-SIX

Oh-eight forty-three hours.

I press the heels of my hands into my eyes. Couldn't sleep at the hotel. Not with Lowri gone. Kept waking, thinking about my trip up the sticks. About what I have to do next. At oh-three hundred I gave up and checked out. Drove home, turned into the street with headlights off to find who-knows-what going on. Panda cars everywhere, blue strobes lighting up the house fronts. Sector plods milling about on my driveway. Looking for me, no doubt. To commend me for all the hard work during my tour of duty. I'm not in this game for the plaudits so thought it best not to interrupt and drove away, drove off quickly and headed for my father's place. Forgot they locked the gates at night so tucked the truck in a nearby lane and toked away on a doobie, mulling things over until I couldn't keep my eyes open any longer.

And now I'm here. The sun is shining for the occasion. Blue sky, Jacob. Got to be March by now. Spring at last. Light at the end of the tunnel.

'Answer me,' I say, but he doesn't. As usual.

My old man. Always the strong, silent type. Hold on to your emotions, boy, he'd say. Stop your grizzling. What are you, a homo? Some skinny weakling, crying just 'cos I'm fighting with your mother? Get me another beer, sonny. Because what do you know? What d'you know about us, boy? What is the truth to you? You bloody pansy. If you knew what I'd been through for you, you'd kiss my spotty arse . . .

I kick him. Kick him good and hard.

You prick. If you knew what I'd been through *because* of you, you'd fall to your knees and implore me to forgive you. You'd smother my feet with drool while you wept and begged for absolution. You *made* me. You've made me what I've become.

'Why?' I ask again and throw a punch, a thumping hay-maker with my right, but he says nothing. I hear nothing. Just feel white-hot pain in my knuckles.

There's nobody else around. Just me and Dad, alone beneath clear sky. I sit down on cold grass, feel damp spread through the seat of my uniform cargos. I look at him, think about all those years ago. My eighteenth birthday. The whole day, in school, worrying about what was going to happen that night. What version of my old man was going to show. The morose, uncommunicative bore or the belligerent drunk. I got the latter. After my guests disappeared and he finished the bottles of booze they'd left behind it was the same old same old. My mother and father toe to toe. Her goading him, him responding in the way he always did. With his fists and feet and forehead. But that night . . .

There's only so much a person can take. Only so many years of pissed-up hammerings before something snaps. Before you lose yourself, grab the first thing that comes to hand and slice up your husband in front of your only child. I was too late to save Mum. Waited too long. It'll never happen again, Dad. Never.

He says nothing, as is the norm. So I stand, pull the aerosol out of my CS pouch. Point it at the gravestone.

NATHANIEL SMITH
HUSBAND AND FATHER

is etched into the granite. The words surrounded by boot prints, rubber scuff marks where I've kicked him over the years. Chips in the stone where I've pummelled him until my knuckles bled, until my crappy old wooden truncheon snapped in two.

I spray luminous green paint in front of the first word of the second line.

I spray the word *BASTARD* there.

'You deserved everything you got,' I say. I watch for a while as watery paint runs down the stone. One of the drips negotiates the carved lines of my father's date of birth, the weather-induced hairline cracks, the dimples and flaws and minute puncture holes caused by my feet and fists and even a penknife I had with me that one time. I will that drip to reach the end, to reach the plinth and the overgrown grass. I find myself urging it on, *you can do it, go on, son, you can reach it, keep pushing, fella* . . . But in the end it runs out of puff and just hovers an inch from the bottom, a tiny green pustule that's achieved nothing.

I walk away.

Ignore the pain in your gut, Jake. Your racing pulse. The fact you can't seem to take a breath. Just keep walking. Stay on target. *Stay on target.*

'Wait,' shouts the receptionist, the bald dude from last time I was here. If he thinks I'm going to hover at the desk again while he arranges his evening dogging session on the phone he's got another thing coming.

'I'm going to see my mother,' I say, zipping up my fleece. 'Bernie, remember?'

'But *wait* . . .'

I'm already in the corridor. Baldy, he's huffing behind his little counter, threatening to ring security, bitching that he knows who I am and what I do for a living and he isn't intimidated, oh no, though he can bloody well do what he pleases because nothing's stopping me now. His voice is fading but I can still hear him bleating about not going without a chaperone, about dangerous patients wandering the building alone, that my mother's only allowed one visitor at a time. But I don't care. I'm on a mission.

There's the boom of a tannoy as I round the final corner. A feedback whine, the receptionist's distorted voice asking for security to attend my mother's room.

'Mum?' I say at the doorway, because she's sitting up in bed and smiling. Smiling at the guy flopped nice 'n' comfortably in her bedside chair next to the sink unit, some leathery old silver fox with a jumper tied around his shoulders, legs stretched out under the bed, arm draped casually behind his head. There's a mirror behind him and above the sink; in it I can see he's wearing a chunky diver's watch, like that Ewing from Professional Standards. Not the sort a patient would be wearing.

It takes a moment for me to place him. It's Ralph, isn't it? Ralph Lauren, the Saga dude. The smoothy with the sailing jacket who almost crashed into me, then legged it before I could have a word. He looks at me, then around as the tannoy blares again. I see his nice jacket hanging on the end of my mother's bed.

Now I get it. He's not some loon. He's Mum's shrink.

'Ah . . . hello, Jacob,' Ralph says, standing.

'How . . . How do you know my name? What's she been saying about me?'

I look to my mother. She's still smiling at him. Like she's in raptures. Her hair's been washed, has been styled and swept back from her face. She's got a cardigan on, some pink thing that looks new.

'It's not . . . we weren't expecting you,' Ralph says.

'Caught again, Keith,' she grins goofily, wet teeth shining in the morning sunlight.

I look at Ralph Lauren. At *Keith*. This is the dude she's been banging on about? Her psychiatrist? But he's so familiar . . . My head begins to hurt. There's a stabbing sensation behind my right eye; I can see bright amber flashes, small starbursts like cheap-arse garden fireworks going off in there somewhere.

I swallow as Keith bends down to place one hand over Mum's on the bed. He pats it gently.

'Mum,' I say, my eyes on Ralph. On Keith. 'What have you been saying?'

'I'm sorry, Jacob,' says Keith, and I'm telling him to shut up, to shut up because I'm speaking to my mother, and I can hear footsteps now, footsteps coming down the corridor. More than one person as well.

'I'd hoped . . . we'd hoped to do this properly . . .' Keith says, looking from me to my mother. 'We've been planning it for so long, but you started coming here unannounced . . .'

He doesn't finish, just checks over my shoulder and I turn, see Baldy and his corduroy-wearing colleague. Two beefy security guards stand behind them just outside the doorway.

'You have to leave,' says a security guy.

'I'm sure we can sort this out,' says Corduroy, apparently to everyone.

'One visitor at a time,' says Baldy. 'It's the rules.'

'*Fuck* the fucking rules!' I scream. 'I have my *list*. And I need to speak to my mother so get this shrink out of here.'

The security guys move forward.

'You have to leave,' one says again. 'Now.'

'Jacob . . .' says Keith softly. I feel his hand on my shoulder. Shrug it off.

'Let's keep everything calm,' says Corduroy, backing away from me while maintaining eye contact.

'I fucking well am calm,' I say. My right eye. Those amber flashes.

'Please, can I have a word?' Keith says then, stepping past me. He gestures for Baldy and his muckers to move out into the corridor. 'It would help if I explained.'

I watch them as they hover, swap glances, mull it over. Keith's doing the placating thing, palms raised, soothing them with little knowing nods. They shuffle out of the room, the taller of the security guys waiting that little bit longer to give me the evil eye before disappearing.

I hear muted conversation from the corridor, Keith crapping away about something. My mother's just smiling. Her eyes haven't moved from the window.

'Is he taking advantage of you, Mum?' I ask her.

'Did you bring me flowers?' she asks, and this isn't really important right now but I think about the tulips and nod. Take a seat on the edge of her bed.

'I did,' I say. 'I wanted you to know I've been thinking about you. About us. What we went through. What *you* went through . . .'

'They were lovely,' she says. 'Died a day later, but the thought was there.'

'Are you listening?' I ask. 'I'm trying to tell you I'm sorry about *everything*. I'm here to show you I'm not Dad.'

'Ahh, your father,' she says.

'You've always said we'd never talk about it because it's too painful,' I say. I reach across, start to place my hand over hers. Stop. Let it hover, thinking about the last time I came here. 'But I don't want to become like him. I'm losing myself. I'm losing everything . . .'

I pull my hand away, lower my head. Wish she'd rub her fingers through the stubble of my hair. I'm waiting for her touch. Willing her to make it all better.

'Don't fret, Jacob,' she says, suddenly irritated. 'You're always *fretting*.'

'Mum,' I say. 'I couldn't bear to think that when you look at me, all you see is him.'

'I don't know what you're getting so worked up about,' she tuts. 'There's nothing wrong with seeing your father when I look at you.'

'But you must hate me then, like you hated him . . .'

'I never hated your father, Jacob.'

I hear a cough, crane my neck around. The bloody psychiatrist's in the doorway. I stand as he walks in and drops back into the chair. Reaches across to Mum. I'm about to stop him, tell him no, don't do it, you can never touch her face or hair, but as I'm opening my mouth to speak, as I'm tensing to dart forward and push his hand away, his fingers brush against her.

And my mother closes her eyes. Tilts her head towards Keith as his fingertips caress her cheek.

He looks at me. 'I've known your mum for a long time,' he says.

Those flashes. Behind both eyes now. Like strobes. My head. It hurts so much.

I swallow. 'What's going on here?' I ask. 'She's your *patient*.'

'She wrote to me,' he says. 'From prison. For years.'

'So you're not her shrink, you're her fucking pen p—'

'But I was living my life,' he interrupts, shaking his head. 'That's why I walked away in the first place. Your mum was already married, I wasn't ready to settle down. I couldn't give her what she needed. But when she started writing, explaining, it changed things. It changed me. And I'm alone now, Jacob. Not getting any younger. And when she told me . . .'

'Told you what?' I ask, looking from him to my mother.

He's squeezing her hand. 'When she told me about you, I had to come back,' he says, staring up at me from the chair. 'But we wanted to do this properly, Jacob . . .'

And he tears up, stretches out his arms, waggles his fingers, beckoning for me to step over and embrace him.

'Oh, for God's sake,' my mother says. 'Just hug each other.'

I stare at her. She's flicking her head from me to Keith. I look away, catch sight of my reflection in the mirror behind him. Blink. Blink again. The fireworks exploding behind my eyes. I glance down at Keith. That face. So familiar. I look back at myself. Down to Keith. To the mirror. To Keith.

So familiar.

My chest. It's too tight. I can't breathe.

I look at Keith, arms outstretched.

I've known your mum for a long time.

I am Luke Skywalker on the gantry in Cloud City.

I'm about to black out.

'Why?' is all I can say.

'Why, why, whine, whine,' she huffs. 'You were always such a cry-baby, Jacob. I couldn't bear the thought of you grizzling about it. Nathaniel *knew*. About Keith. About you. He took you on as his own.'

'Bernadette,' Keith says.

'It ate away at him though. Not being man enough to produce his own kids. And didn't he turn out to have a temper when I reminded him how much more of a man Keith was!'

'Bernie . . .'

'All this time . . .' I say, my mouth sopping with saliva. 'I thought it was him . . . I've spent so long trying not to be like him . . .'

She rolls her eyes. 'You're just like he was. Always whining, always trying to be the good man. That's probably why you took on that silly job of yours, isn't it? Thought you could make the world a better place.'

She swivels her head towards the window, lost in thought.

'I'm sorry, Jacob,' Keith's saying. 'I didn't want it to happen like—'

'You . . . *cunt*,' I say to her.

'Jacob . . .' says Keith, and I'm dropping my hand, reaching into my cargo pocket.

My mother turns back to me, face hard. The face I saw that night, the night of my birthday, the night of an eight-inch Kitchen Devil and the man I thought was my father bleeding out onto the linoleum.

'*I'm* the victim here, Jacob,' she says, voice a forced whisper. She's jabbing her finger at me as she speaks. 'I'm doing my time. I'm the one who needs help.'

My legs give out. The amber flashes become solid amber, I feel cold hospital floor tiles on my face. Hands on me. Keith's voice. Then I'm trying to focus, pushing Keith away. I'm backing away from them both, towards the door. Pushing myself backwards using the heels of my tactical boots, the seat of my job cargos swishing on the floor. I scrabble to my feet and run for the exit, clutching the mouse gun through the fabric of my trouser pocket.

You do not have to say anything unless you wish to do so because you never did anyway, did you? Not all these years. Not until now, Mum. Why, Mum? I don't know him. I don't know you. Not any more. Who are you? Who? Mother? Mum, Mummy, Mama, whatever your name is, whoever you are, Mama yeah that'll do, Mama I want to kill this man. Point a mouse gun at his head, pull the little trigger and he's dead, so what you going to fucking do, eh? Ring us? Who ya gonna call? Eh? No point ringing me, bra. Oh no. Not the law. Not the law. Don't ring the law, bra 'cos we all know that 999 is just an inverted 666. Right? 999 is just an inverted 666999 is just an inverted 666999 is just an inverted 666

999 is just an inverted 666

999 is just an inverted 666

and all work and no play makes Jake a dull boy...

TWENTY-SEVEN

I am a bullet.

A loaded gun. A ready-to-fire hand cannon. A weapon of mass destruction.

No matter how hard I've tried, no matter how hard I've fought, I haven't changed anything. It was always beyond me. So I'm not going to sweat the small stuff any more.

I am who I am whether I like it or not. I am my mother's son.

Nathaniel, I'm sorry.

And there's been a change of plan.

I've been trying to work things out, slumped here in the truck in The Elite car park. Trying to make sense of everything. But all I can think is: there's no mileage in trying to be the good guy. Nobody cares. I don't care. I don't know right from wrong any more. Goodness is something you choose and when a man can't choose he ceases to be a man.

So be it.

I'm tucked into a far corner with a perfectly good view of the gym door. Sweating from the heat of the spring sun. Swapping the mouse gun between sticky hands. You don't want to answer the phone, Sinclair? Want to keep me dangling, not knowing if you've called off the dogs? Well, I've come to you, brother. I'll give you your nine millies back, all right. Every last one of them. Then we'll be square, won't we? But what now? Wait for you to leave, sneak up, shoot you in the nape? Or is it Columbine time? Go in there screaming, teeth bared, lob a couple of ten-kilo plates about, boot a couple of bench-pressing scrotes in the neck, then blow a few caps into your pecs?

I drum my fingers on the steering wheel. Hmmm. It's a toughie.

But then The Elite door opens and my heart starts going triple-time and I don't have to deliberate any further because out steps Young Pacino. Leather jacket. Flat-top. Shades. Tattooed hand pressing a mobile up to his ear. I duck down. Hold my breath. Listen as he barks into his phone, as he yells about Sinclair, yells *no, I'll keep looking, make sure you keep 'em there and keep 'em quiet, we're going to sit tight until this is sorted, until I gets my fuckin' cash*. I hear a car door slam shut, an engine start up.

Initiative comes to thems that wait.

Sinclair, you lucky, lucky bastard. You don't know how close you came, friendo. Because this is miles better. This is further up the food chain. Maybe the top of the food chain. Why kill a grunt when you can go for the colonel? Hoo-aah!

I straighten up as Pacino pulls out onto the main drag. Peels away in some souped-up blue Subaru. I should've whacked him right here. No problemo. Quick adjustment. A nice easy follow, like I've done a hundred times before. Tail him, see if there's someone even higher up at the end of it. Take him out too. Take them *all* out.

I start the truck. Ease onto the street. 'Subject is mobile,' I say. 'On the move in target vehicle.'

He heads south, motoring towards the bay. For a drug lord he's not exactly surveillance-conscious. It's straightforward stuff: no changing lanes, no doubling-back on himself. Nothing. The clown's even teasing his hair in the rear-view as he goes, like he hasn't a care in the world. Like he's untouchable. But it's sloppiness, fella. Your arrogance will be your undoing. I guarantee it.

This is a doddle. I even spark up a cheroot, lower the window. Listen to a bit of radio as I follow the Subaru at a discreet distance, mindful that Pacino might know my truck. I weave through morning traffic, pulling in occasionally to give him time to get ahead before accelerating onwards, catching up, see him take the next bend or rise or junction. It's stuff Frankie and I do all the time. *Did* all the time, I remind myself. I wish he was here, though. Would be nice to have him in a secondary car; we could be swapping behind so Pacino doesn't get spooked.

'Target vehicle now left, left,' I say, continuing the commentary. I have no radio, which is a bummer, so I'm talking to no one via my switched-off mobile phone, which I've clipped to the front of my fleece.

The Subaru leaves the link road, roars up an offslip. I know where Pacino's heading. I've worked this city long enough. There's nothing but those swanky flats overlooking the harbour. I hang back, let him disappear. Give him a minute. No need to worry, no need to be compromised. There's just one way in and out.

The security gates, they're starting to close when I reach the high-rise. I dump the truck at the perimeter wall, lose the fleece because this is full uniform time. Quite possibly for the last time. I nip through the gap in the gates, mouse gun at the ready.

Perfect. Pacino's already parked the Subaru, has his back to me, is strutting towards the entrance whistling 'The Winner Takes It All'. An Abba tune, of all things. I let him get halfway across the car park.

I am Harry Callahan. Dirty, grubby Harry. How lucky does this guy feel? I wonder.

'I'm the winner now,' I say, and he doesn't know what's hit him.

He's pretty strong, I'll give him that. The tattooed hand, it's pulling on my left forearm, trying to yank it free from his neck as I strangle him from behind. I squeeze tighter, pull him closer, dig him in a kidney with the barrel of the PM9 for good measure. His leather jacket's squeaking against my polyester tie, undoubtedly making it even shinier.

'Whaddaferchhh?' he says, voice choked and reedy. Fair do's, he's still having a right go: tugging my arm, elbowing my ribs, stamping on my toes. Good old tactical boots with their steel caps.

Enough. I bring my right hand up and around, around so he can see what I'm holding, and he stiffens as I jam the mouse gun into his cheek.

'Hello, Al,' I whisper into his ear, and squeeze at his throat again.

Pacino stops moving. Shifts his eyes right as far as they'll go, until he's looking along the length of the Kahr at my face hovering near his shoulder.

'*You*,' he phlegms.

'Evenin' all,' I say, and it's probably only lunchtime but, y'know, so what? I glance around. Check apartment windows. Nobody. Drop the gun into my cargos, quickly frisk him. Some drug lord. Just keys, phone, wallet, comb. Not even a tiny cosh. This guy thinks he's invincible. I dump everything except the keys. Put them back in his pocket for later. Pull out the PM9, place it against his right temple.

'You . . .' Pacino says again, clearly getting the hang of this conversing-while-being-asphyxiated thing. 'You took your time.'

'What? Where's my receipt?' I ask him.

'Wha' you on about?'

Arsehole. 'No one's had the decency to give me a receipt for paying my debt.'

Pacino gives a short laugh. 'Receipt? I don't . . . don't know anything about any receipt. And last I heard, people only got receipts when they paid for things.'

'I *paid*,' I say, and thump the butt of the Kahr against his eyebrow. 'See this? I fucking paid, Al. And I've got more money too.' Frank's cash. Still in my pocket. What's left of it, anyway.

He's groaning, squeezing the eye shut. 'Nobody paid, bra,' he says. 'Not you, not Sinclair, wherever he is. You had enough warnings. You knew what would happen. Why else are you here?'

'What the fuck are you on about?'

He pauses. 'Why don't you see for yourself, Superman?'

I try to ignore the awful grin he's got on his chops. 'How exciting,' I say, not feeling excited whatsoever. 'Let's go back to your place then, eh?'

I duck-walk Pacino forward, Kahr gouging his face, my arm locked across his Adam's apple. Reach the entrance. Get him to key in the door code. Nice 'n' cool in the lobby. Air-con. Marbled floor. Stark white walls dotted with original artwork.

'Nothing to see here,' I say to the concierge. 'Police business, move along.'

He doesn't, of course. The only movement is his mouth falling open and his hand slowly going for the telephone on the desk while his eyes bug out.

Then Pacino and I are into the lifts, I'm jabbing his cheek with the PM9, telling him no funny business, telling him to press for the right floor, and up we go, staring each other out in the mirrors, my left arm numb now, aching from holding his neck. He's quiet, gritting his teeth, glancing from me to the digital numbers above the lift doors: three, four, five, six . . .

Ten floors up the doors part and we're out into the corridor. It's like we've become comfortable with each other.

With the situation. He's given up struggling, is just leading me onwards with my forearm nice 'n' tight around his throat. With my mini pistol plugged up against his eye socket.

'Is this it?' I ask him when we stop outside an apartment door.

Pacino nods. Well, nods as best he can.

'You'd better not be pissing me about, Al.'

Shake of the head.

'Anybody else in there?'

No response. I jerk the mouse gun up so the muzzle pokes further into his eyeball.

'You fucker,' he grunts. Then: 'Why don't you look for yourself, hero?'

I take a breath. A shaky one. Legs a little unsteady now. Those amber flashes, they're back again. I squeeze my eyes shut.

'Take the keys out of your pocket,' I say. 'Open the door. Slowly.'

Those fireworks behind my eyes.

Pacino's unlocked the door.

Open my eyes. Still the yellow starbursts. Another deep breath.

I barrel him into the apartment, into a hallway with my arm rammed up against his neck, squeezing at his throat to keep him quiet, switching the PM9 from his face to the open doorway ahead of us, arcing it in a one-eighty, back to his face, to the doorway, grinding my teeth, crushing his windpipe, working out what I'm going to do when we get into the next room; perhaps a tactical sweep while I'm still holding him, maybe pistol-whip the prick so I can free my arm for five minutes, maybe just shoot him on the spot and be done with it because it's not like we can discuss what's happened over tea and biscuits, is it?

Then we're through the doorway into a cavernous rectangular lounge and all these thoughts are lost because sitting on a settee at the far end of the room are Karen and the kids.

'Wife?' I blurt.

And she's up on her feet, hands to her face, *ohmygodohmygod* she's crying and I'm looking from her to my horrified children, my body slack, arm falling from Pacino's throat, I don't know where to point the gun, don't know what to make of all this, it's going too fast and I wish those bloody orange lights would just *go away* because Al's legging it down the hall and out the door, he's getting away and I'm about to go after him when a door opens further down the lounge.

And another guy appears.

Young. Blond. Toned. Handsome. Almost Brad Pitt quality. Bowl in one hand. Spoon in the other. Solitary Coco Pop stuck to his bottom lip, mouth full.

'What the?' he crunches. Milk leaks down his chin.

I point the mouse gun at him and he freezes. Look from him to Karen. Down the hallway after Pacino. To Pitt. To Karen. What's she doing here with these two? Why is she . . .? Oh, no. No no no no *no*. Please God, no.

'You . . .' I say, swinging the PM9 towards her. 'You filthy fucking *whore*.'

The kids sob.

Karen holds out a hand, eyes flitting from me to Pitt. 'Jake, you don't understand . . .'

'Two guys? *Two?*'

I hear a muffled thump. Out the corner of my eye I see a flash. Not amber. Silver this time. I swivel at the waist, see Pitt's dropped his cereal on the carpet, is coming towards me fast and low. It's not a spoon he's holding any more. It's a big fucking hunting knife.

I jerk the mouse gun around, squeeze at the trigger.

Those fireworks. They fill my vision.

TWENTY-EIGHT

Frankie's on his way in, which means I'll have the chance to apologise for that night at his house, and I'm checking the lounge once more, checking the black bin bags I've ripped and taped across windows are secure. That the front door is deadlocked, the heavy oak hallway table wedged against the frame. That the rear kitchen window overlooking the courtyard ten floors below has the blind lowered. Everything battened down. Sealed. Searched. Boxed in.

I pace back and forth on the deep carpet, my tactical boots leaving footprints in the creamy hundred-quid-a-square-metre lushness. I do wish everyone would stop the hysterics. I still have a job to do here and the incessant crying is rather distracting.

I look across at the settee. At Karen, Naomi, Ben. Lined up, sickly faces drained of colour, watching me with fearful eyes. At Brad Pitt, sitting next to my wife, Karen trying to push herself away from him as if all of a sudden he disgusts her. But I'm not buying it, oh no. I'm nobody's mug any more.

'Aw, the new happy family,' I say. 'Everyone comfy?'

Karen shifts forward again, squealing something unintelligible, and I've already warned her about this, warned her what will happen if she keeps on, doesn't she appreciate the situation? That I don't want to hear the *nonoJakeyoudon't getityoudon'tunderstandplease* hysterical pleading bollocks all over again and it's because of her that I shoved the mouse gun in her mouth to shut her up? That she's terrifying our children? That it's because of what she's done that they're in this predicament?

A waggle of the PM9 shushes her. I light a reefer, suck on it. Glance at pretty-boy Pitt, offer him a toke but he says nothing, just stares at me silently, so I exhale and resume walking the floor. He's a handsome sod, despite the Coco Pop still glued to his chin. Probably a doctor, too. A swaggering twenty-something star neurosurgeon. That's why Karen fell for him, isn't it? Swept her off her feet in A and E with his humorous monologues about cranial excavation.

I finger the mouse gun, imagine flying to the US of A and offing the real Brad Pitt for having the temerity to look like the man Karen's shacked up with. Then taking out Brad's missus and all those kids of theirs as well, even the ones they bought off the Internet.

My children are weeping next to their mother. Jesus, guys, it's not like you've had to deal with what I've been through these last few weeks.

'Karen,' I say to her. 'You don't know what you've done.'

'*Please*, Jake, you don't know what you've done . . .'

I hold up a finger when my mobile rings. It's Pamela Howells. Ginge, doing her negotiator thing again. I suck on the reefer, let it ring. Let her wait. Walk over to the window, peel back one sliver of black sack I've sellotaped to the frame and peek down into the car park. They've got the whole world out there this afternoon. Arrived pretty quickly too. Very efficient. Collingwood would've had an erection if he'd been around to see it. There's panda cars. ARV wagons with the crews covering the apartment block. Ambulances. Trumpton trucks. Sector bobbies on cordon. Snipers on the roof of the harbour offices opposite. Television vans. Even Tommy bloody Hall. It's *Dog Day Afternoon* time. *Attica! Attica!* How exciting for the locals. How thrilling for the concierge who clearly dialled 999.

'Frank's at the door,' she says when I finally answer.

'Is he alone like I asked?' I say. 'I need time to explain about wanking over those shoes.'

'What?'

'Never mind.'

'He's alone, Jacob,' Ginge says. 'Like I told you, there's not going to be any nonsense. I'm more than aware you know what you're doing and what we're capable of. We just don't want anyone getting hurt. Anyone else.'

'Lovely jubbly,' I say. 'You enjoying this?'

'Not one iota.'

'No worries,' I tell her, puffing on the joint. 'Everyone'll be happy when it's over.'

I cut her off, out the spliff. There's a knock on the front door. I open it slowly.

It's Frank. My buddy. My partner. I check the corridor, see there's no Tac Team waiting to blow hinges, so relock the door, shift the table back into position, drop the PM9 into my cargos, keep telling him *I'm sorry about what I did in Jessica's bedroom, I'm sorry, Frankie, I'm going to make this right, I'm so glad to see you* and he nods quietly. He's looking very smart today, I see he's bulled his boots and pressed his trousers for the occasion. Even the Glock in his holster is gleaming. Oiled and polished.

When we step into the lounge he takes a quick scan around. A tactical visual sweep. Looks at Karen and the kids. Sees Doc Pitt.

'Jesus fuckin' Christ,' he says, rushing over to him. 'What did you do?'

I glance across at the Doc as Frankie takes his hands, leans over him. See the bullet hole in his left temple. The exit wound behind his right ear, an apple-sized cavity that's ruined his neat haircut. I was as surprised as he was when I fired the mouse gun. It certainly packs a punch for a small weapon.

Knocked him five feet backwards and onto the settee, the hunting knife still in his hand.

'Wondered why he was being so quiet,' I say. 'He's a brain surgeon don't you know? At least . . . I think he is. You'll have to ask Karen.'

'I don't even *know* him,' she cries.

'Can't operate to save himself now though, can he?' I laugh because it's meant to be a joke but nobody else cracks a smile so I stop.

Frank jerks his head. I can see the corner lamp reflected in his glasses. 'Jake . . .'

'We fell out,' I say, shrugging. Mentally count the bullets in the Kahr. Four. Five of us in this room now. What a dilemma. But then that isn't the way this is supposed to go.

Frank hauls himself up, draws his nine millie. He's looking at me, shaking his head slowly. Looking at me, pistol gripped in his right hand as he steps away from Dr Pitt, moves in front of Karen, Naomi and Ben. Blocking them from my view. Shielding them. Like I knew he would.

I pull the PM9 out of my cargo pocket. Look down at it as I hold it in front of my midriff. Glance across at the dead man sprawled next to my family. Think about my mother, my father. About the man I thought was my father. About the only way I'm ever going to make everybody happy again.

'I need you to help me put things right, Frankie,' I say.

'The only thing you need is to put that down and come with me,' I hear him say.

I look up. 'You know that's not going to happen. Not after this. I'd never survive over the wall. This has to stop here.' And it's true. I have made peace with this.

He takes a couple of steps towards me, one hand stretched out. Leaving me with a clear shot at the settee. 'We can take care of you,' he says. His Glock hangs against his trouser leg, finger curled around the trigger. 'You're one of us, Jake. Don't make this any worse than it already is. Please.'

'I can't do this on my own,' I say. 'Set me free. Set *them* free from me.' I wave the PM9 at my family and Frankie tenses. The Glock shakes. 'I love you like a brother, Frank. You're a grunt, just like me. I wouldn't ask this of anybody else. I couldn't take this from anybody else.'

My children are sobbing, faces buried into their mother. 'Please, Frank,' she's shrieking, obviously fed up of trying to wheedle her way out of this with me. 'He doesn't understand . . . these men, they came to our flat . . .'

'Drop the gun, Jake,' he says, voice louder. He's looking a little twitchy now. Glassy-eyed, like he's about to blub behind those awful specs of his. Poor Frank. Such a nice bloke.

I raise the mouse gun, point the muzzle directly at Karen. She screams, pushes herself further into the settee cushions.

'No!' Frank shouts and lifts the Glock. Aims at my chest.

And my hand is hovering in mid-air, the business end of the PM9 levelled at my wife's forehead, my children screeching and covering their faces with their arms, and this is the way it's supposed to be, isn't it? This was how I imagined it. Frankie's got his pistol aimed right at me, the muzzle hole like a gaping maw with a nine-millimetre parabellum just waiting in the chamber. But I know he's not going to discharge his weapon for this; oh no, it'd take a lot more than me waving my miniature gun about to make him do that because we're friends, right? We're brothers, grunts, troopers, cops who've shared beer and smokes, swapped porn films and endless war stories, endured the misery that is our job and even though I'm pointing a shooter at my family, Frank will be completely aware I'd never go through with it, because he knows me better than anyone.

So I swing the mouse gun across and shoot him in his left thigh.

And suddenly I'm on my back on the lovely cream carpet and the room smells of cordite because Frank has fired two rounds into my chest, an instinctive double-tap just like he's been trained to do, a textbook bit of police firearms procedure and well done, Frankie. Good on you. So professional. A classic riposte.

There's more screaming and I tilt my head to the left, see Karen holding on to Naomi and Ben, pulling them to her and hugging them, wrapping them in her arms. Such a good mother, at least. Always so great with the kids.

My chest, it's ice cold, and I've read about this, about gunshot victims and the stages they go through and it's quite intriguing actually, quite interesting to experience it first hand, so I wait for the next part, the agonising part, in a detached kind of way. Tilt my head in the other direction. Check Frank. He's moaning and writhing on the floor, hands on his thigh, blood pissing out of his work trousers, and it's a shame because the jobsworth up in the HQ tailor's department always makes a fuss about giving out replacement slacks.

And then it's not funny any more because I can't take a breath, my sternum feels like someone's dropped a two-hunded-kilo barbell on it, crushing the air out of my lungs and oh, God this hurts, this burns like nothing has ever burned before, and I reach my hands up to my chest, feel warm fluid over my still-green fingertips, can feel hot sticky liquid pooling on the carpet beneath me, and if old Doc Pitt was still breathing he'd be having a coronary about it right now.

I'm coughing blood. Pull open my police shirt, rip those buttons off, send the shiny clip-on tie flying, touch the puncture holes in my flesh, one dead centre, the other above my right nipple, and it's no wonder Frank always topped the target-range classes because this is so impressive. My fingers touch two pieces of metal hanging from my neck and one of them has a hole right through it. My dog tags, man.

But wait. *Wait.* My fingers claw at my shirt pocket, reach in, yank out the contents. I see shredded paper. Bloodied handwriting. Oh, no. Please *no.*

The horror. *The horror.*

'Frank,' I say, my voice odd and thick with blood. 'You've ruined me fuckin' pocket notebook, you muppet.'

He says nothing, just whimpers and calls out for an ambulance, which means he'll be fine because he's grumbling as usual, so I drop my head back to the carpet and stare at the ceiling. This isn't so bad after all. All of this, it's not so bad really.

I can't feel anything now. Can't feel a thing. Don't want to move anyway. I'm just happy to lie here for a while.

Just lie here and wait and feel good that things turned out all right in the end.

My chest isn't working but it's not important. My mouth is filled with blood but that doesn't really matter. I can't keep my eyes open any more but that's fine.

I let them close. Let them go. Let it all go.

Fade out.

Cut.

'Come with me,' I hear Frank say, and it's a struggle but I'm so glad to hear him sounding normal again that I open my eyes. He's standing over me, reaching out one hand.

I squint up at him. 'Aren't you angry?'

He looks down at his left leg. 'Just a flesh wound, bra,' he smiles.

So I smile back, take his outstretched hand. Wait for the

pain as he pulls me up but it doesn't come, then I'm upright, looking at him, and he's grinning, hand still holding mine.

'I'm sorry,' I say.

'No need,' he says and turns to his right. Nods in that direction.

I follow his gaze. Karen's waving at me from the settee. Naomi and Ben are either side of her. They look so happy. So content. It's nice to see it at last.

'Thank you,' she says to me.

'It's my pleasure, sweetie,' I reply.

'Come with me, Jake,' Frank says, his hand tightening on mine. He leads me to the front door where he pushes the table to one side, unlocks the deadbolt and it's only now I can hear some sort of noise coming from outside, a faint musical melody, and Frank looks at me, asks me if I'm ready and I think I am. I nod. *Yes, Frankie. I'm ready.*

He opens the front door and we take the lift to the ground floor, walk through the lobby where the concierge throws me a wink, the concierge who looks remarkably like Brad Pitt, and the sound is growing louder then we're out through the entrance doors and it hits me.

Applause. Music. Wooting, laughing. I see row after row of police uniforms, number one dress with white gloves and everything, a sea of faces looking up at me. Placards. Banners. *Attica!* they chant. Toothy grins beneath helmets beneath clear blue sky.

'Is this . . . is this for me?' I ask Frank.

He squeezes my hand. 'Yes, Jake. All of it.'

So we walk down the steps into the crowd of plods who part like the Red Sea, who clap and call my name, slap me on the shoulder. Frank's pulling me along, the music's getting louder then we're upon a brass band, the force marching band, and I recognise the tune now, it's The

Doors and they're playing 'The End' and look, it's Baker and the rest of the kiddie-cop crew, all of them here with instruments: Two Backs, BMX, Roid, even Plug banging away on the bass drum like a retard. Then I see little old Lapdog parping away on a cornet, so stop and tug at his sleeve.

'I didn't know you played,' I say to him.

He places a hand on my arm. 'I learned just for you, Tee,' he says.

'Well, you're fantastic.' He blushes, then Frank's pulling me along again. We wind our way through this swarm of blue serge, this thousand-strong ocean of titheads, and I don't know where we're going but I'm with my buddy so everything's going to be okay.

I see familiar faces. Sinclair on the fringes of our human corridor, clapping and hooting then draping his arm around Young Pacino who's looking a little sheepish as he cheers me on. Ewing, slick as ever, holding hands with Dwayne Cooper and Tang Yeh, all three of them eyes closed and rocking their heads from side to side in time to the music. Along we go, it takes an eternity to get there, an age to work our way through the massed ranks, but suddenly we reach a platform and everything goes quiet.

'We're here,' says Frank.

I look up at the figures on the raised dais, back to him. Place my hands on his shoulders. 'Thanks,' I say.

'Any time, brother,' he says, and steps away. Melts into the crowd.

I take a breath. Walk up the steps. Feel a thousand pairs of eyes on me. And then I'm up with the dignitaries. A line of people with a table at one end. Dave Collingwood sits behind it, watching me impassively. Seems like he got his desk job after all.

'Welcome back, Smithy,' Collingwood says.

I nod. 'Cheers, guv.' And I walk across to meet everyone.

Frank's worked his way around the back, joined the line-up. Standing there with Mel and Jessica. Next to them are Karen and my children. Then Rachael and Cliff, the happy couple. Ginge. Tommy Hall. Lowri and her parents, along with their yapping dog that I'm pleased to see has been muzzled. The girl from the Clio. Whole again. Uninjured. Grinning. *Thank you*, she whispers as I pass. *Thank you, you were there for me, you did all you could.* All of them waiting, hands clasped in front of them. Like they're about to meet the Queen.

At the far end, dressed in the full uniform of Chief Constable, is Nathaniel.

My father but not my father.

No, my father.

I walk up to him. Look into his eyes.

'I wish I could be like you,' I say to him.

He gives a warm smile. Takes hold of my hand. 'You are, Jacob,' he says, his voice quiet and reassuring. 'You're the son I never had.'

And I lower my head. Begin to cry. His gentle fingers brush the stubble of my hair.

'I'm so tired,' I say.

'I know,' he says softly. 'Rest now. You've done your duty.'

And I look up, look around. Collingwood's climbed out of his chair. He gestures at it.

So I sit, take the weight off my feet. Slump back, look from Nathaniel to the line of people next to him, across to the swell of epaulettes and clip-on ties. Back to the man who gave me everything and said nothing.

I check the crowd. Can't see my mother anywhere. But that's okay. That's all right. It doesn't matter. I'm just so relieved to be here on this beautiful day. To be sitting down. To be off duty at last.

I am Police Constable 754 Jacob Nathaniel Smith, signing off duty.

Signing off duty at last.

At last.

ACKNOWLEDGEMENTS

Personal: my amazing wife (a.k.a. the editor/muse/ nursemaid/ego massager/bullshit detector) and beautiful children; Ma 'n' Pa for the use of the loft and pretty much everything; my Londonista sister (go Joey Deacon, go!); Nats 'n' James; Seiko (if I must); Jackie, Anthony, Richard, Amanda, Scott, Hannah-Marie, Shika, Leanne – this is why I haven't seen you for two years . . .

Professional: super-agent Karolina Sutton and the gang at Curtis Brown; *uber*-editor Jason Arthur and his fantastic team at William Heinemann.

'School': at Glamorgan – Sheenagh Pugh for suffering through countless rewrites, Rob Middlehurst for *getting it* big time, Barrie Llewelyn (this is all your fault, y'know . . .), Tony Curtis for the 'publisher ambush' that fateful December night, Des Barry, Chris Meredith, Cath Merriman, Phillip Gross, Stephen Knight, Gillian Clarke; my oh-so-talented cohort for the advice, encouragement and willingness to let me know when I was talking bollocks – Harvey Marcus (hey roomie!), Caroline Ross, Stephen Elves, Lynda Nash, Rosie Shepperd, Sarah Dunlin, Kate Noakes, Luigi di Castri; all the FNGs who endured the first draft, especially Shauna Busto Gilligan, Caroline Fox Betts and Claire Williams; at All Round – Shelagh, Paul, Lizzy and Colin; at Barrie's Writers – the 'Golden Girls' and in particular Dinnella Shelton for vouching for me all those years ago.

The Morning/Afternoon/Night Job: Neil 'The Decider' Evans, Jevans, Linda Wyer, Sian 'Helga von Sashay' Rees, Li'l Talbwards, Johnkey, Crystal Tips, The Berg, Coxy Coxalino, Bashelle Bowen and Fanjita 'Kwik Suit?' Gravington (apologies for trying out some of Jake's worst lines on you all . . .); the 'Blue Rinsers' of D Relief/Team Two/Whatever.

Miscellaneous: Dave, Mart, Fletch and Alan (and maybe even you, Vince) for the soundtrack to my life; David Kinchen at TWB; Inspector Gadget and his glorious blog; Uncle Jack; Henri Wintermans; Ken 20; Blocky B's; Empire; George, George, Steven, Martin, Brian, Fincher, QT, Francis, Oliver, Woody, Frank, Robert, Ang, Stanley, Abel; CP, JRL, SK, TW, CM, BEE, JF.

And to all the grunts out there in the boonies – may the Force be with you . . . always.

DOUGLAS COUPLAND

Generation A

Generation A is set in the near future in a world where bees are extinct, until five unconnected people around the world – in the US, Canada, France, New Zealand and Sri Lanka – are all stung. Their shared experience unites them in ways they never could have imagined. *Generation A* fizzes with Coupland's trademark wit, invention and vivid understanding of the world we live in.

'With this exceptional sequel to Generation X, Douglas Coupland may be one of the smartest, wittiest writers around . . . He is a terrifically good writer . . . This is a clever, brilliant book'
ESQUIRE

'A delightful Decameron of a book . . . Rich, educative and even consoling'
INDEPENDENT

'One of the most popular serious writers of our time'
ARAVIND ADIGA, FINANCIAL TIMES

'Inventive and unexpectedly moving'
DAILY MAIL

'Highly recommended. Like Murakami in a thriller-trope mode. Go for it'
WILLIAM GIBSON

'Coupland's audacious flights of fancy, his laugh-out-loud dialogue and his magnificent ability to bring it all back to storytelling and orange-flavour tang, they're all here . . . Such a treat'
INDEPENDENT ON SUNDAY

JAMES ELLROY

Blood's a Rover

It's 1968. Bobby Kennedy and Martin Luther King are dead. The Mob, Howard Hughes and J Edgar Hoover are in a struggle for America's soul, drawing into their murderous conspiracies the damned and the soon-to-be damned.

Wayne Tedrow Jr: parricide, assassin, dope cooker, mouthpiece for all sides, loyal to none. His journey will take him deeper into the darkness.

Dwight Holly: Hoover's enforcer and hellish conspirator in terrible crimes. As Hoover's power wanes, his destiny lurches towards Richard Nixon and self-annihilation.

Don Crutchfield: a kid, a nobody, a wheelman, and a private detective who stumbles upon an ungodly conspiracy from which he and the country may never recover.

All three men are drawn to women on the opposite side of the political and moral spectrum; all are compromised and ripe for destruction.

'A writer of visceral power and historical reach ...The plot is fantastically, but satisfyingly, complex ...It's a seedy, erratic, bloody and compassionate masterpiece.'
INDEPENDENT

'A triumph of imagination, both palpably real and overwhelmingly nightmarish'
DAILY TELEGRAPH

'Sensational ... leave you breathless with respect for Ellroy's prose ... still the classiest act around ... stunning sweep and grace.'
DAILY MAIL

Josh Bazell

Beat the Reaper

The doctor will see you now . . .

Meet Peter Brown, a young medical intern in the worst hospital in Manhattan. His job is to save lives. It used to be to take them. When a patient from his past threatens to blow his cover, Peter needs all his professional skills – old and new – just to stay alive.

Hilarious, chilling, and spattered in adrenaline-fuelled action and bone-saw-sharp dialogue, *Beat the Reaper* is a debut thriller so utterly original you won't be able to guess what happens next, and so shockingly entertaining you won't be able to put it down.

'A Firecracker . . . fast and ferocious'
JAMES ELLROY

'A blast . . . blew me away . . . relentless as a bullet'
MICHAEL CONNELLY

'Funny and outrageous'
GUARDIAN

'A roller-coaster ride from the very first page, fast, furious, and – believe it or not – funny . . . breathtakingly accomplished . . . Bazell is a name to watch'
DAILY MAIL

'This is the second funniest health care-based fiction to come out of the United States this year after the Republican Party's descriptions of the NHS'
DAILY TELEGRAPH, BOOKS OF THE YEAR